THE
WICKED ONE

LAURA JORDAN

Find Laura on:

Twitter @Laura_Katie_J
Facebook: Laura Katie
Snapchat: laurakatie_j
Instagram @laura_katie_j
TikTok @laura_katie_j
Youtube: Laura Katie

Also by Laura Jordan:
The Dead King

This book contains scenes of a sexual nature.
Reader discretion is advised.

Potential trigger warnings for this book:
Violence
Torture
Sexual assault
Murder
Satanism
Human sacrifice

By reading on, you will encounter the topics mentioned above, even
if only very briefly. If these are things that you find triggering, please
proceed with caution.

This book is dedicated to the great love of my life.

No. Not my cat.

To *Derek*.

You are my best friend, my greatest inspiration, and my soulmate.

You're also *really* good in bed.

1.

'INCUBUS! I-N-C-U-B-U-S! INCUBUS!'

Olivia watched, bemused, as Professor Flannigan flicked through the various images on his crude presentation, each more grisly than the last..

'Male sex demons that prey on sleeping women. Derived from the Latin "a nightmare induced by a demon". These creatures have a sole purpose of impregnating women in the hopes that their offspring will too have supernatural abilities.'

Olivia felt a headache coming on. She let her eyelids drift closed. Darkness felt good. It was only 10am, and she had barely enough patience to tolerate her Paranormal Folklore professor, let alone take notes on things she already knew. This headache had the potential to become a migraine.

'Some believe that the incubus can be identified by a particularly large, cold, penis,' Flannigan bellowed.

Okay, that made Olivia open her eyes. She picked up her pen and wondered if she should write that down. But did she really want the words "large, cold penis" in her notebook? Probably not. She put her pen back down.

Flannigan glared at the students who dared giggle at the mention of such a word, and went back to his slides. 'Though many accounts claim the incubus to be bisexual, others argue that the incubus is strictly heterosexual, and views intercourse with men as either useless or detrimental. That is where the succubus comes in.'

The slide changed from a squat, ugly imp to a tall, stacked Goddess, and Olivia frowned. Did the demon-lady have to be ridiculously hot? Why would a demon-lady need to be hot? She's a demon. All powerful. She could be a fat little troll like the other guy, it wouldn't make a difference.

Probably painted by a man.

Olivia nodded. True that. She picked up her pen.

Flannigan pointed to the succubus. 'The female counterpart to the incubus. It is said, in folklore, that to penetrate a succubus is like entering a cavern of ice.'

Olivia put her pen down once more.

'Now, who can tell me when the earliest reference to an incubus was made? Come along, it was in your reading assignment.'

Olivia watched all the introverts wilt into their seats, begging not to be called on. The biggest introvert of them all, Kian Kelly, was sat a few seats down from her. He shrank down more than all of them. Olivia knew what was about to happen. She suspected Kian did too.

'Mr Kelly!' Flannigan snapped. A nasty smile bloomed on his wrinkled face. 'Would you enlighten us please?'

In a small voice, Kian said, 'I don't know, Professor.'

'Pardon? Speak up, Mr Kelly. We are humans, not dogs.'

Kian flushed. 'I said, I don't know, Sir.'

Flannigan tried —and failed— to suppress a grin. 'You don't know? Did you not do the reading?'

'Yes, Sir. I did.'

'Did any of the larger words confuse you, Mr Kelly?'

'No, Sir.'

'Then why don't you know?'

Kian looked down at his hands in his lap. 'I just can't remember.'

Olivia couldn't take much more of this. She put her hand up and without waiting to be chosen she said, 'Mesopotamia, 2400 BC.'

Without taking his beady eyes off his prey, Flannigan replied, 'I wasn't asking you, Miss McQueen.'

'I know, you weren't,' she said. 'Because I actually know the answer. You're asking Kian because you know he doesn't know the answer.'

That got his attention.

Bad move. Abort mission.

Flannigan looked at Olivia and licked his thin lips. 'What are you saying, exactly, Miss McQueen?'

Don't do it, Liv.

Olivia sucked in a deep breath. 'Well, Sir, when you asked the question, at least ten people in here put their hand up. That's ten people who think they know the answer. But you didn't pick any of those people, you chose someone who didn't have their hand up. This isn't the first time, either. This is almost every lecture.'

It was around that point that Olivia got the feeling she should stop, because Flannigan had that I'm going to eat you alive look on his face, but she had already dug herself in deep enough by that point. Might as well keep going until she hit China.

'That begs the question,' she continued. 'Do you enjoy watching your own students squirm more than you actually enjoy teaching us?'

Dear God, this parachute is just a backpack.

Olivia continued, 'I don't know if it's a sadistic thing, or a power thing. Probably the latter. Probably the same reason why you make us all call you *Sir* or *Professor* — which no other lecturer does by the way. My guess is it's your way of setting yourself up as the Alpha-male. King of the classroom. Head Honcho. So tell me, Darragh — oops, sorry, I mean *Sir* — did I get it right? Hit the nail on the proverbial head, as it were?'

Flannigan stared at her. So did the rest of the lecture hall. His puckered anus of a mouth opened, as if to come back with some kind of biting retort, and then closed again.

The bell on his desk rang.

Olivia rose out of her seat and slung her bag over her shoulder. She smiled at Flannigan. 'Cool. Also, your fly has been open this whole lecture. Thought you'd like to know.'

Olivia left the lecture hall with a bigger headache than when she'd entered, but at least she was smiling. Well, on the inside, anyway. She made her way down the stairs and out of the Parnell building. It was late afternoon and the Irish sunshine was still beating down strong. It was an unusually warm day for early October, but she wasn't complaining. She had been studying at Dublin Community College for three years now, and she still hadn't adjusted to the weather. She missed the long, warm days back in the South East of England — but that was the only thing she missed.

She made it halfway across the quad before she heard someone call her name. She pretended not to hear. Kept walking. But her pursuer was persistent.

'Olivia!'

She heard the thumping of feet and puffing of breath, and Kian Kelly came into her peripheral vision. His face was still red, this time from exertion. He smiled at her. It was a nice smile. He was a nice-looking boy. Everything about Kian Kelly was perfectly nice. That's what made him such an easy target for people like Flannigan.

'Hey,' he puffed. 'You didn't hear me calling you?'

Olivia kept up her pace. 'Sorry. Uh… I was thinking.'

'Oh,' Kian said, struggling to keep up with her long legs. 'Right. Well, anyway, I just wanted to say thanks. You know, for back there. Flannigan's a dick.'

'That he is.'

'I don't think anyone's ever stood up to him like that before. Ever. After you left he just stood there, staring at the door. Then he went berserk! He threw his laser pointer on the ground and screamed at us all to leave. Just as I was walking out he picked up that Lilith bust he has on his desk and drop-kicked her into the wall. Well, he tried to. I think he may have broken his foot. Anyway, it was *deadly.*'

Olivia smiled. 'Cool. Hope it hurt.'

'Yeah. Anyway, I figure I owe you a drink or something? You know, as a thanks.'

Uh oh.

Olivia shook her head. 'You don't owe me anything.'

'Sure, I do. That look on Flannigan's face was worth at least a first round. Maybe a second one too.'

'Seriously, Kian. It's fine. Forget about it.'

'Well… maybe not a drink then? Maybe lunch? There's a café just off campus. Domhnall's. They do everything. Full Irish, Spanish omelette, cakes, pastries—'

'Kian, stop,' she said, pausing.

Kian trundled on a few steps more before he realised they had stopped walking. He turned and looked at her, a hopeful smile on his perfectly nice face. Olivia knew that it wasn't going to last, because she was about to be unforgivably rude, because that's just what she did. She didn't enjoy upsetting people — she wasn't a twat — but it was easier to deal with people's disappointment at her rather than their expectations of her.

'I don't want to go for lunch with you,' she said, flatly. 'Or drinks. Or an open mic night, or whatever other thing you're about to suggest. You don't need to thank me, alright? I know what you're trying to do here, you want to start something. A friendship. Whatever. I don't know. But I'm not interested.'

Kian frowned. 'You're not interested in having friends?'

'Not really, no.'

'I was just trying to be nice.'

'Well, I don't want you to be nice to me.'

Ouch. Even she knew that was harsh. But everyone knew what happened to Icarus. Not that Olivia was arrogant enough to think of herself as the centre of the solar system, but she was certainly as destructive as the sun. Maybe more so.

Kian's forehead only creased more. 'I don't understand you. We've been in Paranormal Folklore for three years together, and you've never spoken to me. Not once. Or anyone else, as far as I know. You keep to yourself, you only speak when spoken to, and even then it's like it's too much effort. And then today you swoop in and save the day, and when I try to say thank you, you blow me off? You just go back to being the moody loner who doesn't talk to anyone? Why? I don't understand.'

Olivia started walking again. 'I never asked you to.'

Kian fell into step beside her once more. 'You want to know what I think?'

'No, but I can tell that you're going to tell me anyway.'

'This? The whole too-cool-to-care thing? It's an act. A façade. You push people away so that you don't have to let them in, because that would make you vulnerable. And the last thing that the moody loner — who spends six nights a week at the campus gym lifting dumbbells — wants, is for anyone to think that any part of her is vulnerable.'

He's kind of got you there.

'Kian, I think you're wasting your time in Paranormal Folklore. You're much better suited to psychology.'

'It wouldn't kill you, you know,' he said. He stopped walking and watched her go. 'To let people in. What's the worst that could happen from having a friend?'

You have no idea.

Olivia was no expert at makeup — not by any stretch — but she knew enough to get by. She could apply mascara without smudging black all over her nose. She could fill in her brows without looking like a cartoon character. Most importantly she could cover up her scar. An angry slash across her left cheek, curving like a waning crescent moon. A bit of foundation and powder and it was gone. Magic.

You didn't need to be particularly dolled up to get into The Betsy. As long as you had a shirt and proper shoes, that was good enough. The bar was small, and packed well over legal capacity, and the jukebox played eighties pop while the band set up on stage. The vibe was good. It always was.

Olivia made a beeline for the bar, and waved her favourite bartender over. If she had anything even close to a friend, it was Tadhg. He saw her and stopped flirting with a cute guy. He sauntered over in jeans tighter than Olivia's and dropped his elbows to the counter, his head in his perfectly manicured hands.

'The Prodigal Daughter returns,' he said.

Olivia smiled. 'I think the expression is "the Prodigal Son".'

'Nu-uh. Gilmore Girls, season six, episode nine.'

'You're so gay, it hurts.'

'So, what will it be?' he asked. 'Sex On The Beach? Pornstar Martini? Slippery Nipple?'

'Diet Coke with lemon, please.'

Tadhg rolled his eyes. 'You're so boring.'

'No, I'm just sober.'

And if you drink, you're not one hundred per cent in control.

'As a judge,' he said, filling a pint glass with draft cola. 'Why exactly do you even want to be sober anyway?'

'I like to be prepared. For anything.'

'Expect the unexpected?' he asked, popping a lemon slice into her glass and handing it over.

'And then some.'

Tadhg smiled. 'So, I heard you practically bit Flannigan's head off today?'

Olivia took a sip of her drink. 'Where'd you hear that?'

'Aoife told Niall, Niall told Cara, and Cara told me. Is it true you called him a Wankenstein?'

'Not even remotely.'

'Shame. Because he is.' He reached out and turned Olivia's necklace over in her hands. 'Sell this to me.'

'It's priceless.'

'Then give it to me.'

'Family heirloom.'

He sighed and let go. 'Your family has taste. My nanna collects thimbles.'

Olivia looked down at the necklace. It was simple, just a gold disc on a thin chain with a squiggle engraved into it.

Not a squiggle. An insignia.

'The symbol means alliance,' she said. 'My mother gave it to me. She said to remember its meaning when faced with confrontation. Alliance breeds triumph.'

'Looks kind of like a pair of titties to me.' Tadhg's gaze flickered to something over Olivia's shoulder and his eyes widened. 'Oh my God.'

Olivia stiffened. 'What? What is it?'

'Oh my *God.*'

'Tadhg, what's wrong?'

'Behind you.'

'What? What's behind me?'

'He's a ten. *Definitely* a ten. Maybe even an eleven.'

A guy.

It took everything in Olivia's power not to hit him.

'It's just a guy?' she asked.

'Total hottie.'

'So, there's nothing wrong? It's just an ordinary man?'

Tadhg snorted. 'I wouldn't call him ordinary. Oh my God, he's looking at you.'

'No, Tadhg, he's probably looking at you wondering why you're gawping at him.'

'He's coming over!'

'Brilliant.'

Tadhg looked at the guy in the seat beside Olivia who was minding his own business and smiled. 'Hey, sweetie. Why don't you show me your best banana impression?'

The guy looked up from his phone, his game of Candy Crush on pause. 'Pardon?'

Tadhg's smile dropped. 'Split.'

Before the guy could argue, Tadhg was shooing him away with his tea towel. The guy gave Olivia a confused look, and she tried to smile apologetically before glaring at her —kind of— friend.

'Did your last two brain cells die?' she snapped.

'I love it when you talk dirty to me.'

'I'm going to kill you.'

He winked at her. 'You can thank me at your wedding.'

The seat beside her was only empty for the briefest of moments before the mystery man sat down. Olivia didn't look at him, kept her angry gaze on Tadhg who was giving the new guy his best smile.

'What'll it be?' he asked. 'We have signature house cocktails. Juicy Lucy? Grow-A-Pear? Sand In The Crack?'

'Just a Diet Coke please,' said the man, his voice like liquid velvet.

Tadhg's smile disappeared. 'God, you're made for each other.'

He slung his tea towel over his shoulder and meandered off. Olivia counted how many seconds it would take before the man said hi. She got to eight.

'I think we're being set up,' he said.

Olivia huffed a laugh. 'Don't feel special, he does this every weekend.'

'I'm Roman,' he said, holding out his hand. 'Roman Wylder.'

And so it begins.

Olivia turned on her stool and met his eyes. She was pleasantly surprised. Tadhg was right, he was attractive. A shock of copper hair and green eyes. Early thirties. Leather jacket. She shook his hand.

'Olivia McQueen.'

'Nice name. Is it real?'

'I guess you'll never know.'

Tadhg returned with Roman's Diet Coke. 'Don't drink it too quickly now.'

Roman paid for his drink and offered to pay for Olivia's too, but she declined. They sipped in silence, while Tadhg looked between them, clearly unimpressed.

'So,' Roman said, putting his glass down. 'What do you do, Olivia McQueen?'

'I'm studying at DCC,' she said. 'Paranormal Folklore. Masters Degree.'

Roman arched an eyebrow. Not sceptical, but interested. 'Paranormal Folklore?'

Olivia nodded. 'The study of paranormal events and entities in folklore throughout history.'

'Sounds interesting.'

'It's alright.'

'Do you believe, then?'

Olivia frowned. 'Believe in what?'

'In paranormal events and entities?'

She smiled. 'You don't have to believe in a subject to study it.'

Roman nodded. 'True. Though it might make it more interesting.'

'True.'

'At any rate it makes my psychology degree sound boring.'

Olivia shrugged. 'Well, at least you're licenced to tell women that we all secretly want a penis.'

Roman laughed. 'God bless Freud, and his sick little brain.'

'He should have known that it's not the appendage we're after, it's the equal pay.'

'Well said.'

'That and the penis.'

Roman laughed again. It was a nice sound. Deep and smooth. West End Girls by the Petshop Boys came on the jukebox, and his smile quickly melted into a frown.

'I hate this song,' he said.

Olivia gave him a look. 'If it's eighties music you don't like, then you won't like it here. It's only ever eighties tracks.'

'The eighties are fine,' Roman said. 'It's the Petshop Boys that I hate.'

Olivia grinned. 'Blasphemy.'

'How's about a deal, Olivia McQueen?'

Olivia sipped her Coke. 'Hm?'

'If I change the song, and it's something that you like, you have to dance with me.'

Olivia considered his offer with vague interest. 'And what if it's a song I don't like?'

'Then that should be punishment enough, surely?'

Before Olivia could answer. Tadhg leaned in between them. 'She'll do it.'

Roman Wylder smiled. It was a shark's smile. It was infectious. 'Perfect.'

2.

Olivia waited until Roman was out of earshot, before grabbing Tadhg's top and growling, 'What did you do that for?'

'Firstly,' he said, uncurling her fist from his favourite shirt. 'This is assault. You're assaulting me right now. I could press charges and then you'd be completely friendless, which would be, obviously, a travesty. Secondly, you were *vibing* with him.'

'I was not.'

'You were. You were already considering his offer.'

'I was humouring him.'

'You like him.'

You do kinda like him.

'*You* like him,' she snapped.

Nice.

Tadhg sighed. 'Liv. Honey. Baby. Listen to me. It's been a long time since Cillian.'

Olivia closed her eyes. She didn't want to think about Cillian. She nodded. 'I know.'

'You've got to move on.'

Olivia opened her eyes when she was sure she wasn't going to tear up. 'I have moved on.'

'Shutting down doesn't mean you're moving on. The only way to get over trauma is to confront it. Talk about it.'

'I know.'

Tadhg laid a hand over hers. 'It was an accident.'

No it wasn't.

'It's not your fault.'

Yes. It is.

'Nobody blames you.'

Because they don't know the truth.

Tadhg pulled away from her and nodded over her shoulder. 'Hottie McHotcakes is coming back. Be nice, Olivia McQueen, or I'll make your life hell.'

Already there.

Olivia turned and saw Roman smiling. To her surprise, she smiled back.

'What did you pick?' she asked.

'You'll see.'

West End Girls finished up with its last few robotic chords on the synthesiser. There was a hesitation before the next song queued up. There always was. The jukebox was older than The Betsy itself. Then, *As The World Falls Down* by David Bowie came on. Olivia's mouth fell open. Her parents had danced to that at their wedding.

God rest their souls.

'How did I do?' Roman asked.

'Suspiciously well,' Olivia replied.

He shrugged. 'I have a knack for these things.'

Tadhg appeared at Olivia's shoulder, like she'd grown a second head. 'Do you have a knack for anything else?'

Olivia swatted him away. Roman held out his hand and raised his eyebrows. When Olivia didn't immediately take it, Tadhg gave her a not-so-subtle shove. Olivia toppled off her stool and grabbed Roman's hand to steady her. She threw a nasty look at Tadhg as she was led away to the pathetically small dance floor.

It wasn't until Roman reached for her waist, hesitating, waiting for approval, that Olivia realised this was a slow dance.

'We could two-step?' Roman offered. 'Madison?'

Olivia didn't answer. Instead, she squared her shoulders, looped her arms around his neck, and stepped in close. His hands settled on her hips, and they danced. He was a good dancer. He had rhythm.

You know what they say about men who have rhythm.

'I know exactly what you're thinking,' Roman said.

Olivia tilted her head. 'Very much doubt it.'

'You're scoping out the exits,' he said. 'Checking to see if you have a clear path to safety in case this all suddenly goes wrong.'

Seriously, is this guy a mind reader?

Olivia didn't reply, just watched him with a guarded expression.

Roman smiled. 'Sorry. I used to be a self-defence instructor. I can spot a fellow fighter when I see one. We have a… way. What did you train in?'

'Brazilian jiu-jitsu,' she said. 'And don't take it personally. I always check my escape routes when mysterious men ask me to dance.'

'Happens often does it?'

'Actually, no.'

Roman surprised her by lifting her right arm and spinning her before pulling her back in. 'Their loss.'

Olivia smiled, but something over his shoulder caught her eye. Her feet fumbled. It was *him*. The actual guy she'd been hoping to find tonight. The man she'd been stalking for weeks. The one she'd been vetting. The man she was going to kill.

He glanced up, saw her looking at him, and quickly looked away, backing into the crowd. Olivia's arms fell loose around Roman's shoulders.

Don't lose him, Liv.

Roman looked at her, cocking an eyebrow. 'Everything okay?'

'Ladies' room,' she said, excusing herself.

He went to speak, but she didn't give him the chance. She untangled herself from Roman's arms and weaved her way through the dancefloor. Following her prey. The man peeked over his shoulder, saw Olivia following him, and picked up his pace. So did she.

Does he think we can't walk any faster? Is he dumb?

He tried to lose her by ducking out through the side exit that the band were using, but she had keen eyes. She followed and stepped through the door just in time to see him disappear around the side of the building into an alleyway.

Ah. A trap.

'He's so smart,' Olivia mumbled.

Isn't he just?

Olivia squared her shoulders and continued.

Ditch the jacket. It's too restricting.

Olivia obliged and let her jacket drape over a wheelie bin as she passed. She turned the corner, anticipating the ambush that was coming. She ducked a sloppy punch to the head, and as she came up, brought an elbow with it that rocked her assailant's world. He stumbled, putting enough distance between them for Olivia's heel to connect with his breastbone, and the man went sprawling. She followed.

The man held up his hands in surrender.

Why do they always wait until they're on the floor to surrender?

'Cormac O'Connor?' she asked.

Cormac looked up at her. 'Yes, you know I am.'

'Tidy. Just checking. I've come here to kill you.'

Cormac blinked. 'What?'

'Are you deaf as well as stupid?' she asked. 'I'm here to *kill* you, Cormac.'

24

'Why?'

'You know why.'

'I actually don't, though.'

Olivia stepped forward, and Cormac scrambled back through the dirt. 'Alright! Alright!'

'Why do you guys always play dumb first?' she asked, genuinely interested. 'You know what you've done. You know that *I* know what you've done. Why all the preamble?'

'Maybe we think of it like foreplay?'

'Yeah, because men are so good at that.'

'Can I at least stand up?'

Olivia considered it. Then said, 'No.'

'Why not?'

'Murderers don't get to stand up.'

'They don't?'

'Not around me, they don't.'

Cormac sighed. 'Look, do you even have any proof?'

Olivia held up her hand and showed him her palm. His name was carved into her flesh, fresh and raw but not bleeding. Cormac nodded, and she smiled and let her arm drop down again.

'Devil's debt,' he said. 'Not much arguing with that, is there?'

'Not really.'

'Can I ask you one thing, though? Before you do it?'

'Go ahead.'

'How did you know I was a demon?' he asked.

Olivia smiled. 'Intuition.'

'Come on. Have you been watching me? Spying?'

'A little.'

'Do I have a tell?'

'Kinda.'

'Was it when I ate that baby?'

She nodded. 'That was my first clue.'

'What about when I ate that other baby?'

'That was my second.'

Cormac sighed. 'Well, no point hiding it anymore.'

Olivia agreed, 'Probably not.'

Cormac changed. His skin turned as black as his coal, red veins blossoming beneath it, like lines of magma flowing through rock. From his sloping forehead, two horns sprouted, bursting through the skin and curling round on themselves. His nails fell off, making way for his talons that grew in, long and sharp, and his teeth lengthened into fangs. Last to change were his eyes. A flicker, and then they were completely red. He rose to his haunches, a good two feet taller than he was previously, and grinned.

Olivia took great joy in watching that smile disappear as she did the exact same thing. Her skin was the colour of fresh blood, dotted with black scales over her softer spots like chainmail. Her eyes blacked out, little charcoal veins spreading from their corners and blossoming across her cheeks. Her incisors had elongated into fangs that protruded over her crimson lower lip when she smiled. And she did smile. Because that *I've shit my pants* expression on grown men literally never got old. Especially when she showed them her horns, which were always bigger than theirs.

Why do they never expect that either?

'Are you alright?' Olivia asked. 'You look like you've seen a ghost.'

He blinked. 'You're... a demon too.'

'You have good eyesight.'

He licked his lips. A pause. Then, 'This is the part where you run away.'

Olivia tilted her head. 'Are you quoting *Shrek*?'

'I'm going to kill you.'

'You can *try* if it makes you feel better.'

For the second time that night, Cormac lunged at her. For the second time, she dodged. She slapped his arm away, stepped in, and landed a punch to his gut. Winded him. He doubled over and she clamped her hands together and brought them down on his neck in a double fist. He dropped to his knees and his face collided with her knee. His nose exploded, blood drenching his face.

Olivia lifted her foot and booted him, and he fell back onto his ass. She kicked him again and he skidded right back to where he originally was. His hands clutched at his face, at where his once straight nose had been, howling.

'You broke my nose!' he squealed. 'You broke my nose, you bitch!'

'Flattery will get you nowhere,' she said, reaching down to her boots and slipping the dagger free. It was an ugly thing. A sharp blade and a gnarled black handle. It did the job, though. 'Any last words?'

'You bitch!' Cormac spat. 'You bitch! You stupid, ugly, *bitch*!'

'Come on now, only one of those is true.'

'I'm going to kill you! I'm—'

Olivia opened her palm and let the dagger do the rest. It trembled in her grip for a moment, then shot out of her hand and plunged itself deep into Cormac's neck. Olivia watched his eyes bulge in surprise. He tried to speak — probably to call her a bitch again — but all that came out was a gurgle. His hands wandered from his busted nose and reached for Olivia. He swiped at her through the air, like a cat playing with string, and then they fell by his sides. Dead.

A few moments later he evaporated, leaving nothing but ash in his wake, and the dagger clattered to the ground. Olivia watched it for a few moments. Hoping it would disappear. Hoping her debt would be cleared. But nothing happened.

She sighed and fetched the obnoxious thing, stuffed it back into the hidden slot in her boot. She counted down from ten, felt herself calming, returning to her normal self. She turned to head back into The Betsy—

—and saw Roman watching her from the street, mouth agape.

Oh shit.

3.

You have to kill him.

'Shut up,' Olivia murmured.

He saw you.

'I know.'

He saw what you did.

'Yeah, I know.'

And now he thinks you're talking to yourself.

'Why is he just standing there? Why isn't he running away?'

I think he's frozen.

'Good. Frozen is good.'

Olivia put on her warmest smile. She gave Roman a little wave, and when he didn't bolt, she dared to stroll over. She stopped a few feet back, keeping that kind, well-rehearsed smile fixed into place. Roman just stood there, unblinking. An uncomfortable silence fell.

'So,' she said. 'You're probably wondering what you just saw there.'

No response.

Get rid of him, Liv.

Olivia cleared her throat and tried again. 'I can explain everything.'

Roman blinked. 'You killed a guy.'

She nodded. 'Yes. Yes, I did.'

'You stabbed him.'

'That's right.'

'And then he disappeared.'

'Poof.'

'You were like a… a…'

'Monster?' she suggested.

He nodded again. 'Yeah.'

'Well, actually, I'm a demon.'

'Oh.'

'You're taking this all remarkably well.'

'I think I might faint.'

Olivia pulled a face. 'You're pretty tall, that would be a long drop.'

'Am I in shock?'

'Quite possibly.'

'I feel like I'm going to start panicking.'

'I'd really rather you didn't.'

Roman looked down at his hands. They were shaking. 'I'm doing it. I'm panicking.'

'Please don't.'

The shakes intensified. 'Oh God, I'm freaking out.'

Olivia took a step forward, 'Roman, listen—'

Roman held out his shaking hands and stumbled back. 'Stay away from me!'

'I'm not going to hurt you!'

'Yeah, I'm sure Ted Bundy used to say that all the time.'

Olivia frowned. 'You're comparing me to Ted Bundy?'

'Who would you prefer? Jeffrey Dahmer? John Wayne Gacy? Buffalo Bill?'

'That last guy wasn't real.'

He stopped and looked at her. 'You're a murderer.'

'It's not like that.'

'You kill people. That makes you a murderer.'

'Honestly, there's more to it than that.'

Roman's hands went to his head. 'Oh my God, I'm going to be sick. I'm going to throw up. And you're probably going to kill me to keep me quiet. Then I'll just be lying here, dead, in my own sick.'

Liv, put the man out of his misery.

She shook her head. There was another way.

Oh, come on! That hardly ever works.

It was worth a try.

So was caviar, but we're never trying that again either.

It could work.

Strongly disagree.

Olivia let out a big sigh, then said. 'Roman Wylder, stop panicking.'

He wasn't listening. He was still babbling to himself.

Told you.

She tried again. 'Roman Wylder, stop panicking right now.'

Roman stopped talking.

Well, shit.

Olivia let out a long breath she hadn't realised she'd been holding. 'Roman Wylder, you will remain calm.'

Roman looked at her, wide-eyed, and nodded. 'I am very calm.'

'Good. You are very relaxed.'

He nodded again. 'Yes, I am.'

Olivia took a deep breath. 'You didn't see anything here tonight. You came outside for some fresh air. You didn't see me. You didn't talk to me. Nothing unusual happened, okay?'

Roman smiled. 'Pretty uneventful night, to be honest.'

'Yes, it was. Now you're going to go home, go to sleep, and forget all about me. Don't remember my name. Don't remember my face.'

Roman's smile melted into a frown. 'Who are you?'

'Perfect. Roman Wylder, goodnight.'

The smile was immediately back. He gave a little wave before turning and strolling away, hands in his pockets. Olivia was amazed to hear him whistling *West End Girls* without a care in the world.

That was a close one.

Olivia nodded. Far too close, indeed.

Olivia's flat was nothing shy of dilapidated. A student loan and a zero-hours contract at the student union could hardly set you up for anything greater than a crap-shack in inner-city Dublin. And a crap-shack it definitely was. The front door needed a kick to open, and a miracle to lock. Mould festered in the corners on the ceiling, and the brown carpet looked as though it may have once been white.

We need to move.

'We have no money,' Olivia said, heading to the kitchen.

You should start charging people for demon hunting.

'You know I can't.'

Because it's morally wrong?

'No, because I'm repaying a Devil's debt.'

Oh yeah.

Olivia chose not to think about how talking to an imaginary voice in her head that was probably, most likely, definitely not there was not exactly a paragon of a healthy and sound mind. She chose not to think about how this voice had been with her for as long as she could remember, or about how, when she mentioned it to her parents as a child, they had exchanged worried looks and then told her *not* to worry about it. About how, in her teens, therapists had told her it was most likely a sign of psychosis or something similar. And she *definitely* did not think about how it was her longest, oldest, and truest friend.

And whenever she accidentally *did* think about how talking to a made-up voice in her head was probably a bit Not Good — capital N, capital G — she gave herself an exception. She was a demon. Well, *half* demon. She had a soul, after all. It was expected for her to have a few quirks. Having a conscience that actually voiced itself in her head like having headphones in and cranked up to full volume at all times, was another one of her little peculiarities. Besides, it had always been there for her. Where most people turned away, the voice turned towards her. Guided her. Comforted her. In a way, it was like self-soothing. Home therapy. And most likely, absolutely nothing to worry about.

She hoped.

Olivia wrenched open the fridge door, nose wrinkling as the awful fridge smell hit her. The starkness of the shelves made her frown.

'When did I last go shopping?'

Two weeks ago.

'Ah.' A pause. 'Pizza?'

Pizza.

As much as she wanted to order from Dominos, the moths in her wallet were not so keen, and so Olivia ordered from the local pizzeria. *Eatily.* She didn't know what made her cringe more, the name or the one-star reviews on the *Chomp* app. Nevertheless, she ordered something called a "Mighty Meaty," took to her lumpy sofa, and put on the latest episode of *Crime Line*.

The pizza was going on fifteen minutes late when the doorbell rang. Olivia leapt from the sofa with enthusiasm that she could only ever muster for a food delivery. She raked through the dish on the table by the door and counted out €8.50 then rounded it up to €10 for a measly tip.

You can't afford to give a tip.

'But the nice man is bringing me pizza.'

She braced herself for small talk and opened the door. To her surprise, she found Roman Wylder looking at her, eyes wide.

Uh oh.

Before she could speak, he came crashing over the threshold. His arm shot out, launching a palm into her chin. She staggered back, and he swung for her again. She stepped in, arms braced over her head, and absorbed the blow before it even had time to gain momentum. She wrapped one arm around his, and her free hand sent hammer fists into Roman's face. Once. Twice.

On the third time, he caught her hand in his and twisted. Olivia yelped and her grip loosened, and Roman was able to untangle his arm from hers and crack an elbow into the side of her head. The world swam for a few moments and Roman grabbed her, wrapped her up in a clinch. Olivia squirmed, turning in his grip and used the momentum to throw him over her hip. He landed on his back with a thud and she immediately mounted him, keeping her head low, wrapping him in a headlock. She tried to pin his arms down with her knees, but he thrashed beneath her and wrenched them free.

Pain rocked through her side as he landed punch after punch in her ribs. Sweat beading on her brow, she tried to manoeuvre him into an Americana armlock. A dislocated shoulder would slow him down — or at least she hoped it would. The blows to her ribcage stopped for a blissful moment, giving her head just enough time to clear for her to realise that wasn't a good thing.

She saw the knife right before she felt it slide between her ribs. She screamed before she even felt the pain, and when it hit her, she screamed some more. Beneath her, Roman bucked his hips and easily rolled Olivia off him. This time, he mounted her. She tried to crunch up, tried to hide her head against his chest so he couldn't hit her, but her ribs screamed at her when she moved. He pinned her down.

'Who are you?' she screamed.

'Never you mind,' he replied.

Roman gave what Olivia could only describe as a perfectly polite smile before curling his hand into a fist. He reeled his arm back, ready to let her see stars.

Your necklace, Liv! Tell him that you sire him!

Without questioning, Olivia grasped the necklace at her throat and held it out to him.

'I sire you!' she shouted, having no idea what it meant. 'I sire you!'

Roman's eyes grew wide, his face falling flat. His fist uncurled and his arm dropped to his side.

'Oh shit,' he said.

4.

O livia and Roman stared at each other for the longest time. Nothing was said. Olivia was fully aware of the throb in her side, but equally aware that it was already healing. Demon blood was both a curse and — on occasion — a blessing.

'Shit,' he repeated.

With all her force, Olivia bucked her hips upwards sending Roman flying forwards. His hands shot out to catch himself and Olivia wrapped her legs around his waist. She wrapped one arm around his and flipped them both. Suddenly she was on top, brandishing her necklace at him like a weapon.

Roman blinked. 'Shit.'

'Start talking, Irish boy.'

Roman swallowed. 'Do you have any idea what you've just done?'

'Do you have any idea who you just stabbed?'

'Do *you*?'

Her brow furrowed. 'Talk. Now.'

Roman shrimped out of Olivia's grip, toppled her and sat back. She glared at him, sitting up. They stayed like that on her filthy carpet, watching each other like vipers, waiting to see who would strike first.

'Who the fuck are you?' she asked.

'Roman Wylder.'

'And *what* the fuck are you?'

'A demon,' he said. 'Like you.'

'*Half* demon,' she corrected.

He snorted. 'Sure.'

Her jaw tightened. 'How would you know?'

'I do my homework,' he said, getting up.

Olivia sprang to her feet, arms already up in a fencing stance. 'Stay the fuck still.'

Roman arched an eyebrow. 'I'm just standing up.'

'You don't get to decide what you're doing until you tell me what the fuck you're doing here.'

Roman leaned back against the sofa, crossing his arms. He looked so infuriatingly nonchalant. Olivia wanted to hit him again.

'I came here to abduct you,' he said, very matter-of-factly.

She *really* wanted to hit him. 'Why?'

'Someone is paying me to.'

Olivia grabbed a dish from the side table and threw it at him. He barely dodged.

'Fuck you!' she shouted.

Roman glared. 'Fuck me? Fuck *you*! That would have hurt!'

'More than being stabbed?'

Ask who sent him, Liv.

'Who sent you?' she asked. 'Who's paying you?'

'We're not on a first name basis.'

Olivia snatched up the fruit bowl from the coffee table and hurled it at him. He ducked.

'Will you stop that?' he snapped.

'Names!' she barked. 'Now!'

Roman uncrossed his arms and stuffed his hands into his pockets. 'They call themselves the Brotherhood. They're a fanatical group of wannabe Satanists devout about bringing forth the end of the world by Awakening the long dormant hell-beast inside the Wicked One.'

'What the fuck has that got to do with me?' Olivia asked.

Roman cocked an eyebrow. '*You're* the Wicked One.'

There was a long pause. Then she laughed. 'Wow. You're funny. You're fucking *hilarious*.'

'It's the truth,' he said. 'Well, as far as they're concerned. They've sent me to retrieve you so they can worship you. Or sacrifice you. Or something. I don't know, I wasn't paying attention. Basically there's a Big Bad living in your head and they want it out.'

Olivia was strong but she doubted she could throw a coffee table at him. Instead she said, 'You're a psychopath.'

'What's your point?'

'Am I going to have to explain to you how that's one hundred percent *not* going to happen?'

'Well not anymore,' Roman said, nodding to the necklace at her throat. 'Thanks to that.'

Olivia blindly reached to touch it. Her mother's words echoed somewhere in the back of her mind. *Alliance means triumph.* She looked up at Roman and didn't say anything. Slowly, a smile crept across his annoyingly calm face.

'You don't know what that is, do you?' he asked.

'Shut up.'

Great comeback, Liv.

'How much do you even know about your heritage?' he asked. 'You *are* a demon, after all.'

'*Half* demon.'

'And yet you don't know what a sigillum is?'

They watched each other in a silent stalemate. Finally Roman sighed and crossed his arms again.

'That little trinket you hold there, is beyond ancient and equally as binding as a Devil's debt,' he said, taking on a TV commercial narrator tone. 'In the Infernal realm a sigillum was used to owe favours between demons. When presented with one, the demon is sired to do the wearer's bidding for seventy-two hours. One time usage only. Failure to comply ensures punishment. Eventually they were wiped out because they were being used more and more for blackmail. Side effects may include itching, diarrhoea, blindness and death. Consult your GP before use.'

Olivia blinked. Two of her few-and-far-between talents were pretending not to be shocked when receiving shocking news, and pretending not to be confused when she had absolutely no idea what was going on. Which, right then, covered about everything Roman had said. And even she was having a hard time keeping her face neutral. Because, what the fuck? She didn't feel anywhere near important enough or well versed enough on her own species to be trusted with something so important. And yet, her mum had left it with her anyway.

A horrible idea really.

Truly, *spectacularly* horrible. And, of course, instead of admitting that she had very little to absolutely no idea what any of that even meant, she indignantly lifted her chin and said, 'What do you mean *sired?*'

'Exactly that. For the next 72 hours I'm all yours, otherwise it's curtains for me.' He smiled, but it was hollow. 'Make the most of it, because once it's up I'm hauling you to the Brotherhood and asking for double my pay.'

Olivia needed to sit down. The backs of her legs hit the armchair and she sunk down into the uncomfortable couch cushions. She braced her hands on her knees and folded over, taking in a deep breath.

Don't freak out.

'Did you know about this?' she murmured.

Liv...

'Did you?'

Yes.

'Is he telling the truth? Am I this… Wicked One?'

Maybe? Possibly? I don't know?

Roman cleared his throat. 'Who… uh… who are you talking to?'

Olivia held a hand up but didn't look at him. 'Be quiet.'

He's telling the truth about the sigillum. He's essentially your bitch for the next three days.

'So what do I do with him?'

Well…

Olivia groaned and sat up. Roman had joined her, sitting in the armchair opposite. He tilted his head quizzically.

'Talk to yourself often, do you?' he asked.

'You're mine for the next three days?' she asked.

'I am.'

'For anything I want?'

'I draw the line at pegging, but essentially yes.'

Olivia pulled a face. 'I can't believe I thought you were cute.'

'Of course you did,' Roman said, pulling out his phone and typing. 'Don't feel too bad. I wanted you to like me — to trust me — so I was my most charming self.'

'That's sick. What are you doing?' she asked.

'Setting an alarm seventy-two hours from now. So I'll know exactly when to turn you in.'

'Wow, I actually think I hate you.'

Roman put his phone away. 'Love me or hate me, I'm all yours. Now what do you want to do with me?'

Olivia stood and stepped closer to him. 'Okay. Okay, here's what we're going to do. You're going to help me find a way to stop these assholes that want to sacrifice me.'

Roman snorted. 'I'll bite. What's your big plan?'

'You're going to help me with that too. Consider yourself my Mr Miyagi and bodyguard for the next three days.'

He frowned. 'You realise Mr Miyagi wasn't a life coach?'

'Fine. You're my Obi Wan.'

'Have you *ever* seen a movie?'

Olivia jabbed a finger at his chest. He was unsurprisingly rock solid beneath his shirt. Demon bodies had a certain durability that put mortals and their soft bellies to shame. Olivia thought that it should be some kind of a crime that someone could be so objectively attractive while simultaneously also being so objectively fucking awful. It messed with the stereotypes that *Disney* had instilled in her as a kid that all evil-doers had to look as ugly on the outside as they were on the inside. This man was just... unfair.

'Here's the plan, fuck-head,' she said. 'We're going to leave here. This place is compromised and surrounded by innocents that I want to keep out of the crossfire. You're going to take me somewhere safe — somewhere that you *trust* — and we are going to sit down and plan what to do. And then we're going to do it. Questions?'

Olivia was surprised at her own decisiveness. The assuredness in her tone. Because she absolutely, positively did not feel decisive or self-assured in the slightest. She actually felt a little bit sick. And stupid. How had she not known any of this? How had she let herself get compromised into a situation where she was making bargains with a stranger who had just tried to kill her? Plus, she was also really fucking annoyed at herself for maybe, potentially, *possibly* thinking that he was an okay guy at The Betsy. Wow.

Not your best judge of character, I'll give you that.

Roman tilted his head. 'You really thought I was cute?'

Olivia gave him a hard shove that barely moved him. 'I want these people dead, understand me? Or as good as. They think I'm some sort of messiah? Well, they're wrong. I'm Olivia Fucking McQueen, and once we're done flaying these bastards alive, you and I are going to go our separate ways and never cross paths again. And if we do, I'm going to kill you on the spot. Understand?'

Roman's mouth twitched up into a smile. 'Understood.'

There was a shuffle behind them and the sound of someone clearing their throat. Olivia looked over her shoulder sharply to see an almost prepubescent pizza delivery boy at her door. His eyes were wide, his mouth agape. For a long stretch there was silence. Then Roman broke into a friendly smile.

'Hi,' he said, raising his hand in greeting.

The pizza boy dropped the box he was holding and ran away. Olivia blinked. She turned back to Roman in time to see his smile drop, his face settling back into utter indifference.

Bloody psychopath.

'Alright,' she said. 'Let's go.'

Roman's car was not what Olivia expected. She didn't know what she was expecting — perhaps a motorbike to match his leather jacket — but she found herself, nonetheless, in the passenger seat of a matte black Mercedes G Class with tinted windows. Not the most inconspicuous car in the world, but she admired the way other cars on the road yielded for it.

A mouse isn't going to play chicken with an elephant.

Olivia nodded. 'True.'

Roman glanced at her. 'You talk to yourself a lot.'

She frowned. 'I never talk to myself.'

'Then who are you talking to?'

'My inner monologue.'

Roman kept a straight face. 'And people call *me* a psychopath.'

Olivia turned in her seat to look at him. His profile was annoyingly perfect.

Yeah, so was Patrick Bateman's.

'Tell me about the Brotherhood,' she said. 'Everything you know.'

Roman sighed as he followed a sign for Dublin city centre. 'Can't we listen to the radio?'

'Talk. Now.'

'Very well,' he took a deep breath. 'The Brotherhood are a group of right-wing white supremacists and self-proclaimed Satanists. It started originally with just a few, none of them actually brothers, and over time they've obtained a cult following. They've dedicated their entire lives to seeking out the Wicked One so they can free their messiah from her captive bonds and usher in a new apocalypse.'

'Well, they *sound* delightful,' Olivia said. 'And how did they come to the conclusion that I'm their messiah?'

'As far as I'm aware you strike an incredible likeness to the one they've been looking for.'

'Seems legit. I don't suppose I could tell them that they've got the wrong girl? Or that that's not how Satanism works?'

'They have their ideals and their messiah and they're sticking to them,' Roman said, exiting the motorway and pulling onto a B road. 'At least they're consistent.'

'Brownie points for that,' she mumbled.

A few minutes of silence ticked by where Olivia watched Dublin city build up slowly around them. Firstly the outskirts: a mish-mash of council flats, side streets, and graffitied shop fronts. This slowly gave way to wider streets, housing estates, mini-supermarkets, and schools. Then they were in the city. The traffic ground to a jarring halt as the roads — not built to handle this many cars — were packed with green busses, tacsai cabs, and tourists. The suburban world fell away and in its place reared up a pseudo-London, forced clumsily into Irish culture, neither needed nor wanted but there all the same.

Georgian architecture tried its best to obliterate any traces of the charming medieval city Dublin had once been before England had rudely interrupted. But you could still see it there in smatterings: the Liffey river, the Ha'Penny Bridge, Dublin castle. And most of all in Temple Bar, which seemed to be where they were heading.

Olivia looked at Roman. 'Who the hell are you?' she asked.

Roman looked at her. 'Are you sure that's a hill you want to die on?'

'Absolutely.'

He hesitated. Then said, 'I'm a serial killer.'

Olivia looked at him for the longest time. She blinked. 'No, really.'

'Really.'

What?

'What?' Roman turned off the humming city streets and onto a much narrower road. 'I kill people. Serially.'

Olivia frowned. 'That's not funny.'

'I am aware.'

She paused. 'You're being serious.'

'Why would you think that I'm not?'

Olivia stared at him for a very long moment. Then said, 'I think that is something you should have told me earlier.'

'Would it have really changed anything?'

'Hugely.'

Roman pulled up in a side street and cut the engine. Olivia recognised the narrow passage and knew the main square of Temple Bar was just down the road and around the corner. They walked in silence and Olivia hugged her jacket tighter around her bracing against the cold Dublin breeze.

Roman shrugged out of his coat and offered it to her. She declined.

Why'd you do that? It's cold!

She marched on, teeth chattering.

Midweek and gone midnight, and the city was ready to party. It didn't seem to matter what time of the day, or what day of the week it was, it was always a party in Dublin city. Live music carried down the cobblestones, accompanied with shouts, laughter, and tuneless singing.

They turned a corner and Temple Bar opened up before them in all its charmingly quaint glory. A main square, boxed by pubs on all sides, thrummed with people spilling from one bar into the next. Live music blared from each establishment, and buskers performed on the square, struggling to be overheard by the merry crowd. It all blurred into one ear splitting cacophony. And yet, it somehow worked.

Roman led the way through the square and into an alleyway that had always reminded Olivia of *Harry Potter*. It felt like she was walking through Diagon Alley. The ground was uneven, and the buildings on either side slumped into each other, almost creating a tunnel. They came out on another side into a much quieter dead end. Only a few people milled about, and they were far less jovial to say the least.

Olivia had only been back here a few times, and then it was just usually to corner someone on her list. She had never taken much notice of the narrow, slightly slanted, building in the North West corner. It looked like it had been in a fire long ago, the wood and stone charred black. The windows were boarded up and a sign on the door read "closed permanently." Over that, hanging on a shamrock shaped signpost jutting out from the masonry:

Shenanigans

Roman knocked on the door and for a long moment, nothing happened. Then the door inched open a crack. Olivia couldn't see the person on the other side but she could tell from his tone that he wasn't especially happy to see him.

'What the hell do you want?' the gruff voice said.

Roman smiled. 'Hello, old friend.'

'I'm not your friend, Wylder.'

'Very well,' Roman replied, not at all offended. 'My associate and I are looking for a place to stay the night.'

'You've got a flat. Use it.'

'Somewhere secure.'

'Not interested.'

The door started to close but Roman put his hand out to stop it. His other hand fished out something from his coat pocket and showed it to the innkeeper. It was a small coin, the size of a euro, thin and brass. There was a long silence. Then the door swung open and the light of the streetlamp fell across the man's face. Or what was left of it.

He stepped aside to let them in and the shadows eclipsed him again. Roman beckoned her to follow, and the darkness of the building swallowed them whole. Olivia's body tensed, ready to spring into action at any moment.

There was a soft clicking sound, then a hum, and the lights overhead flickered to half-life. Much to her surprise, Shenanigans was — to put it delicately — a dive bar. One that had come and gone a long time ago, by the looks of it. There had been a fire; that much was obvious. It was as if the place had been poisoned and now it was rotting from the inside out. Semi-new furniture had been added to try and dress the place up a little, but it was the equivalent, in Olivia's opinion, of hanging a used condom on a gallery wall and calling it art.

Olivia looked round to see Roman looking irritatingly indifferent. Her stomach rolled at the sight of the man standing next to him. Half of his face was gone. An almost perfect line traced down his face, splitting it in two halves. The right side was normal. Handsome, even.

But the left side was disfigured with angry scars. He reminded Olivia of a Ken doll with a partially melted face. Only his mouth seemed unafflicted — perfectly ordinary on both sides.

Harvey Dent comes to mind...

The man scowled. 'Something you'd like to say?'

Olivia shook her head. 'Not particularly.'

'Good,' he said.

The man looked at Roman and held his hand out. Roman placed the coin into his palm with a smile. The man grunted, pocketed the coin and turned. He strode out a door behind the bar, slamming it shut after him. Olivia wondered if the rest of the building was as sad as this room.

'Well,' Roman said. 'That was Alastair Knox.'

Olivia turned to him. 'Why does he hate you?'

Roman frowned. 'He doesn't hate me.'

'Well, he sure as shit wasn't happy to see you.'

'Very few people are.'

'Shocking,' she said, crossing her arms and looking around the building. 'What is this place?'

'It used to be Alastair's pub before the fire,' Roman said, walking behind the bar and helping himself to a can of Diet Coke and passing another to Olivia. 'Now it's an inn for irreputable scallywags like myself.'

'A B&B for demons?' she asked.

'Minus the breakfast, yes.'

Olivia sat on a creaky barstool and looked up at Roman. 'Is that how his face got like that? The fire?'

'Yes and no. Actually, it was kind of my fault.'

'Why am I not surprised?'

'It was an accident. A job gone awry. He doesn't like to talk about it though, and I choose to respect his wishes.'

'Convenient.' She paused. 'What was that coin you gave him?'

Roman crossed his arms and lent forward on the bar, bringing himself and Olivia face to face. 'You ask a lot of questions.'

Olivia tilted her head. 'You deflect even more.'

Roman smiled. 'A token. A promise of one killing by yours truly, no questions asked, to be used whenever the gifted should so please.'

'So you just gave Alastair an I.O.U. for murder?'

'Yes. And when I finish the job he gives it back.'

'Your currency is killing?'

'I prefer to call them favours, but sure.'

Olivia watched him for a long moment, searching his eyes for a trace of the warm, funny, sweet guy she had met earlier that night. She came up blank.

'How do you do it?' she asked. 'The way you were at The Betsy tonight. You just turn it on and off like your humanity has a switch.'

Roman shrugged. 'I'm a good study. I watch people.'

'You said you'd been doing your homework on me,' Olivia paused, not sure if she wanted to know the answer to the question she was about to ask. 'Have you been watching me?'

Roman cocked an eyebrow. 'Would you like it if I *had* been watching you?'

'No.'

Liar.

Roman took a sip of his Coke. 'Olivia Ivy McQueen. Born in Canterbury, Kent and promptly abandoned by your god-fearing Christian parents when they realised you were cursed with demon blood. Maybe you spoke backwards, maybe you burped fire. Who knows? You stayed in foster care until you were adopted by Lorna and Jackson McQueen, both demon hunters and paranormal investigators.

Seeing that you weren't fully a demon, they took pity on you and decided to raise you to fight on their side. One of the *good* guys.

'Flash forward eight years, you were orphaned at the age of ten after a tragic car accident. Your father swerved off Nelson's Bridge and your car plummeted into the river. You were the only survivor. Without any other family members alive, you were sent to live with your godfather: Russell Hall. At age sixteen you moved out and hopped from one hostel to another while you studied history at Canterbury Community College. Once you were eighteen and you had your qualifications, you moved to Ireland to start afresh.

'By day you are standoffish, stoic, no-nonsense Olivia McQueen — just your average Master's degree student who spends six nights a week at the gym training and punching dummies. By night, you turn into Olivia McQueen: demon hunter. Fuelled not only by your need to do right by your dearly departed mammy and daddy, but by that mark on your palm. A Devil's debt if I'm not mistaken? Tell me — am I getting *any* of this right?'

For a long moment Olivia did nothing. Then she hit him with all her might, her knuckles cracking as they made contact with Roman's jaw. He barely staggered and she went to hit him again, but he caught her fist in his hand and gave her a scalding look.

'I won't be much use to you if I'm unconscious,' he said, evenly.

'You're a sick bastard, you know that?' she said.

'So you keep telling me.'

Olivia wrenched her fist out of his grasp and inspected her hand. Not quite broken. Even if it was, it would heal. Bloody hurt though. Roman rifled around in the freezer and found a bag of ice. He wrapped it in a dirty rag from the bar and offered it out to Olivia.

'A peace offering,' he said. 'We stop hitting each other. For the next seventy-one hours and thirty-five minutes at least. Deal?'

Olivia grudgingly took the ice pack and gently rested it against her hand. She groaned in both pain and relief. She looked up at Roman and resisted the urge to hit him with her good hand. Instead, she nodded.

'Deal,' she mumbled. 'Until your timer goes off. Then I'm killing you.'

Roman smiled. 'Not if I kill you first.'

5.

Olivia couldn't sleep. Sleeping seemed so banal after everything that had happened. And every hour she spent sleeping on the rock-hard bed in the matchbox-sized room in Shenanigans was an hour of Roman's forced loyalty to her wasted.

She looked at the time on her phone and saw it was 4:13am. She groaned, covered her face with her hands and sat up.

You're not going to be able to sleep all the while you're worrying about not being asleep.

'Yes, thank you. I do realise that.'

Have a walk. Make a cup of tea.

Olivia nodded. Tea and a little plod around the bar would help her. It *had* to help her. If she didn't sleep tonight then she would never be ready for Roman's plan tomorrow — whatever that was. Part of her was dreading to find out.

She rolled out of bed, slipped her trainers on, and padded downstairs. Shenanigans, it turned out, was three stories high. The ground floor was the bar, the first floor had the rooms for paying customers, and the top floor was Alastair's home. Only the bar remained as it was since the fire. The upper floors had been returned to their former, debatable glory.

Olivia reached the bar and fumbled around blindly for the light switch. There was a hum and a flicker as the ground floor grudgingly came to life. She nearly screamed at the sight of the man sitting at the bar. Alastair however, looked at her, one eyebrow cocked.

'You can scream if it makes you feel better,' he said.

Olivia took a deep breath and willed her heart to sink back down into her chest where it belonged. 'Sorry. I thought it would be empty down here.'

'So did I,' he mumbled.

'Oh. Right. I can go.'

She turned to leave, but stopped as Alastair stood up. He walked around to the other side of the bar, slung a dirty tea towel over his shoulder and watched her.

'What'll you have?' he asked.

Gratefully, she took a seat. 'Tea please. Milk, two sugars.'

Alastair grunted and turned to the kettle. They sat in silence while the water boiled and normally Olivia wouldn't have minded the quiet, but tonight her mind was far too loud.

'Can I trust him?' she asked, suddenly. Blurted out, really.

Alastair made a noise that was close to a laugh. 'If you have to ask then you already know the answer.'

'Do *you* trust him?'

'Not in the slightest.'

'You took his token, though.'

Alastair turned to Olivia and unceremoniously placed the mug of tea in front of her. 'He makes good on his word when it comes to payment.'

Olivia wrapped her hands around the mug and shivered as its warmth jolted through her. 'Will he betray me?'

'The first chance he gets.'

Olivia took a sip of her tea. She tried not to let it show on her face that he had forgotten the sugar and chose her next words carefully. 'How did he betray you?'

Alastair nearly smiled. 'Figured that one out did you?'

'I go to university, like a big brainy girl.'

Alastair sighed and crossed his tree trunk arms across his broad chest. 'We used to work together. We were known as highwaymen for hire. If you had a problem with something supernatural you came to us. We used to kill the bad guys. I thought we were doing something good. Something noble. Then I found out what he really was. He wasn't doing it because it was the right thing to do. He wasn't trying to help people or make the world a better place. He was in for the kill. He *likes* killing people. It satiates some hunger inside of him that nothing else can. When I discovered his true nature, I ended it. And yet, he keeps showing up.'

'Maybe you should stop letting him in when he does.'

Alastair scrubbed the good side of his face with his hand. He suddenly looked very tired. 'Roman has a… way about him. He gets under your skin. Once you've got him, you can never really get rid of him.'

'Like herpes.'

'Herpes doesn't kill people.'

'Not for the fun of it, at least.'

A silence fell. Olivia sipped her tea and Alastair stared down at his bar with an unreadable expression.

'Are you like us?' she asked finally. 'A demon?'

This time Alastair really did smile. 'No.'

Olivia smiled back. 'Good.'

'I'm a vampire.'

The morning rolled around far too quickly, and not soon enough, both at once. Olivia stared down into her coffee cup, blinking heavily. Alastair placed a ham and cheese bagel down in front of her and she smiled appreciatively. He sat opposite her at the table, a mug of warmed-up blood in front of him. She tried not to cringe as he took a long swig.

I try not to judge, but that is nasty.

Alastair tilted his head. 'I can go somewhere else?'

Olivia shook her head. 'No. No, please, it's fine. I've just… I've never met a vampire before.'

They watched each other for a long moment. Silence stretched out. She was almost glad when Roman joined them, annoyingly chipper — as seemed to be his way.

'It's a surprisingly sunny day,' he said. 'What shall we do first? The Spire? The Liffey? Ooh, what about the Viking Tour? Alastair, you would like that. You were there when the Vikings came to Ireland, weren't you?'

Alastair scowled, which — as it turned out — wasn't all that different to his usual expression. 'I'm not that old.'

Roman nodded to the mug in his hands. 'Still drinking from the blood bank, I see. Good to know that moral superiority doesn't have an expiry date.'

'We don't all enjoy killing people, Roman.'

Roman scoffed. 'You liked killing people as much as I did. You're just better at lying to yourself.'

Alastair's jaw tightened. 'I liked killing people who deserved it.'

'And did all those villagers from when you first turned deserve it?'

Alastair stood up, his chair toppling backwards. Olivia jumped to her feet and held her hands out diplomatically. Roman stayed seated in his chair, the picture of calm, watching with thinly veiled amusement.

'Not at the breakfast table please, boys,' she said.

Alastair looked from Roman to Olivia. 'I'm done with him. Get him out of here.'

'I will,' she said. 'We'll finish up here and go.'

Alastair nodded and made for the door behind the bar. He paused, turned to look at her. 'Don't let your guard down. Never forget what he truly is.'

He gave her one last look before showing himself out. Olivia sighed and looked at Roman.

'Why did you do that?' she asked. 'He's been good to us. Better than you deserve at least.'

Roman frowned. 'He's a big boy. He can handle it.'

'Thanks for telling me he's a vampire, by the way.'

'I assumed you'd figure it out.'

Olivia sat down and crossed her arms. 'What's your plan? The Brotherhood are expecting you to deliver me to their doorstep and I obviously don't want that to happen. So, what do we do?'

Roman watched her with mischievous eyes. 'The Liffey really is beautiful this time of year.'

'Roman, I swear to God—'

He sighed. 'Relax. I have a plan. For a demon, you're very uptight.'

'*Half* demon.'

'Sure.'

'Plan,' she prompted. 'Now.'

Roman sighed. 'The Brotherhood are too big to take on. Think Flat Earth Society Facebook group then triple it. Only the High Esteemed Ones wanted to see you, but that's still twelve plus, and that's about twelve more than I want to take on at once.'

'So what do we do?'

'We stop you from being the object of their desires.'

'How?'

Roman leaned back in his chair and crossed his arms. 'They want you because you're the Wicked One—'

'Which I'm not.'

'Because they think it's your destiny to be the big bad harbinger of doom. So, we just take away that part of you.'

Olivia watched him for a long moment. 'Are you dumb?'

He frowned. 'Not even a little bit.'

'So your answer is to just... what? Change my fate?'

'Exactly.'

'Cool. Great. Done,' she said. 'While I'm at it, I also think I might make myself a princess.'

Roman's eyes narrowed. 'For a demon you're also very grumpy.'

Her jaw clenched. '*Half* demon.'

'It's easy,' he said, standing. 'We go to the Celestial realm, meet with Fate and make a bargain to let you change your destiny. Simple!'

He shrugged into his leather jacket and smiled. Olivia didn't even have time to question him before he strode out of the bar and into the harsh morning sun. She cursed, fished a ten euro note out of her pocket — it was all she had — and left it on the table before she followed.

Roman was right, it was unusually warm. The city was just after waking up. Temple Bar — for the most part — was empty. It wasn't until they hit the main streets that the traffic slowed with the congestion of the work and school run. Horns blared. People shouted. Kids laughed as they walked in their packs, shoving and jostling each other, dragging out their time before school as much as possible.

The G Wagon drew looks of all kinds. Awe, bemusement, jealousy. Kids waved at them, signalling for Roman to honk the horn. He ignored them. Either that, or he just had no idea what they wanted. He didn't strike Olivia as a natural with children. Then again, neither was she.

Roman seemed to have unwavering patience with the stop and start of the traffic. Olivia watched as his face remained the perfect picture of calm. It was almost like he had unplugged. Stepped outside his body. It was like this that he looked most terrifying. When there was absolutely nothing there. Just emptiness. And she knew that at any moment he could pull the façade back on, animate his face and smile like he really meant it.

Bloody psycho.

'Tell me about vampires,' she said.

Roman glanced at her. 'What do you know?'

'That they exist,' she said. 'I never paid much attention to them past that.'

Roman turned down a side road and the traffic eased a little. 'Ask away.'

'Sunlight?'

'Burns them.'

'Reflections?'

'Yes.'

'Coffins?'

'Personal preference.'

'Holy water, crucifixes, and vervain?'

'All fallacies.'

'How do I kill one?'

Roman smiled. 'Same as demons. Take the heart or the head.'

Olivia watched as the city started to melt away around them. After twenty minutes, rural county Dublin steadily reclaimed the roads. Everything became narrower. Bumpier. The buildings were few and far between, and those that *were* there were old and crumbling. The roads freed up, empty save for the occasional tractor. The greyness of the city was overtaken by the soft, hazy greens and yellows of the countryside. Even with the windows shut, Olivia could still smell the leeks growing in the fields. She noticed Roman's nose wrinkle slightly at the scent, and she smiled to herself.

LAURA JORDAN

Don't be petty.

They drove for another fifteen minutes through fields and rolling hillsides. A paranoid voice in the back of her head pointed out to her that he could be driving her out here to kill her, but she ignored it. He couldn't kill her all the while he was sired to her.

Still, he could be taking you out here to kill time.

Olivia straightened and turned to Roman. 'Where are we going? You're being suspiciously cagey about the *where's* and *how's* of all this.'

Roman turned right and onto a dirt road. 'We need a specific landmark to cross to the Celestial realm. This is the closest one I know of.'

'Have you ever been to the Celestial realm?'

He shook his head. 'Only the Infernal.'

'Do you know how to pass through?'

'Of course I do.'

Olivia watched him for a long moment, then sighed.

Blood out of a stone.

She nodded. It really was.

They reached the end of the dirt road that opened up into a clearing. It was as vast as it was empty, and in the middle of the overgrown grass and weeds, alone and crumbling, was a set of archaic stone stairs leading to absolutely nowhere.

Roman parked and got out. He headed for the clearing and she followed, arms crossed over her chest. It reminded her of something from a Brothers Grimm story. It was halfway between a fairy tale and a nightmare, and she approached with apprehension. She watched as Roman circled the staircase to nowhere and tried to bite back the painfully obvious question that was fighting to break free.

She sighed. 'What the fuck is this?'

Roman didn't look at her, kept examining the steps. 'This is a gateway. One of many into the Celestial realm.'

60

'All I see is an old staircase.'

'That is because you are remarkably smooth-brained.'

Olivia watched as he tested the first step with his boot. Satisfied that it wasn't going to topple beneath his weight, he ascended the staircase. When he reached the top he turned and looked at her.

'Coming?' he asked.

Olivia arched an eyebrow. 'After you.'

Roman shrugged. He turned back to the empty sky and stepped off the stairs and into thin air.

Olivia's eyes widened.

Well, I wasn't expecting that.

She ran around the back of the staircase to see if he'd just fallen down, but he was gone.

'What the fuck...' she mumbled.

Remember when our life was normal?

'No, not really.'

Me neither.

She strode back to the base of the staircase and looked up. It wasn't particularly high. About twenty steps. Still high enough that she didn't want to fall from it though.

Before she could chicken out, she climbed up. The stones wobbled under her boots, and her sense of equilibrium wavered with each step. Her balance had never felt so off and she wished she had a railing to cling to. A fear of heights she never knew she had before crept into her peripheral vision. At the top, she hesitated, unsure what to do next.

Roman just... walked off.

'Yes, but do I have to think of something? Visualise something?'

I have no idea.

'You are absolutely no help at all.'

Just do it. Worst case scenario you fall twenty feet.

'And break a leg.'

Probably not a leg. An ankle, sure. But not a leg.

Olivia peered over the edge. Nothing but grass below. She stood straight and looked at the empty space in front of her. Nothing but air. And yet…

Is it me or is the air shimmering?

Olivia nodded, slowly. It was like a heatwave — when the air flickers. It was warm for October, but seldom a heatwave. She reached out with a tentative hand, and she surprised herself by how nonchalant she was as her hand disappeared.

Your life got weird in a hurry.

Olivia drew her hand back, and it reappeared. She turned it over, looking at her palm. She was unscathed.

Groovy.

Olivia nodded. 'Groovy,' she agreed before stepping of the staircase—

—and into something that she could only liken to sparklingly white reception. It was barren, and so bright it hurt her eyes. The only thing in the vast room was a receptionist desk with a pretty red-haired girl behind it.

Roman looked at her as she stepped up beside him. 'What took you so long?'

'You didn't exactly leave an instruction manual.'

'All you had to do was follow me. It seemed fairly straight-forward.'

'Excuse me?' the receptionist said, smiling. 'Fate will see you now.'

Roman plastered on a big, believable smile. 'Excellent. Thank you.'

Before Olivia could ask him what was going on, Roman was already striding down the hallway, hands in his pockets. She ground her teeth together and caught up to him.

'Nice of you to join me,' he said as she fell into step beside him.

'Why do you always act like you're in charge?' she snapped.

'Because I *am* in charge.'

'Um, no. You're not.'

'Don't be dense, of course I am.'

'My necklace,' she reminded him. 'My sigillum. You have to do what *I* say.'

Roman smiled. 'And yet, here you are, following me.'

'We're walking down the same corridor. I'm hardly spoilt for choice.'

'Face it. I'm Batman in this scenario and you're Robin.'

Olivia looked at him with something akin to disbelief. 'I'm not Robin.'

'Yes you are. You're the Robin to my Batman. The Rodney to my Del Boy. The Ron to my Harry.'

'More like the Voldemort to my Hermione.'

He glanced at her. 'I really get under your skin, don't I?'

'Yes.'

'Good.'

They reached the end of the hallway and the only door in sight. Olivia went to knock but Roman beat her to it. She glowered at him.

'Please,' a voice said from within. 'Come.'

Olivia practically dove onto the handle and gave Roman a look of sheer playground pettiness. She opened the door and Roman smiled and walked past her.

'Thank you,' he said.

Olivia's hands balled into fists and she stuffed them into her jacket pockets so that she wouldn't hit him.

You can hit him later.

Olivia nodded and followed Roman into the room. Much like the reception, it was sparkling white, and bright enough to make her eyes ache. They were in, what appeared to be, an office. Everything was clinical. The furniture, the décor — all as crisp and clean as fresh snow, and painfully dull.

Looks like an IKEA showroom.

Behind a dull, perfunctory white desk sat a beautiful blonde woman that was the absolute spitting image of an actress Olivia loved.

Fate.

Fate stood and smiled. She wore a white pantsuit and matching heels. Her hair was immaculate, her makeup sparse but perfect. She smiled and it was a smile that Olivia had double tapped thousands of times on Instagram fan accounts.

'Hello,' she said. 'You must be Olivia McQueen. It's lovely to meet you.'

Fate approached her and it took Olivia a moment to realise that she was coming to shake her hand. She blinked, paused, and thrust her hand out. They shook and she tried her hardest not to stare. Tried and failed.

'Are you...' Olivia said. 'I'm sorry, but... are you Jennifer Lawrence?'

Fate smiled. 'No, no. My true form is so beyond your comprehension that it would blow your mind. Quite literally. You would be not only brain dead upon the sight of me, but your body would likely combust. So I appear to those who seek me in a form that they would most find aesthetically pleasing.'

Olivia stared. 'Oh. Okay. So, you like, read my mind and turned into Jennifer Lawrence?'

'Merely just a perfect image of her,' Fate said. 'But yes. If you don't like this I can change? I can be anyone or anything you want. HRH Prince Harry? Tim Curry circa 1975? Simba?'

Roman frowned and looked at Olivia. 'Simba? The lion?'

Oliva ignored him. 'No. Nope. This is perfectly fine. This is great.'

'As in the cartoon lion? From *Lion King*?'

'So I guess I'm not really standing in an office block right now?' Olivia said, looking around.

Fate smiled. 'Not quite. The Celestial realm is a lot more... how would you put it?' She paused as if reading Olivia's mind for the right word and settled on, 'wiggy.'

'Seriously?' Roman asked. 'The big animated cat from Disney?'

No one paid attention to him. Instead, Fate took her seat behind her desk and gestured for them to sit. Olivia took a seat but Roman remained standing, arms crossed over his chest.

'So,' said Fate. 'I would ask you why you've come to see me, but, of course, I already know absolutely everything about you.'

Olivia arched an eyebrow. 'Everything?'

She nodded. 'Everything past, present, and future.'

Olivia grinned. 'Suppose you can't tell me if I pass my final exams?'

'Unfortunately not.'

'Worth a shot.'

Stop flirting. It's not really Jennifer Lawrence.

Fate laughed. 'Your passenger is right, you know. I'm not really her.'

Olivia felt herself pale. 'You can hear her?'

Fate leaned back in her chair and shrugged. 'I know—'

'Everything,' Olivia said. 'Right yeah.' She paused before her next question, not entirely sure if she wanted to know the answer. 'What do you mean *passenger*?'

'It's not a part of you,' Fate explained.

Olivia felt something like ice slide down her chest and settle in her stomach. She'd always thought she'd had a pretty good handle on who she was, on the voice in her head that she'd always told herself was just her conscience. An inner monologue. Some kind of power she had as a demon that allowed her to organise her thoughts separately enough so that she could actually sit back and have a conversation with them.

And now that she was thinking about it — *really* thinking about it — she realised how ridiculous that sounded. She wasn't special. She wasn't smarter than anyone else. She had, for lack of a better word, a parasite.

Oi.

Panic threatened to bubble and boil over like a pot of water left on the hob. However, she drew on her talent of taking bad news with exceptional aplomb, and said, 'Can you tell me what it is?'

'I cannot.'

'Oh.'

'You will find out later. It is not for me to set new plans in motion. What I *will* say is: the people we carry in our hearts leave a lasting impression on us.'

'That is… vague.'

'It is as much as I can interfere.'

Roman snorted. 'Then you're really not going to like what we came here to ask.'

Fate looked at him. 'I know what you came to ask of me, Roman. I cannot help you.'

'Because you can't meddle with destiny?'

'Because I cannot help those who do not have a soul.' She looked at Olivia. 'Destiny is set in stone for those without a soul. You are a demon. The path that is set for you is treacherous and unchanging. It is how the natural balance of order is equalised. Humans are free to pick their future. You… are not.'

'So, I'm stuck like this?' Olivia asked, feeling a yawning pit in her stomach opening up even as she said it. 'I am the Wretched One, or Wicked One, or whatever the Brotherhood wants me to be?'

Fate gave her a sympathetic look. 'You are a demon. It is your destiny.'

'Half demon,' Olivia mumbled.

'And you have half a soul. That is not enough. I am sorry. Truly, I am.'

Roman was already heading for the door. Olivia turned to him, incredulously.

'You're leaving?' she asked.

'*We're* leaving,' he clarified. 'Plan A is a bust. That means we move onto plan B. Failing that, plan C, and plan D, and… well, you know how the alphabet goes.'

Olivia turned back to Fate. 'Please. Is there anything you can do to help me?'

Fate hesitated for only a moment. She held out her hand and beckoned for Olivia to take it. She took it with her hand that wasn't used for her Devil's debt. The moment their skin made contact, there was a spark. It didn't hurt, but Olivia felt the sensation flash through her body, like electricity.

Fate drew her hand back and smiled. 'There. I owe you one favour. Should you ever need me — anytime or any place — call on me and I shall come. Use it wisely though. It will only work once.'

Olivia looked down at her hand. On the palm, already fully-healed, was a scar in the shape of an intricate sigil.

'*Debitum Placabilis*,' Fate said. 'Basically an I.O.U.. Don't waste it.'

Olivia nodded. 'I won't.'

6.

Olivia looked at the sigil on her palm while the G Wagon made easy work of the country lanes. She traced the lines and curves with her fingertip, and wondered — not for the first time — how her life had gotten so complicated.

Of course, she knew when. Birth. It had *always* been complicated. A demon born to good Christian, god-fearing parents. Given up and adopted by demon hunters. Raised to be human with the half a soul she had, and kill demons alongside her adoptive parents. And to top it off, apparently destined to be the bringer of the apocalypse.

The Wicked One.

Olivia ignored her passenger and looked out the window at the unchanging scenery. Fields, farms, glasshouses, repeat.

You can't ignore me forever. I live in your head.

Olivia turned on the radio. Roman scowled.

'I'm thinking,' he said.

Olivia found *80s FM* and settled back in her chair. She crossed her arms and looked back out the window.

'Are you sulking?' Roman asked.

'Yes.'

'Why?'

'Because Fate was a bust.'

Roman indicated left and turned down a road, where the traffic seemed to pick up.

'I have a plan B,' he said. 'I already told you.'

'Your plan is to hand me over to the Brotherhood.'

'Under the guise of being on their side,' Roman clarified. 'We go, you put up with a little fanfare, they do their spooky juju and unleash your inner Hulk — then we turn on them. Easy!'

She looked at him. 'And for the last time, Roman, I'm telling you that's not going to work.'

'Why not?'

'Firstly, we have no idea how I'll be received. They could throw me in a prison cell or a dungeon for all we know.'

'I doubt they have a dungeon.'

'Secondly, we don't know if whatever ritual or sacrifice they have planned will even work. It might just kill me.'

'How much do you really enjoy your life anyway?'

She glared. 'And thirdly, if it does work and I *do* Hulk out — there's no guarantee what will happen after. What if this thing that's inside me turns me evil? Full demon, no half a soul. I could be like Angel when he finds a moment of pure happiness, or Damon Salvatore when he turns his humanity off.'

'You watch too many vampire shows.'

'What if I turn into a monster, Roman?'

The words were out before she had time to stop them. She immediately wished she could snatch them back and stuff them back down her throat where they belonged. She could feel Roman watching her, unsure how to proceed. Like the conversation was careening far too close to actual-talking-feelings territory. Neither of them wanted that. The *last* thing Olivia wanted was for Roman to know that she was fucking terrified. And she was fairly certain that the last thing *Roman* wanted was to hear about it.

Roman cleared his throat. 'A metaphorical monster or a literal monster?'

Oh, it was uncomfortable. Painfully uncomfortable. Olivia felt like a dick. So, naturally, she lifted her chin and looked directly at him. 'Either. Both.'

Roman shrugged. 'If you go full blown Magneto, I promise I will kill you before you can hurt anyone.'

Olivia sunk down into her seat. 'Thanks.'

They drove in blessed silence for a few minutes. Olivia felt a sharp sting on her palm — not the one with Fate's sigil — and uncurled her fist to watch a name carving itself into her skin.

Aoife Teague

Olivia groaned. 'Not now. Please not now. We don't have time for this.'

Roman frowned. 'What's wrong?'

Olivia waved her hand at him. 'Devil's debt. He's calling in a favour.'

'Well, tough. Tell him you're busy.'

'You think I haven't already tried that?'

Roman took one hand off the wheel and grabbed her wrist. He spoke into her fist like it was a microphone. 'We're a little busy at the moment. Call back later.'

Olivia snatched her hand away. 'Don't piss him off.'

'I'm not afraid of the big bad wolf.'

'You should be.'

'Well, we're not going.'

Olivia sighed and waited patiently for—

Roman cried out in pain, both hands flew from the steering wheel to his head. His eyes screwed shut and his forehead scrunched up. Every vein in his neck stood out, his face steadily turning purple.

Olivia reached out and grabbed the steering wheel, stopping them from veering off into a ditch. Roman snarled and twisted in his seat. He slammed his hands on the dashboard before bringing them back to his forehead.

He's so stubborn.

'Roman!' Olivia shouted. 'Say sorry before he fries your brain completely!'

'Alright!' he yelled. 'Alright, I'm sorry! We'll do it! Fuck me!'

Almost as suddenly as it had started it stopped. The colour of his face went back to normal, and his white-knuckled fists uncurled. He took the steering wheel from Olivia and blinked hard.

'Asshole,' he muttered. 'How do I know where to go?'

Right on cue, the G Wagon indicated by itself and took them off a ramp. Roman cocked an eyebrow and let his hands off the wheel, watching his Mercedes drive itself to their destination. He gave Olivia a look of bemusement and she shrugged.

'I hope he pays for petrol too,' he mumbled.

They sat back and watched as the G Wagon took them North-West, from Dublin into County Meath. Motorways melted into A roads, which meandered into country lanes, and civilisation rose and fell around them. After thirty minutes they pulled up at a small cottage with a thatched roof, sitting alone at the end of a dirt driveway.

The G Wagon parked and the hand break wrenched itself up with an awful squeal.

Roman looked at her. 'If my brakes are damaged, I'm blaming you.'

Olivia got out and made sure to slam the door behind her. It was childish but it made her feel better. She strode up to the house, Roman in tow. She knocked on the door and waited. The cottage was old, but charming. It reminded her of the one she grew up in, except there was no trace of Tudor architecture here. Just stones, hay, and cobbles.

A pretty blonde woman in her early thirties opened the door and smiled warmly. Her hair was in pigtails. Her dungarees had flour on them.

Oh God, it's like killing Fraulein Maria.

'Hi,' she said in a thick Cork accent. 'Can I help you?'

Olivia smiled. 'I hope so. We're looking for Aoife Teague.'

'That's my wife. She's out back, in the glasshouse. I can get her for you?'

Thank God. I don't think I could handle the guilt of killing someone with dimples.

'That would be great, thanks.'

The woman closed the door and Olivia and Roman shared a look. Roman's face was infuriatingly impossible to read. A few moments later the door opened and a punky-looking woman with black hair and smoky eyes looked out at them.

If the other one was Fraulein Maria then this one is The Crow.

'Aoife Teague?' Olivia asked.

Aoife nodded. 'Yeah?'

Olivia smiled apologetically. 'Sorry about th—'

Before Olivia could finish, Aoife's fist came swinging at her. She lunged, bringing her arms up over her head and blocking Aoife's attack. Olivia wrapped her left arm around Aoife's and her right hand landed a palm shot under the woman's chin. Aoife's head snapped back and Olivia followed up with a knee to her stomach. Aoife's legs buckled and she sank ungracefully to the floor. Olivia grabbed her head by her hair and rammed another knee into her nose, hearing the bone and cartilage crunch as it made contact.

Aoife fell onto her side, rolled onto her stomach and tried to crawl away. Olivia sighed and pulled the dagger from her boot. Standing over Aoife, she kicked her over onto her back and crouched so she was straddling her.

'Sorry again,' she said. 'I was trying to make it quick and painless, but you hit me first.'

Aoife grinned and the blood streaming from her nose trickled into her mouth, staining her teeth. Olivia arched an eyebrow but didn't question it. She raised the dagger in both hands, ready to plunge into her chest—

—Then Aoife opened her mouth and a long, spiked tentacle shot out from within and clamped it's lamprey-eel-style-claw, or head, or whatever it was, around Olivia's face. Despite herself, Olivia screamed. Or she tried to. She dropped the dagger, heard it clatter away somewhere. Her hands clawed at her face, trying to rip the thing off, but it only sunk its teeth in deeper.

Instead she grabbed the tentacle arm, ignoring how the barbs bit into her palms. She twisted her hands in opposite directions and felt a rip, heard the tear of flesh. The claw-head-whatever-the-fuck-it-was let go of her face with a piercing shriek and flailed wildly. Olivia scrambled back and brought her feet back underneath her, watching as Aoife sucked the tentacle back inside her mouth.

Aoife was still for a moment, then she sprang forward off her back and onto her feet. Olivia had only seen people do that in movies. She rose to standing and Olivia copied her, wiping her own blood from her eyes. She was already healing and so was Aoife.

Aoife ran at her. Olivia waited until the last moment and side-stepped, grabbed her, and hauled her back, flipping her over her hip. She went down and Olivia went with her, raining elbows onto her face. Each strike made a satisfying crunch. Aoife slammed a fist into Olivia's side and tried to roll them but Olivia dug her hooks in tighter, securing her ankles around the backs of Aoife's knees.

Aoife bucked her hips up and Olivia shot forwards, her hands splaying out to catch herself. Aoife wrapped her arms around Olivia's body in a bear hug and shrimped her way out of Olivia's hooks. She tightly wrapped her legs around Olivia's waist, and brought her head in close to Olivia's chest so that she couldn't strike her again.

Olivia reared back, trying to shake Aoife free but she held on tightly, waiting patiently for Olivia to tire. So, instead, Olivia sat up on her knees, grabbed two fistfuls of Aoife's hair and wrenched back. She screamed, her head snapping back. Olivia slammed her forehead into Aoife's nose, breaking it all over again. Aoife's arms went slack and Olivia untangled herself from the woman's limbs, scrambling back.

She watched Aoife roll on the floor, unsure whether to clutch her nose or the back of her head, and eventually deciding on both. Spotting the dagger under a side table in the little hallway, Olivia rose to her feet. She grabbed the dagger and a hand weakly grabbed her ankle. She looked down at Aoife, watched her open her mouth. The head of the tentacle thing reared up from the back of her throat. It hesitated for a moment, as if unsure it wanted to follow its master's commands, before leaping at her.

Olivia brought the dagger round in a clean sweep and the blade cut through the slimy, barbed-tongued snake. Blood spurted and Aoife screamed, the tentacle falling limp. Olivia crouched over her and raised the dagger once more. This time it plunged deep into Aoife's chest and she barely had time to scream again before she disintegrated.

Olivia looked at the name on her palm, watched with relief as it faded away.

Relief was quickly overcome by rage as she stood and turned to the door, expecting to see Roman. To her surprise, he was gone.

Shit.

She marched down the hallway and out of the cottage. She spotted Roman halfway down the drive holding the blonde woman in a chokehold. She saw Olivia, and for a fleeting moment hope blossomed across her features. Then she saw the blood. Her wife's blood. Olivia was covered in it. The woman began to sob.

'What the hell are you doing?' Olivia asked. 'Where were you back there?'

'I caught this one trying to escape through the back door,' he said.

'Let her go. We came here for Aoife, not her.'

'Please,' the woman begged. 'Please, I'm human. My name is Ciara. I've never hurt anyone. And neither has Aoife since we met. She stopped killing for me. She loved me. I loved her. Please, let me go, I swear I won't tell anyone.'

'Let her go,' Olivia repeated. 'We're done here.'

'She's a loose end,' Roman said. 'We let her go and she goes running through the town square screaming "demon".'

'She doesn't even know who we are.'

Roman nodded at Olivia. 'Her name is Olivia McQueen and I'm Roman Wylder. Oops.'

'Roman, no!'

He took Ciara's head in his hands. Olivia ran forward to stop him, but he twisted and with a snap, she went limp. He let go and she fell to the ground, her face in the gravel.

Olivia stared at him. She didn't say anything for a long moment.

'What the fuck is wrong with you?' she shouted.

Roman turned to go back to the G-Wagon. 'Like I said, she was a loose end.'

She followed him. 'She was a *human*! She didn't do anything!'

'Apart from shack up with a murderous demon. A *gifted* one, at that.'

'Like you care! Just admit it! You *like* killing people.'

Roman stopped and turned to face her. His eyes were dark, his expression black.

'I will if you will,' he growled.

'What are you—'

'I saw how you looked when you killed Aoife,' Roman said, stalking closer. 'The look in your eyes when you ended her life. The same as when you killed Cormac. You *like* it, Olivia. You're gagging for it. The first chance you get to drive that dagger through a demon's heart, and you leap. Of course *I* like killing people. I'm a serial killer — it's what I do. What's your excuse?'

She hit him. He barely reacted. She went to strike him again and he caught her fist in his hand. He grabbed her roughly, and pulled her in close to him so that their noses were nearly touching. His gaze bore down on her.

'Do not,' he said, 'ever try that again.'

He shoved her back, turned and climbed into the jeep.

I want him dead.

Olivia nodded. 'So do I.'

7.

The ride back to Dublin was awkward at best. The silence grew increasingly stagnant to the point where Olivia had to turn the radio on. To her relief Roman didn't argue, and they listened to irritatingly upbeat eighties pop all the way back to Temple Bar. The clock on the dashboard said it was already 13:24pm, and the thought of already losing so much time and gaining absolutely nothing made Olivia antsy.

Alastair looked unsurprised to see them arrive and Olivia wondered just how many times Roman had returned there over the years, tail between his legs. Probably more times than either of them were letting on. He immediately took residence behind the bar and made them each a strong cup of tea.

Forgot the sugar again.

When neither Olivia nor Roman spoke first, Alastair signed and asked, 'What happened?'

'Fate was a bust,' Roman said. 'She can't tell us anything because Olivia only has half a soul, which apparently is a thing.'

Olivia held up her hand with the mark left by Fate. 'She gave me an I.O.U. though.'

Alastair grunted. 'How generous.'

'Then Roman killed an innocent woman for no good reason.'

Alastair looked at Roman, cocking an unsurprised eyebrow. 'Oh?'

Roman shrugged. 'Covering our tracks.'

'She did nothing wrong.'

Alastair frowned. 'Is that true?'

Roman looked between the two of them, incredulously. 'Yes. Obviously it's true. Why are you both acting so surprised? I kill people, that's what I do.'

'What happened to only killing demons and vampires?' he asked, gruffly. 'You said it kept you off the radar.'

'And to keep me off that radar, every so often I have to kill a human,' he said, voice rising. 'She saw us. She knew what we were. I protected us. Get over it.'

Olivia opened her mouth to retort, but a look from Alastair told her not to. Instead, Alastair waited a moment, cleared his throat, and changed the subject.

'So now what?' he asked. 'What's plan B?'

Olivia sighed. 'He wants me to hand myself over to the Brotherhood, let them unleash some ungodly evil within me and hope that it doesn't end the world. And then afterwards go for milkshakes.'

Alastair hesitated. 'I… don't think that is a good idea.'

'She added the bit about milkshakes herself,' Roman said.

'I think that's a really bad idea,' said Alastair.

'Me too,' Olivia agreed.

Me three.

Roman finished his tea and stood up. 'Does anyone have a better plan?'

Olivia and Alastair exchanged glances but said nothing.

Roman smiled. 'Brilliant. Now, if you'll excuse me, I'm going to make a call to the Brotherhood and tell them that we'll meet them first thing tomorrow.'

Olivia frowned. 'Why can't we go now?'

'Because we have to meet someone first.'

'Who?'

Roman grinned. 'A witch.'

Imelda Crane was not what Olivia expected. The young woman was tall, toned, and covered in piercings and tattoos. Her skin was a rich mahogany, her eyes a startling blue. Her dreadlocked hair was a mixture of pastel pinks and purples, and pinned high atop her head in a messy bun. She wore a *Cry Baby* t-shirt and had a quote from *The Rocky Horror Picture Show* on her inner bicep. *Don't dream it. Be it.* Olivia liked her instantly.

She looked up from her client as they entered the tattoo parlour, grimacing when she saw Roman. Roman smiled and waved back cheerfully.

'You seem to have that effect on most people,' Olivia murmured.

They took a seat on the couch, opposite a nervous-looking young man who was flicking through a book of tattoo ideas. His leg bounced uneasily. He looked up at them and smiled.

'First time,' he said.

Olivia smiled. 'I hear it's not as bad as childbirth.'

'I'm Kevin,' he said.

'I'm Randy,' Roman said before Olivia could answer. 'This is my girlfriend Joan. We're getting each other's names tattooed on our faces.'

Kevin blinked. 'Oh. Right.'

Roman nodded and smiled some more. 'I wanted to get it done on our asses, but I already have my widow's name tattooed there.'

'Oh, God,' Kevin said. 'Oh, I'm so sorry.'

'God rest her soul.'

'How did she die?'

'Alcohol.'

Kevin looked at him sympathetically. 'My mother was an alcoholic too.'

Roman frowned. 'Oh, she wasn't an alcoholic.'

'Oh.'

'She was crushed by a giant wine barrel.'

Kevin paled. 'Oh God…'

Roman sighed. 'I know. One moment you're alive and well, taking a tour through France's best winery, and the next… Sauvignon bonk. Dead.'

Kevin watched him for a long moment, eyes wide. Suddenly he stood, mumbled something about changing his mind, and left in a hurry. Olivia looked at Roman disparagingly, who picked up the discarded book and began flicking through its pages.

'You're impossible,' she said.

'He was annoying,' Roman said. 'He kept bouncing his leg. And he was chatty. I hate small talk.'

'So instead of ignoring him, like a normal person, you scared him off?'

Roman sighed. 'I'm not a normal person. I'm a demon. Humans bore me.'

'Do you think humans are just your playthings?' she challenged. 'Here to amuse you, and to push around, and break when you're bored of playing with them?'

Roman glanced at her. 'Do you really want me to answer that?'

Olivia hesitated then looked away. They sat in silence.

Imelda finished up with her client and showed him to the mirror. The burly man smiled at the depiction of a naked alien woman with three breasts now permanently inked onto his bicep. He winked at Olivia as he left and she scowled.

'What'll it be?' Imelda asked as she approached. 'Mom? Your dead cat's name? The word *peace* in Chinese, but it actually translates to *soup*?'

Roman stood, smiling. 'Actually, we've come for a favour.'

'You're so sweet,' she said. 'No.'

Olivia stood and smiled. 'Actually the favour is for me, not him, if that helps?'

'Depends what it is.' Imelda held out her hand. 'Imelda Crane.'

Olivia shook her hand. 'Olivia McQueen.'

'And what is it I can do for you, Olivia McQueen?' she asked. 'Because I doubt you've come for a tat.'

Olivia looked at Roman who moved to the shopfront and changed the sign on the door from *open* to *closed*. Imelda arched an eyebrow but waited patiently for an explanation.

Roman flashed his shark's smile. 'We need your witchy powers.'

Imelda sighed. 'For the last time, Wylder, I'm not a witch.'

'You're as good as.'

'I'm a *seer*.'

'A seer?' Olivia asked. 'Like a psychic?'

'In a way,' she said. 'I get glimpses here and there. Just fragments. The past is easier to see than the future, and the future is always subject to change.'

Roman crossed his arms. 'Tell her the catch.'

Imelda's mouth twitched up into a smile. 'I can only read you while I tattoo you.'

Olivia frowned. 'What, really?'

'It's like a witchy sonar,' Roman said, passing Olivia the big book of tattoos. 'It lets her hone in on her powers by making a connection with you.'

Imelda glared. 'I'm not a witch.'

Olivia looked at the binder in her hands. She'd always considered getting a tattoo but had always, at heart, known she was far too indecisive. Her mother had told her it was the curse of being a Libra. The inability to make decisions and the power to hold grudges for a lifetime.

Olivia smiled. 'I think I have an idea.'

8.

Olivia sat in the seat that felt far too much like a dentist's chair and willed the butterflies in her stomach to wither and die. Her left forearm faced the ceiling, the back of her hand resting on a stool. She watched Imelda prepare the needle and ink, and clean the area of skin on her wrist. She looked at Olivia and gave her an encouraging smile.

'You'll be fine,' she said.

'Of course you will,' Roman said from where he watched in the corner of the room. 'It's like a bee sting.'

Olivia nodded. 'Okay. Okay that's fine. I can handle that.'

'But a thousand of them at once.'

Olivia glared. Roman quickly lost interest in her and looked at the various photos of tattoos and piercings on the wall with absolute disinterest. Olivia almost envied him. There had been more than one occasion in her life when she wished she could shut it all off. Turn off her emotions. Her parents. The Bridge. Cillian. The Fire. Her grief was always there, in the back of her mind. It never got any smaller, but she instead got bigger and so could handle it better. Sometimes it minded its own business, keeping quiet and tucked away. And sometimes it drowned her.

She closed her eyes and breathed deeply, counting back from ten. When she opened her eyes she saw Imelda, poised and ready to ink her.

'Ready?' she asked.

'Will demon healing affect it?' Olivia asked.

'Not the actual ink,' Imelda explained, patiently. Like she got demon clients all the time. Maybe she did. 'You'll just heal pretty much immediately. No scabbing or aftercare needed. It's still going to hurt though.'

Olivia couldn't answer. She just nodded. Roman appeared at her side and reached for her other hand. She snatched it away, glowering.

He rolled his eyes. 'So that I can see what Witchy-Woo sees,' he explained. 'We need to have a physical connection. I can hold somewhere else if you'd like?'

Olivia glared and held her hand out. Roman took it, his fingers enveloping hers. His hands were strong. Callused. Hands of someone who punched a lot. It felt strangely intimate. Olivia realised, with some surprise, that the only skin-to-skin contact she had these days was when she was beating someone up, or vice versa.

Well, that's depressing.

Imelda bowed her head over Olivia's wrist, the drill switching on. It was shrill and high pitched. Olivia's jaw clenched. She knew it was silly. She fought demons on the daily. She had been in more fights than she could count. She had trained in mixed martial arts ever since she was seven and she could deadlift 120kg. And yet she was scared.

The needle touched her skin and she was pleasantly surprised at the lack of pain. Then it hit her all of the sudden, sending spasms up her arm. It felt like she was being carved open. Her body tensed and she felt Roman give her hand the tiniest of squeezes. She looked up at him but he was looking away, lost in his thoughts.

Olivia peeked at her wrist. It was messier than she thought it would be. Every few seconds Imelda had to stop and wipe the ink and blood away. She could feel the start of a migraine coming on. She winced, closing her eyes, and rested her head back.

'Are you alright?' Roman asked.

'Head hurts,' Olivia mumbled.

'That's just me,' Imelda said. 'Try to relax and let me in.'

Olivia nodded. She focused on her breathing. For a moment her headache worsened, but slowly it began to drift away. She frowned. No, that was wrong. It wasn't fading. It was… softening? Like it had once been jagged and sharp, and now all the points were slowly rounding out. After a while — she had no idea how long — the pain was gone. She felt like she was floating. She was weightless. Relaxed, almost. The pain and noise of the drill was a faraway memory. She knew it was there but it wasn't important anymore. The only thing that was important was this. Floating. Floating. Float—

She heard the sound of her mother's voice and she opened her eyes immediately. She was no longer in the tattoo parlour. She was in her front room back in England. On the sofa sat her mum and dad. They looked younger than she remembered. Her dad's hair had only the faintest trace of silver, her mother's face unlined. They looked worried.

Opposite them on the armchair sat a handsome man in a slate grey suit. His hair was a shock of black, his eyes a soft amber. He was young and Olivia could tell that beneath his clothes he was strong. He smiled at her parents. They did not smile back.

'Mum?' Olivia asked, stepping into the room. 'Dad? Everything okay?'

They either ignored her or they couldn't hear her.

'Please,' Lorna said. 'Please take this away from her. She has the chance to live a normal life. She *deserves* a normal life — she's just a child.'

Jackson put his hand on his wife's knee. 'We would be forever in your debt if you could help us. Please.'

The man sighed. 'I came here because I thought you wanted to negotiate, not beg.'

'There must be something you can do,' Lorna pleaded. 'Please.'

'You know the Story, Lorna,' said the man. 'The Wicked One, born of the bloodline of the First, will carry with her the antichrist until the day of reckoning. The Wicked—'

'Olivia,' Jackson said, firmly. 'Her *name* is Olivia.'

The man smiled. 'Of course. My apologies. *Olivia* was chosen by the First to carry the antichrist until she is ready to be awakened. That could be ten years from now. It could be twenty. We don't know. But until then, the Wicked One must remain on this plane. She is only half demon. The First wanted her to have half a soul so she could at least experience human life here. Joy. Sorrow. Rage. Love — these are our gifts to her. This is how the antichrist will decide if the world is worth saving when she rises.'

'Why my baby girl though?' Lorna asked. 'Pick anyone else. There must be others that share the blood of the First.'

'Her blood sings,' he said. 'She is the one. The mirror image. I knew it the moment she was born. I could feel it. And when the antichrist is ready to rise, she will call to us again.'

'This will destroy her,' Jackson said. 'No one can carry this evil inside them. It will ruin her.'

'And one day she will be free of it.'

'And what will happen then?'

The man shrugged. 'She will die. Pass on. Be at peace.'

Lorna choked back a sob. Jackson wrapped his arms around her and held her close. Olivia stepped between her parents and the man, but he seemed to look right through her.

'That's enough,' Olivia said. 'I think you should leave now.'

There was a nose in the hallway and Olivia turned to see her three year old self appear at the door, cradling her *Thomas O'Malley Cat* teddy in her pudgy arms. She looked between her parents and the strange man, unsure. The man stood and Jackson mirrored him. The man gave him a warning look, however, and Jackson reluctantly sat back down.

Olivia watched the man. He crossed to her younger self and crouched beside her, taking her chubby face gently in his hand. She watched herself frown.

'Hello, Olivia,' he said. 'My name is Lucifer. You and I are going to be very good friends.'

Olivia's legs gave way beneath her. Suddenly she was falling. She barely had time to scream before her eyes snapped open. She sucked in a huge gasp of air and both Imelda and Roman came into her line of sight. She glanced around her and saw she was back in the tattoo parlour. Looking down at her hand she saw she was still clinging onto Roman, her fingernails biting into his skin, drawing blood. She let go and his hand immediately began to heal.

Imelda placed a gentle hand on her shoulder. 'Are you alright?'

Olivia looked at her, eyes wild. 'What the hell was that?'

'A memory from your past,' Imelda said. 'That's all I could see before I finished your ink. I wasn't sure what I was looking for when I went in until I saw it. It was buried deep in your subconscious. The moment I found it, it tried to fight me off. That's how I knew it was important. Are you okay?'

Olivia looked at Roman. 'Did you see?'

He looked at her, expression unreadable. He nodded.

'What the hell are we going to do?' she asked.

Roman paused. Then said, 'I really don't know.'

Olivia looked at her tattoo. A small Libra sign, no bigger than a one euro coin, sitting neatly in the centre of her wrist. Imelda had applied some aftercare cream and wrapped it up in clingfilm. Olivia had tried to pay her but she'd refused. Before they left she'd wrapped Olivia up in a tight hug and put her number into her phone. She realised, with some sadness, that she would miss Imelda. She tried not to think of it.

They took the M50 heading out of the city centre and into Swords. Olivia hadn't been in an airport since she arrived in Ireland three years ago. She hadn't been back to the UK since leaving. There was nothing left for her there. And yet here they were, on their way to catch a flight to London Gatwick.

Olivia was quiet, her leg bouncing the whole journey.

Do you want to talk about it?

Olivia shook her head.

Roman glanced at her. 'Do you want to talk about it?'

She sighed. 'And say what? The Brotherhood is right? I really *am* the Wicked One? I'm descended from the First — whoever that is — and that I'm responsible for carrying the antichrist around inside me — whatever that means — until she decides to pop out and destroy the world — whenever that might be — and there's nothing I can do to stop it? Sure, you start.'

Roman was silent for a long moment. 'It might not be that bad.'

She turned in her chair to stare at him. 'I'm sorry, but what traumatic repressed memories were *you* watching?'

'I just mean… nothing is concrete.'

'Except that it is. We're on our way to hand me over to the Brotherhood so they can call out the antichrist from within. And that's not even the worst part. Say that, for example, your idea isn't completely batshit, and they don't realise we're completely playing them, and by some divine miracle they *don't* murder us… then what happens? We kill them, and then what? I'm still the Wicked One. The antichrist is still running loose.'

'It could be worse.'

'How the *fuck* could it be worse?'

Roman shrugged. 'You could be ugly.'

'I hate you.'

He sighed. 'At least *you're* not the antichrist. This isn't really you, just a thing inside of you, hitching a ride. This darkness, this evil — none of it is you.'

Something about that touched all the tender places inside of her that Olivia had long forgotten about. Or, at least, *forced* herself to forget. It was raw and the gentleness of his tone made her chest ache. Like, actually ache. That was the thing about Roman. He had the annoying habit of saying the *exact* thing she needed to hear at the *exact* time she needed to hear it. She was certain that most of the time he wasn't even trying to make her feel better, that he was just being logical. But what was logical for him was painful for her, and she had to swallow down a feeling that was nauseatingly close to heartache. It was so much easier when he was just being a dick.

She said, 'Thank you.'

'Welcome.'

'Do you really think it will kill me?' she asked. 'If they release the antichrist? Will I die?'

Roman looked thoughtful for a moment. 'I don't know.'

'I don't want to die.'

'I'd be worried if you did.'

Olivia turned and looked out the window. Dublin airport rose either side of them, a honking mass of modern architecture that didn't fit its humble surroundings. She shifted nervously in her seat. Instead of heading to the car park, they veered off, taking a small side road that said *staff only*. She looked at Roman but he said nothing. They were met by no barriers and the G Wagon rolled freely into a small parking lot. A tall blonde woman in a teal airhostess uniform greeted them as they got out.

'Mr Wylder and Miss McQueen?' she asked.

Roman plastered on his very best counterfeit smile and shook her hand. 'Yes, thank you for helping me to arrange this on such short notice.'

'Lovely to meet you both. My name's Zara. Ariel sent me to collect you. If you'd like to follow me, the private jet is on standby.'

Olivia looked at Roman incredulously. He merely shrugged and followed Zara. She took them through a small walkway and they appeared on the side of the tarmac. Olivia eyed the row of planes waiting in their parking spaces to be boarded. Zara led them to a caddie and she drove them across the blacktop. In the distance, the airplanes took off and landed on the runway at perfectly timed ninety-second intervals. The knot in her stomach tightened.

Zara pulled the caddy up beside a small private jet. A security guard met them and scanned them with a handheld metal detector before giving them a quick pat down. Zara beckoned them to follow her onboard and Olivia's eyebrows rose at the jet's interior.

It was less of a plane and more of a private room at a club. Everything was effortlessly pristine and modern. The seats were thick, over-plumped armchairs and at the back of the cabin was a small bar with two barstools. It was, surprisingly, open plan.

So the billionaires can all argue amongst themselves about who has the most money.

Inside the jet, seated and reading something on an iPad, was a well-dressed man in a blue suit. He looked up as they entered and smiled. His face was sharp and attractive. He wore his shoulder-length hair down. His gaze lingered on Olivia, expression indescribable.

Roman shook his hand. 'Ariel. You look well.'

Ariel laughed. 'Don't I always?' He was American, his accent from New York.

Roman turned to her. 'Ariel, this is Olivia. Olivia, this is Ariel. He's an old friend.'

Ariel cocked an eyebrow. '*Friend* might be pushing it somewhat.'

Olivia stepped forward and shook his hand. 'Hi. Thank you for letting us use your plane.'

Ariel smiled. 'Well, how could I decline? Roman made an offer I couldn't refuse.'

Olivia looked at Roman. 'Tokens?'

'And then some.'

'Sit, please,' Ariel said. 'Relax. Zara will bring some wine.'

Olivia sat down, and politely refused Zara's offer of chardonnay, opting for a Coke instead. Roman followed suit.

'She's like you,' Ariel said, sipping his wine.

Olivia frowned. 'No I'm not.'

'I meant it as a compliment.'

'Compliment not taken.'

Ariel smiled. 'Forgive me, I misspoke. Alastair told me all about you, Miss McQueen. The long awaited Wicked One.'

Olivia tensed. 'What do you know?'

'Oh, I know everything. I've been studying you my whole life.'

She frowned. 'Me specifically?'

Ariel grinned. 'Not quite. The Wicked One. Your legacy. I never thought I would actually meet you. It is an honour.'

'Um… thanks?'

'Ariel studies demonology,' Roman said. 'His business fronts as a clean energy company, but in reality he's a collector.'

'Collector?' she asked.

'All things supernatural,' said Ariel. 'Tomes, talismans, antiquities. All in the vaults beneath *Levine Corp.*'

'So he is a fountain of knowledge,' Roman said.

The intercom crackled and Zara asked for their attention while she ran through the safety brief. Shortly after, the plane taxied to the runway. Olivia's nails dug into the arms of her chair. She looked straight ahead, refusing to look out of the window. She could sense Roman watching her, trying to figure her out. When he couldn't, he simply looked away.

The small jet thundered down the runway. Olivia screwed her eyes shut as they lifted off. She stayed that way until they stopped climbing. The plane levelled out and she cracked an eye open to peer out the window. They were well above the clouds. Her stomach rolled.

'Bad flyer?' Ariel asked.

Olivia pulled a face. 'It's less the journey and more the… destination.'

'Ah yes,' he said, nodding. 'England. Home to the second largest faction in the Brotherhood, closely following behind America.'

'Tell me about them.'

'They were formed in 1864 in Georgia by a small and stupid band of Devil worshippers. They view themselves as superior to Satanists because they know about the existence of your kind, and therefore they thought they had a purer idea of hell, and Lucifer, and the First Demon. They made it their life's work to watch over any and all descendants of the First's bloodline, in the long awaited search for the Wicked One.'

'And how did they know it was me?' Olivia asked. 'How do they know *I'm* the one carrying the antichrist? It could have been any of her descendants.'

Ariel reached for his briefcase. He laid it on the table, opened it up and pulled out a leatherbound journal. He passed it to Olivia who looked at the inscription.

'The First…' she read.

'Open it,' he said.

Olivia opened it to the first page and froze. Looking up at her was an uncanny charcoal drawing of herself. Except she looked like she was from another time. Her hair was longer and braided. Her clothes looked archaic. She looked older too, but that could have just been her grave expression.

Olivia couldn't speak, so Roman asked the obvious question. 'What is this?'

'That,' Ariel said, taking the journal back, 'is the First Demon.'

'No…' Olivia said slowly. 'No, that is me.'

'No, Miss McQueen,' he said. '*You* are the doppelgänger.'

She shook her head. 'I don't understand.'

'When Lucifer and the First decided to give life to the antichrist, they wanted it to be obvious to their disciples who the Wicked One would be. They decided to introduce the doppelgänger. The Wicked One would be a perfect double of the First. That way their people would know when it was time for the antichrist to rise. The Brotherhood have eyes and ears on all descendants of the First since her demise. They began to lose hope of ever finding the Wicked One until they found you. Your parents did a good job of hiding you. Shielding you. But they still found you.'

'Fast-forward to them getting in touch with me and asking me to bring you to them,' Roman said. 'Far too self-important to get their own hands dirty, of course.'

'Naturally,' Ariel agreed. 'Besides, they are likely scared of you. You have the most evil, all-consuming, world-ending power within you, after all.'

'If they're so scared of it, why do they want to release it?' she asked.

Ariel waved a hand. 'Oh, it's your usual, mindless, Devil worshipper logic. They free the antichrist from her earthly bonds and in return she'll spare them when she destroys the earth.'

Roman quirked an eyebrow. 'So they're hoping for… a pat on the head?'

'Essentially.'

Olivia frowned. 'People keep saying *her*. How do we know the antichrist is female?'

Ariel smiled. 'We know a lot about her, actually, thanks to seers. Her name is Pandora. She is prophesised to open hell on earth and unleash all a manner of unspeakable evil.'

She arched an eyebrow. 'Pandora? As in *Pandora's Box* Pandora? Is that really who we're talking about?'

'Essentially. The Greeks stole it and twisted the story completely. But yes.'

Olivia felt her insides go cold. Without another word, she stood up and walked to the airplane bathroom, the door locking automatically behind her. She gripped onto the sink and breathed deeply. She looked at herself in the mirror.

Doppelgänger. She was the *doppelgänger* — whatever the fuck that meant. There was no escaping it. This was who she was born to be. She would never be in control of herself, of her future, because it had already been written by someone else. She felt sick.

Liv... calm down...

'It's you, isn't it?' she asked quietly. 'You're her. You're Pandora.'

A hesitation.

Yes.

'You're the antichrist.'

Yes.

Olivia ran her hands through her hair. 'Oh fuck. Fuck, fuck, fuck, fuck, fuck.'

Liv, relax. Breathe.

'Stop it!' she hissed. 'Stop talking to me like you're my friend! You've been there this whole time! For as long as I can remember! You've been lying to me!'

Livvy, what did you think I was?

She shrugged. 'I don't know. My conscience? Fuck me, I'm an idiot.'

No you're not.

'All this time you've been manipulating me. You never really cared about me.'

Of course I care, Liv. I've been helping you. Guiding you. I only want what's best for you. For both of us.

'Like the apocalypse?'

I would never let you get hurt. I love you, Liv.

'When you're released, it will kill me,' Olivia said. 'Won't it?'

I'll try not to let it.

'Not good enough.'

There was a knock at the door.

'Miss McQueen? Are you alright?' Zara called.

Olivia splashed some cold water onto her face and patted it dry with a paper towel. She re-emerged from the cubicle and came face-to-face with a smiling Zara. She recoiled and placed her hand over her hammering heart.

'Jesus,' Olivia said. 'You made me jump.'

Zara said, 'Sorry.'

Then she punched Olivia in the face.

Olivia reeled back falling against the toilet. She heard Roman shout her name. Zara moved to hit her again and Olivia launched forwards, grabbed her waist and barrelled them both backwards. They smashed into the drinks trolley and careened down the aisle, Olivia landing on top. She slammed a palm into her chin and Zara's head snapped back. The air hostess went limp as she passed out.

Olivia sat back and looked at Roman and Ariel.

'Thanks for helping!' she snapped.

Roman waved a hand dismissively. 'You had it under control.'

Olivia stood and glared at Ariel. 'What the hell was that about?'

Ariel shook his head, his eyes wide. 'I have no idea. Zara is like me. She's human. She's worked for me for several years. This is the first time something like this has happened.'

Olivia was inclined to be suspicious of people she'd just met — especially men — but there was something in his expression, the slackness of his face, that said he was just as shocked as she was. Well maybe not entirely, but close.

He has an honest face. An honest nose.

Olivia peered at Zara. 'Well whoever she is, she doesn't like me.'

'I don't see why,' Roman said, moving to join her. 'You're a delight.'

'What do we do with her?'

He shrugged. 'Question her?'

'She's unconscious.'

'When she wakes up I mean.'

Olivia turned to Ariel. 'Have you got anything we can tie her up with?'

9.

The plane had begun its descent by the time Zara came around. They had tied her to a chair using a seatbelt extension. She was gagged with her own necktie. Her eyelids fluttered, her eyes rolling. She groaned.

Olivia roughly patted her cheek. 'Wake up.'

Zara looked at her with groggy eyes. After a few moments, they sharpened. She glowered and struggled against her restraints, but Roman put a firm hand on her shoulder. She tried to scream but the gag muffled it. Roman caught her chin roughly in his hand and tilted her face up to look at him.

'I'm going to take your gag off,' he said. 'If you scream, Olivia is going to hit you again. Hard. Do you understand?'

Zara glared and nodded. Roman untied her gag. She opened her mouth to scream and Olivia slapped her. She stayed quiet.

'Oh, Zara,' Ariel said, hunkering down in front of her. 'Why?'

She looked at him with hatred. 'You know why.'

He sighed. 'Who are you spying for?'

'I'll never tell.'

Olivia slapped her again. Harder this time.

'Alright!' Zara spat. 'Alright! The Knights Of Lux.'

Roman and Olivia looked blankly at Ariel.

'A radical Catholic group,' he explained. 'Fighting against the Brotherhood.'

Olivia frowned. 'Wait. So she's with the good guys? Oh my God, are we bad guys?

'They're as bad as each other,' Ariel said.

Olivia looked back to Zara. 'Why'd you attack me?'

Zara sneered at her. 'Use your brain, half-breed.'

'You really fancy me?'

'Don't be disgusting. I'm not a queer.'

Ariel sighed. 'Zara, we don't tolerate homophobia at *Levine Corp*.'

Olivia arched an eyebrow. 'But assault is just dandy?'

'No, that's frowned upon too.'

'So,' Roman said, crossing his arms. 'You came to *Levine Corp* to spy on Ariel. That would mean that the Knights Of Lux know about this. But you chose *now* to strike. That means you were either told to look out for me or Olivia. Seeing as you attacked her and not me, I'll assume she was your main target.'

'She's the Wicked One,' Zara said. 'She is an abomination.'

'Easy,' Olivia warned.

'She must be killed before Pandora can be set free.'

Roman held up a six-inch dagger. 'That explains why this was in your jacket.'

Ariel stood and beckoned for the others to follow him. They regrouped by the bar, speaking in hushed tones.

'What do we do?' Ariel asked.

Roman shrugged. 'We kill her.'

Olivia glared. 'Stop murdering people.'

'I'm a serial killer. It's what I do. Besides, she came here to kill *you*.'

She turned to Ariel. 'She's your employee. It's your call.'

Ariel sighed. 'Roman, would you?'

He snorted. 'Not for free.'

For the first time, Ariel looked annoyed. Nevertheless, he reached into his jacket pocket and pulled out a token. He handed it to Roman who pocketed it with a smile.

'Now what?' Olivia asked. 'You're just going to kill her right here?'

Roman looked at her like she was thick. 'Of course not. I'm not prepped. I don't have a way to dispose of her. How is it going to look if we land and leave a dead air hostess behind us? The police will get involved. An investigation will open. She's human, people will *care* about her death. Not to mention the Knights Of Lux will know what happened.'

'You just left that dead woman at the cottage,' Olivia pointed out. 'She was human.'

'I had someone go in after us and get rid of the body. Not my favourite way to do things, but it was unexpected.'

'So what do we do?' Ariel asked.

Roman just smiled. 'Leave it to me.'

Olivia couldn't shake the feeling that this just wasn't right. Sure, Zara had tried to kill her — but a lot of people had. Roman had stabbed her and she was still alive. They had worked through it. Surely she and Zara could do the same? Talk through their differences? Maybe. Maybe not. Nevertheless, it was too late now. Zara was lying naked on a table, arms and legs secured in place with copious layers of saran wrap.

She screamed and cursed and threatened to kill them all. Olivia looked at her sceptically when she promised to save her for last. Eventually, Roman had resorted to stuffing her mouth with her own balled up socks.

The vaults between *Levine Corp* were deep and sound-proofed. It had been easy enough to get there. Ariel's security had picked them up when they landed. Zara had been bundled into the trunk, no questions asked — it was worth more than his security teams' jobs than to ask questions — and took them to his HQ in Canary Wharf.

Instead of going up into the offices, they had gone straight down, through the underground car park and deep into the bowls of *Levine Corp*. There, it was a warren of clinical-looking corridors. They had passed a series of rooms displaying all a manner of weird and wonderful oddities that Olivia promised she would come back and look at once this was all over. If she was alive, that was.

Instead, they had wound up in a padded cell. It was all set up for them. The operating table in the middle. The plastic sheets covering the walls. The rolls and rolls of cling film. And above all else, three bodysuits for them to wear. Beside the surgeon's table was a small workbench, and top of that lay a long, sharp knife.

Olivia turned to Ariel. 'Why do you have a kill room in your basement?'

Ariel half-smiled. 'Roman and I… we have an agreement. When he's away from home, I let him use my facilities. In return, he acts as my security detail on the rare occasion I need him.'

She looked around the padded cell. 'This is all very… *Dexter.*'

Roman picked up the knife and turned to face them both. 'Are you staying or leaving?'

Ariel sighed. 'She was my employee. I should stay.'

They looked at Olivia.

'Well?' Roman prompted.

'I'm conflicted,' she said.

He frowned. 'About what? She tried to kill you, so now we kill her. It's easy.'

'Why do we get to decide who lives and who dies?'

'You literally kill people every day,' he pointed out.

'I have to,' she said. 'Because of the Devil's debt.'

He sighed. 'In or out, Olivia. She's dying either way.'

Olivia ground her teeth together but stayed put. Roman turned to Zara who glared at him. He beamed.

'I'm going to take the socks out of your mouth,' he said. 'I'm sure you know the drill by now. Speak when you're spoken to, or I'll cut your tongue out. Nod if you understand.'

Zara nodded and Roman removed the socks. She snarled at him but remained silent.

'Now,' he said, twirling the knife in his hands as if it were a baton. 'Who else knows about Olivia?'

'No one,' Zara said. 'I didn't even know she existed until I saw her today. I knew straight away it was her. She's the exact image of the First.'

Roman watched her for a moment. Then said, 'You're lying.'

'I guess you'll never know.'

He rested the tip of the knife against her cheek and she stiffened. He loomed over her, his forehead nearly touching hers.

'Tell me the truth,' he said softly. 'How many know about Olivia?'

'No one, I swear! I didn't have time to contact anyone. I didn't even know what I was going to do with you. I panicked. I thought I could take her out on my own.'

Roman snorted. 'How did that work out for you?'

'Not well, obviously.'

Roman pointed at Olivia with the knife. 'She's the Wicked One. She is harbouring the antichrist in her half-demon body. She is strong, and powerful, and that is without being supernatural. She is a fighter. She is your worst nightmare. And you thought you could take her down yourself? Are you stupid? Or just optimistic?'

Olivia shifted uncomfortably where she stood but stayed quiet.

The knife went back to Zara's face. 'I want names of your leaders. And where to find them.'

'I'll never—'

She was cut off by her own scream as the tip of the knife bit down into her skin. A crimson red tear trickled over her cheek, thick and syrupy, and pooled on the table under her ear.

'Names,' Roman prompted. 'Locations.'

Zara nodded hurriedly. 'Okay. Alright. Adrian Locke, America. Sienna Raines, New Zealand. Aurora Russo, Italy.'

Olivia pulled out her phone, tapped down the names in her notes. Roman took the knife away from Zara's cheek and smiled. She let out a long, shaky breath.

'See?' Roman said. 'How hard was that? That's all I wanted to know.'

'Are you going to let me go now?' she asked.

'Most assuredly not.'

Zara blanched. 'But... but I gave you the names...'

'Yes. But you still tried to kill Olivia.'

Zara glanced at her. 'What is she? Your girlfriend?'

He laughed. 'Don't be ridiculous. I don't even particularly like her.'

Olivia glared but said nothing.

Roman continued, 'But for the next forty-eight hours or so she is under my protection. Pesky little sire bond, and all. Which means that if someone kills her and I fail my duty to keep her safe, I get penalized. That, naturally, makes me a little grumpy. You can understand that, can't you?'

Zara looked at Ariel. 'Are you just going to let him do this? I'm human! Like *you*!'

Ariel sighed. 'You betrayed me. You lied to me. You tried to kill Olivia and you would have probably tried to kill me too.'

'She's a monster!'

'She's my guest.'

Zara looked at Roman. 'I have money. Lots of it. You can have it all.'

'Don't like money,' Roman said.

'Wait! Wait! I can give you more names! Other people are involved in this.'

'You're such a liar.'

'Please! *Please!*'

Roman held the knife in both hands and raised it to his eye level, aiming it directly over her heart. Zara turned her head and looked at Olivia with unrestrained hatred. Roman plunged the knife deep into her chest and her eyes went wide. For a moment, nothing happened. She opened her mouth, as if to speak, but all that bubbled out was blood. Her face fell vacant and Olivia knew she was gone.

Olivia looked at Roman and paused. His eyes were closed, the knife still buried up to the hilt in Zara's chest. He didn't move. The blood trickled down Zara's naked body, rolling in rivets off the table and pooling on the floor. Olivia wasn't used to this part of killing. When she killed demons they turned to ash. There was no blood. No corpse. They returned to hell and she didn't have to think of them again. But this? It was sickening. Even worse was the look of absolute peace that came over Roman's face as he opened his eyes.

You're not safe with this man, Liv. You're safe with me. You can trust me.

Olivia's stomach rolled. She turned and marched out of the room. In the privacy of the hallway she doubled over, hands grasping her knees, sucking in huge gulp of air.

He's a serial killer. He doesn't kill because he has to, like us. He kills because he wants to. Because he likes it. He's sick. He's a monster.

'We're all monsters,' she murmured.

He would still be a monster even if he was human.

Olivia straightened as she heard a door open behind them. Roman and Ariel emerged, both looking disturbingly nonplussed.

Even the people who surround him are psychopaths. This isn't how normal people behave, Liv.

'You'll have full access to the suite,' Ariel said. 'A driver will take you there. I've arranged a dinner with you both and Cordelia tonight. I'll be there too.'

Roman frowned. 'I feel like I'm supposed to know who that is.'

'You are,' Ariel said. 'Cordelia Fox. A demon born gifted with the ability to cause agonising pain at a single glance. Head of the UK division of the Brotherhood. You met her before at that thing in Bruges. She shot you.'

'Doesn't ring a bell, but alright,' Roman said. 'And all this…?'

'Will be taken care of. Thank you again.'

Roman smiled. He looked at Olivia and cocked an eyebrow. 'Coming?'

You cannot trust him. Either of them. He's spent the last twenty-four hours stalling you. He's working against you, not with you. The only person who's ever going to look out for you is me.

Roman looked at her, quizzically. 'Everything okay?'

Don't go with him.

Olivia nodded. 'Yeah. Everything is fine. Let's go.'

10.

Ariel's idea of *simple accommodation* was far from any dictionary definition that Olivia had heard of. The Aphrodite Hotel was so beyond luxurious it had left decadence in its wake long ago. Olivia felt like she wasn't supposed to be there. Like she might burst into flames at any given moment. The polite woman at reception called her *madam* which made her wince. Everyone was so polite and friendly. Everyone smiled as they passed. She'd never been more uncomfortable in her life.

All very Stepford Wives *in here…*

Their suite was bigger than her entire flat. Everything was ultra-sleek and modern, all with clean lines and sparkling surfaces. The balcony afforded them a stunning view of Canary Wharf and, in the distance, Greenwich University. Olivia was sure she would have appreciated it had she not suddenly developed a nauseating fear of heights. Well, not so much heights. More so the act of *falling* from heights. And she still wasn't sure if she trusted Roman not to throw her over the edge, sire or not.

She sat on the overstuffed super-king bed and watched Roman raid the mini fridge in the kitchenette. He found a packet of trail mix and claimed it, along with a can of Diet Coke.

'Remind me,' Olivia said, 'what the point of all this is? Why can't we just go straight to the Brotherhood?'

'Because,' he said, popping open his can. 'There is a particular way these things are done.'

'Yes, but why do we have to waste time like this?'

Roman sat on the armchair by the desk. He opened the bag of trail mix and popped a peanut in his mouth. He looked like he didn't have a care in the world. Olivia supposed that he probably didn't. He didn't care. At all. About anything. He had no emotions, no feelings, no empathy. He was just... empty.

'We're not wasting time,' he said. 'This is how the Brotherhood wanted the trade to go ahead. The leader of the British sector wants to meet you formally. Assess you. Make nice and some small talk before escorting you back to HQ where they will, promptly, sacrifice you. It's called having a bit of decorum.'

'Sure. I never let anyone sacrifice me without buying me dinner first.'

'Well, exactly.'

She sighed. 'So who exactly are we meeting tonight?'

Roman shrugged. 'Cordelia Fox. Apparently she shot me in Bruges.'

'She sounds fun.'

Olivia reluctantly got up off the bed. She looked at herself in the full length mirror. She had seen better days. She'd seen worse, sure. But she'd definitely seen better.

'How formal is this thing?' she asked. 'Because I get the feeling jeans and a t-shirt aren't cutting it?'

'Ariel said someone will be by to drop off a change of clothes.'

'Do you trust Ariel?'

'I don't need to. I just need the *Levine Corp* resources.'

He appeared behind her, watching her reflection. She jumped, spinning to face him. Despite herself, she flinched. Roman frowned.

'What?' he asked.

Olivia pushed past him, crossing to the far wall. 'Nothing. You're just creepy.'

'Are you... are you frightened of me?'

'No, Roman, I am not *frightened* of you.'

He followed her across the room. She turned sharply to look at him. They stayed that way for a while, watching each other in a stalemate. Roman took a step forward and she took a step back. He tilted his head, quizzically. Olivia's jaw tightened, her muscles coiled and ready to strike.

'You are,' he said. 'You're scared of me. Is it because of earlier?'

'Earlier? You mean when you stabbed a woman in the chest as if it was nothing?'

He frowned. 'It *was* nothing.'

'To you.'

'Yes, to me,' he said, crossing his arms. 'Obviously that's not how you feel though.'

'You just… killed her,' she said. 'You didn't even care what it meant. You just killed her. And the look on your face… Roman, it was…'

Roman's eyes hardened. 'Go on. Say it.'

'It was evil,' she said, softly.

'Newsflash, Olivia,' he snapped. 'I *am* evil. Are you expecting to see something else? Some kind of change? Growth? You've known me for barely twenty-four hours! This is who I am! Now can you just get over it so I can go back to saving your life?'

'Do you really feel nothing?' she asked.

'Nothing at all,' he said, stepping forward again.

Olivia took another step back. An expression she couldn't place flashed across Roman's face, gone as fast as it appeared. If she'd blinked, she would have missed it.

'I'm not going to hurt you,' he said, tightly.

'Because of the sire,' she said. 'But what about once that is over? What happens then?'

Roman didn't answer. There was a knock at the door. He gave Olivia one last unfathomable look before turning and answering.

She couldn't see out into the hallway but she heard Roman talking to someone with all the flawless social skills of a man who wasn't a raging psychopath. There was laughter. A joke. The sound of the bellboy thanking Roman for a tip.

Doesn't it freak you out? The way he does that? He can just pull the façade on whenever he wants. He can have everyone around him fooled. He is dangerous, Liv.

Roman returned holding two garment bags. He offered one to her. 'Get dressed.'

Olivia took the bag into the bathroom, sceptical that whatever was in there would even fit. She unzipped it and tilted her head at the black, knee-length dress staring back at her. In the bottom of the bag were a pair of modest kitten heels.

You won't be able to walk in those, let alone fight.

'It's just dinner,' she said. 'I won't be fighting anyone tonight.'

You hope.

Olivia studied the thin heels on the shoes. At the very least they'd hurt if cracked into someone's temple. She showered and washed her hair. It felt good to wash away the last twenty-four hours. She felt gross and tired. Holding her face under the water, she closed her eyes and forced her mind to go blank. For a small moment, there was peace.

Out of the shower, she dried her hair and slipped into the dress. To her surprise, it was a perfect fit. The shoes too. There was no makeup, but she rarely wore it anyway. Inspecting herself in the mirror she realised, with a sharp pang in her chest, that this is what she might have looked like if she was normal. If she wasn't a demon. If she wasn't a descendant of the First. If she wasn't the Wicked One.

If you weren't all those things you wouldn't be you.

'Exactly,' she muttered. 'Think how nice that would be.'

She left the bathroom and walked into the main area. She found Roman on the balcony and paused. He was in a black suit with a matching black shirt and tie. His face was clean shaven, his hair combed back. He looked out over the city, his expression unreadable. She cleared her throat and he turned and smiled.

'Ready?' he asked.

'As I'll ever be to meet an evil demon who wants to sacrifice me.'

'That's the spirit!'

They'd agreed to meet Ariel in the lobby but when they arrived she couldn't see him anywhere. A beautiful strawberry blonde woman in a red dress approached them with a smile. Olivia figured it was probably Roman that had caught her attention. He seemed to do that with most women. And men.

Don't let the good looks fool you.

'Shall we go?' the woman asked.

Olivia frowned, about to tell her they were waiting for a friend. Then paused.

'Ariel?' she asked.

The woman smiled. 'That would be me. Shall we go?'

Olivia nodded wordlessly, and they fell into step behind her.

'Ariel is genderfluid,' Roman said softly. 'Sometimes he is a man. Sometimes she is a woman. And sometimes they are neither.'

Olivia nodded. 'She is… really hot.'

'That, she is.'

Ariel led them to the restaurant. When the Maître d' saw them, he hurried over to say hello and show them to a private area at the back reserved for them. The dining table was needlessly grand and had too many seats for what they needed. They were blocked off from view of the rest of the restaurant by Japanese-style partitions. Olivia and Roman sat down on one side and Ariel sat on the other. Their guest had yet to arrive.

'So what exactly happens tonight?' Olivia asked. 'We eat canapes and make pleasantries?'

'Cordelia wants to make sure you're the real thing,' Ariel said. 'She also doesn't want this to be any more traumatising for you than it need be.'

'How thoughtful of her.'

'You need to be as calm and as willing as possible for Pandora to be released,' she explained. 'It makes the transition easier.'

'So, I'm like one of those pigs that's really well treated before it's sent off to slaughter,' Olivia said. 'Good to know.'

The Maître d' approached, a tall blonde woman following behind him. Olivia tried not to stare but it proved difficult. She was statuesque. Her hair swished behind her in a long platinum ponytail and her royal blue dress hugged her toned frame. Her arms and shoulders were strong — her legs even more so. She smiled and it was impeccable.

I would let her run me over. Then back up and run me over again. Repeat until fade.

Roman and Ariel stood as she joined them, and Olivia copied. She wasn't sure what the proper etiquette was when meeting a demon cult leader, so she figured she would let the others lead the way.

'Cordelia,' Ariel said, smiling guardedly. 'You look beautiful.'

She smiled again. 'You're only saying that because it's true.'

They sat and Cordelia's gaze immediately fell to Olivia. She looked at her with something akin to hunger and Olivia had no idea how to feel.

Horny?

'Wicked One,' Cordelia said. 'It's a pleasure.'

'Just Olivia is fine,' she replied.

'Of course.'

'You don't look like a cult leader.'

Cordelia smiled. 'Oh? How should a cult leader look?'

'Probably more like Charles Manson.'

'Would you feel more comfortable if I had a penis, Olivia?'

She shrugged. 'Either or is fine by me.'

Cordelia finally looked at Roman. 'And what about Mr Wylder? I would say he doesn't much look like a serial killer.'

Roman's mouth twitched into a grin. 'And, pray tell, what should a serial killer look like?'

'Probably more like Ed Gein. Lovely to see you again, by the way.'

Roman nodded. 'Last time was in Bruges, I believe?'

Olivia resisted the urge to roll her eyes. Roman's level of being able to bullshit his way through a conversation rivalled even hers. She settled for kicking him under the table but he just kicked her back.

'It was, indeed,' Cordelia agreed. 'You certainly leave a lasting impression on a woman.'

Roman's lips twitched into a smile, but he didn't reply. Olivia and Ariel exchanged looks as if asking each other if they were still a part of this conversation. A waiter approached, a welcome reprieve from the thick silence that hung over the table. He took wine orders and Olivia stared blankly at the menu realising she couldn't read French. She picked the easiest thing to pronounce and the waiter smiled and nodded, leaving them to it.

'So,' Ariel said. 'You asked for proof of the Wicked One in the flesh. Here she is. I trust she exceeds expectations?'

Cordelia smiled again, radiantly. 'She is the image of the First. But I knew she would be. That's not what this is about. This is about making a good first impression. If we are to work together, Olivia, we must reach an understanding.'

Olivia frowned. 'An understanding? Is that what you call sacrificing me?'

'Don't be so melodramatic. There is no guarantee you won't survive the ritual. You are strong. The blood of the First runs in your veins. With any luck Pandora will be freed and you will be left to live the rest of your life as you please.'

'And without luck?'

Cordelia sighed. 'Historical moments are not without their casualties. But your sacrifice will be duly noted.'

'And say I do survive?' Olivia said, prickling. 'What happens then?'

'Then you are free.'

'I find that hard to believe.'

'We have no use for you besides Pandora,' she said, assuredly. 'Once you fulfil your duty as the Wicked One, your life will be of very little consequence to us.'

The waiter returned with red wine for Ariel and white for Cordelia. Roman and Olivia both had   Diet Cokes. The conversation resumed when he retreated.

'How do we know you're not lying?' Roman asked.

Cordelia eyed him, intrigued. 'Why do you care?'

'Because for the next two days, give or take, I'm sired to her,' he jerked a thumb at Olivia. 'Meaning she's under my protection. Meaning I can't let her die.'

Cordelia tutted. 'Oh dear. Then we really must hope Olivia survives the ritual. If you break a sire—'

'I realise,' he said, quickly.

Olivia frowned. 'He gets in trouble. A slap on the wrist. We know.'

Cordelia glanced at her. 'That's certainly *one* way to downplay an eternity in hell.'

Olivia looked at Roman, eyes widening. 'You didn't tell me that.'

Roman shrugged. 'It didn't seem important.'

'So it would seem more integral than ever,' Ariel said, evenly, 'that we all work together. The last thing we need is half the people at this table dead.'

'Quite,' Cordelia said. 'Olivia, I'm here to answer all of your questions and calm any nerves you may have.'

'Alright,' she said, putting her elbows on the table and leaning forward despite Ariel wincing at her poor table manners. 'Why do you even want Pandora released?'

'Because she is our messiah. She will reshape this world in her vision.'

'I can never understand why you cult types want Armageddon so much. What do you suppose she'll do to you once you've released her?'

'She will be grateful.'

'So you're doing this all for some brownie points and a gold star?'

Cordelia's composure proved infallible. 'I'm doing it because I have faith in her. As does the Brotherhood.'

'And what about the rest of us who like the world as it is now?' Roman asked. 'You know, non-doomsday.'

'You will learn to love the new world.'

He regarded her. 'I am nothing if not adaptable.'

'And how many people will die?' Olivia asked. 'I don't expect the apocalypse to come free of charge.'

'Naturally,' Cordelia said. 'Non-believers will be eliminated. For the greater good.'

'Yeah, *your* greater good.'

Ariel cleared her throat delicately. All eyes on the table went to her.

'It seems,' she said diplomatically. 'That there is an obvious difference of opinion when it comes to Pandora's Awakening. You hired Roman to bring you the Wicked One. Olivia has agreed to come willingly in an act of self-preservation. She cannot fight you, and therefore, she understands that to make the Awakening as smooth as possible, she needs to cooperate. This will, naturally, grant her a higher chance of survival. This we can all agree on. As for what happens after Pandora rises—'

'Is none of your concern,' Cordelia said.

'It is if I don't come willingly,' Olivia said. 'Promise that you will keep Pandora in check or I will fight you every step of the way.'

'All that will do is grant you a swift and painful death.'

'I'm not stupid,' Olivia said, hotly. 'I talk to her all the time, you know. Pandora. She's right in here with me, giving a running commentary.'

This took Ariel by surprise. As for Cordelia, the hungry expression returned.

'She's vocal?' Cordelia breathed. 'What does she say?'

'She says you're a bellend.'

Easy.

'But it's not about what she says,' Olivia continued. 'It's about what she feels. What she shares with me. Because right now we're not two separate entities. We are one. If I die in the Awakening, so will she. I'm right, aren't I? That's the real reason why you want this alliance so badly. If I die, I'm taking Pandora down with me.'

Cordelia said nothing, her face the perfect picture of calm. And yet there was something behind her eyes. A flicker of fear, gone as quickly as it came.

'Very well,' she said calmly. 'What are your terms?'

'No mass genocide,' Olivia said. 'Actually no genocide at all — mass or minor.'

Spoilsport.

Cordelia nodded. 'Alright.'

'Don't end the world.'

'It wouldn't be the end of the world, it would be the start of a new one.'

'None of that either.'

Cordelia sighed. 'You want me to put the Wicked One on the naughty step?'

'Worship her,' Olivia said. 'Kiss the ground she walks on. Put her on a throne and give her a sceptre for all I care. Just don't end the world.'

'And how do you know she will listen to us?'

'I don't,' Olivia said. 'But I have to trust that she values me enough to do this for me.'

Liv, come on...

'Is it a deal?' Olivia asked, ignoring Pandora.

Cordelia broke into a slow grin. 'Oh, I like you. It's a deal.'

The two women shook hands across the table just as the waiter brought their food over. To Olivia's dismay — and Roman's obvious delight — she had ordered the calf's brain. Nevertheless, she forced a tight smile as Cordelia raised her wineglass in a toast.

'To Pandora,' she said.

Roman and Olivia shared an uneasy look.

'To Pandora,' they echoed.

11.

Roman and Ariel had decided to go to the bar after dinner. Cordelia was long gone — far more pressing issues demanded her attention than a night cap — and Olivia saw no reason to continue being sociable. Her social battery had run dry long before dessert, and all she wanted now was blessed sleep, so she left them to it. Plus, this meant that she could claim the bed and leave the sofa to Roman. That thought alone gave her an immense sense of petty joy.

Drifting off to sleep was easy enough. It was *staying* asleep that proved hard. When she woke just after three in the morning and saw that Roman had not returned, she tried to ignore the gnawing sensation in her stomach. He was probably still at the bar with Ariel. Or in Ariel's room. No need to worry.

He's a grown demon. He can take care of himself.

Olivia didn't reply.

Ah. So you're still not speaking to me.

'Why should I?'

You said it yourself. We are one.

'Except you're the antichrist,' Olivia pointed out. 'You want to destroy everyone on the planet.'

Not everyone.

'Just everyone that doesn't suit you.'

You and your friends are safe with me, you know. I wouldn't let anything bad happen to you. I'll protect you.

'You'll protect me from yourself? How comforting.'

It's not what you think it will be, Liv. It's not all fire and brimstone. It's not hell on earth. It will just be different. Demons will be in charge. We won't be a secret anymore. We won't need to hide.

'And what about the humans?'

They will have their purpose.

Olivia closed her eyes. 'Please. Please don't hurt anyone. I don't want you to die. I don't want to die either. I'll take out the Brotherhood if I have to but not you. Just… don't hurt anyone.'

Livvy…

'Please? God, please, I am begging you.'

A pause.

Alright. I'll try it your way.

Olivia opened her eyes and let out a long breath she didn't realise she had been holding. She realised, grudgingly, that she wasn't going to be able to sleep now. Groaning, her tired body protesting with every movement, she hauled herself out of bed and slipped her jeans and t-shirt back on.

It was a long ride down to the ground floor. The lobby was empty, as was most of the hotel. To Olivia's annoyance, the night staff were just as cheerful as the day staff. She found the bar and saw that it too was empty, save for a figure alone at the bar. Roman.

She sat on the stool beside him and he glanced at her. In his hand was a non-alcoholic beer. She flagged down the bartender who was busying himself with cleaning the counters and ordered the same.

'Where's Ariel?' she asked.

'Headed up about an hour ago,' Roman said. 'Couldn't sleep?'

'Not much. You?'

120

He shrugged. 'Sleep bores me.'

'How would you know? You're asleep.'

'Oh, I know.'

The bartender put her beer down in front of her and she smiled as a thank you. They sat in not comfortable, but not *uncomfortable* silence, sipping their drinks. Olivia couldn't remember the last time she'd had a real drink. She didn't miss it either. Initially, she'd thought she would miss alcohol more, but was proved pleasantly wrong. The anxiety drinking brought with it was just not worth the temporary buzz.

'So,' Olivia said. 'Cordelia fancies you.'

Roman shrugged. 'Most people do.'

'I don't.'

'Don't lie to yourself.'

Olivia scowled but it went unnoticed.

'You didn't tell me you could hear Pandora in your head,' Roman said, his tone almost accusing.

Olivia frowned. 'You didn't tell me that if you broke the sire bond you'd go to hell.'

He looked at her. 'You first.'

She rolled her eyes. 'In my defence, I didn't know it was Pandora. I thought it was my… I don't know? My conscience? And then when I realised — which was literally only today — I didn't know what to say. But she promised me she'll try not to destroy the world after she's released.'

'How comforting.'

'Now you,' she said. 'Why didn't you tell me about the sire bond?'

He sighed and took another sip. 'Would it have made a difference?'

'Yes.'

'No it wouldn't.'

'I don't wish hell on anyone,' she said, shortly. 'Not even you.'

He cocked an eyebrow. 'Spoken like someone who's been before.'

Olivia looked down at her drink and didn't say anything. Roman sat a little straighter on his stool.

'Oh,' he said. 'You have.'

'Leave it, Roman,' she mumbled.

'Not likely.'

'I don't want to talk about it.'

'And I don't want to be sired to you,' he said. 'Suck it up.'

'Roman…'

'Is it to do with your Devil's debt?'

She took a deep breath and looked at her palm, half expecting a name to appear on cue.

'I was born gifted,' she said, quietly. 'Like Cordelia. Except my gift was fire. I asked for it to be taken away and we made a deal. My gift would be taken and in return I owe a Devil's debt until I take my gift back.'

Roman watched her, frowning. 'Why did you want your gift taken away?'

'Does it matter?'

'Obviously, yes.'

She looked at him. 'I couldn't control it. One night my boyfriend and I got into an argument. I exploded. Literally, exploded. The fire killed him and didn't leave a scratch on me. The police said that Cillian's death was an accident — a gas leak, most likely. No one knew what really happened but I think his parents still blamed me somehow. I never wanted to use my gift again after that. I didn't even want to *risk* using it. I killed the only person I had left—'

Olivia's voice caught and she closed her eyes, counting down from ten.

You're okay, Liv.

Roman was silent for a moment. She opened her eyes and saw him watching her with a look of complete and utter calm. She didn't know if that made her feel better or worse, but at least the lump in her throat had passed.

'I'm sorry for your loss,' he said after a long moment. It was sincere but rehearsed.

'Thank you.'

They drank again in silence, Olivia focusing on thinking about anything other than Cillian. It proved difficult. She steeled her jaw and stared ahead, eyes hard.

'I lost someone too,' Roman said after a while. 'A few someones, actually.'

She looked at him, surprised. 'Oh. I'm sorry.'

'Thanks.'

'Is that why you're…?'

The question hung in the air between them. He laughed.

'It's not a bad word,' he said. 'You can say it.'

'A serial killer,' she said, softly.

He shrugged. 'Maybe. Maybe I was born like this.'

'What happened?' she asked.

He looked at her. His face was uncharacteristically open, his eyes as close to vulnerable as Roman Wylder got. 'You weren't the only one with God-fearing biological parents. Eamon and Fiadh Byrne were devout Catholics and raging bigots. I was their eldest, followed by two sisters and a brother.' He paused to half-smile at the memory of them, but it was fleeting. 'We never particularly got on, but you can imagine the rift caused when I turned twelve and accidentally set my bed on fire. The realisation that their son was a demon justified their predetermined hatred of me.'

Olivia watched him. Watched his hands tighten on his pint glass. Watched him at war with himself, fighting to ignore an onslaught of repressed feelings he didn't understand or even *want* to try and understand.

'So they decided to kill me,' he went on, mouth set in a grim line. 'But not just me. They thought all of their other children were born with the same affliction and decided they needed to die too. They saved me for last. They rounded us up, tied our hands and took us to the barn. I watched them shoot my siblings.' He swallowed. 'Eabha and Nuala went down easily. Daithi was young and terrified. He struggled and the bullet clipped the side of his head. Took out half his face. He didn't die immediately, though. He just laid there, face down in the muck, slowly bleeding out.'

Olivia wanted to reach out to him but she didn't think he'd appreciate it if she did. And she had no idea what she'd do once she did. Instead she waited, watching as his lips twisted into a grimace.

'Then it was my turn. I attacked first though. I'd managed to loosen my ropes — Eamon was a terrible farmer, the man could never tie a decent knot to save his life — and I went for them. I'll save you the details and skip to the end. I shot my mother and beat my father to death with the butt of his shotgun,' his voice was hoarse now. 'They were the first people I ever killed. My siblings died because of me. Because of what I am.'

Olivia stared at him. She had no idea what to say, so she didn't say anything.

'I changed my name and ran away. I was homeless for a while. Then Alastair found me. He took pity on me and brought me home with him. He raised me as his own. I kept my true nature from him. It started slowly, and then all at once. The need to kill, it was… unbearable.' A pause. A flicker of pain so brief that Olivia wondered if she'd imagined it. 'I thought Alastair would understand, but as it would turn out, he is the only vampire in the world with a conscience. He only fed on blood bags. So, instead, we went after the bad guys together. That way I could control my urges, and no one innocent had to die.

'Then of course, when I was eighteen, he came home one night to find me dissecting one of his ex-patrons that had sexually assaulted a woman a few days prior. He was human, but barely. An absolutely vile excuse of a man. But he was still human and it was still against Alastair's rules. He saw me for what I really was. A monster.'

Olivia sucked in a deep breath. She didn't want to feel sorry for Roman. And she knew Roman didn't want her to feel sorry for him either. Yet here she was, doing it anyway. Because if anyone could understand family drama, and being stuck in a shit-show of a home life, and being let down by the people who were supposed to care for you, it was her. And maybe she felt a little guilty too for never bothering to consider that he was like this for a reason. Most of all, she just felt really fucking sad. For both of them.

'Jesus Christ, Roman,' Olivia breathed. 'Fuck.'

Roman didn't look at her. 'I've never told anyone that before. I have no idea why I just told you.'

'Have you ever killed someone that didn't deserve it?' she asked.

He glanced at her. 'You mean an innocent?'

She nodded. 'Apart from the woman at the farm.'

He shrugged. 'I try not to, unless it's unavoidable. That woman would have created trouble had I let her go. If I go after the bad guys, it keeps the focus off me. *Rapist Gone Missing* doesn't evoke quite the same reaction as *Soccer Mom of Five Brutally Beaten To Death*. People don't care if the bad guys disappear. It keeps me undetected. I never regret killing someone, Olivia. But I always make sure there is a reason.'

Once again, she didn't know what to say. Instead she stood and pulled him to his feet. Before he had a chance to ask what she was doing, she put her arms around him. He tensed instinctively, his arms remaining by his sides.

'Olivia…?' he asked.

'I'm sorry for everything that's happened to you,' she said, holding on a little while longer.

After a moment, she stepped back. Their eyes met.

'Goodnight, Roman,' she said.

He blinked. 'Goodnight, Olivia.'

12.

Her sleep was fitful and restless, and when the wakeup call roused her, Olivia felt as though she hadn't slept at all. She glanced at the sofa and saw evidence that Roman had come up at some point in the night. He was gone now though — probably with Ariel. With a groan, she forced herself out of bed and pulled her clothes on.

The bathroom came with all the sundries she needed, and she washed her face and brushed her hair. She pulled her hair up into a ponytail and took stock of herself. For the first time since she could remember, she looked ill. Her face was pale and gaunt, her under-eyes rimmed with blue semi circles. She needed proper sleep. She told herself that she would sleep for a solid twenty-four hours once this was all over.

She pulled on her boots and slid her sheathed dagger inside, sitting it snugly against her inner calf. She always felt better with the knife on her. It was gruesome to look at, its purpose equally as ugly, but it afforded a kind of protection that she couldn't provide for herself. One tiny nick of the blade and a demon would crumble to ash, banished to hell.

It could kill Roman.

Olivia ignored her and headed downstairs. It was early and the restaurant wasn't yet busy. Olivia spotted Roman and Ariel at a table at the back. They looked up as she approached. Roman was in his usual garb: black jeans, a black t-shirt, and a black leather jacket. Ariel, however, wore an impeccable pale grey suit. He smiled at her and motioned for the waiter.

Before she'd even taken a seat, fresh coffee was put in front of her. Looking briefly at the menu she ordered Eggs Benedict and a plate of fresh fruit. She figured that once she was back in her apartment in Dublin she would be back to eating off-brand ramen and cereal again and that she should make the most of this.

'The helicopter will pick you up at eight,' Ariel said, not bothering with small talk. 'It will take you to Ashmoore.'

Olivia sipped her coffee. 'Ashmoore?'

'The Brotherhood's UK base. It was once an asylum but has long since been abandoned and henceforth turned into a fortress.'

'So I'm going to be sacrificed in a creepy abandoned hospital? How on brand.'

'Cordelia left late last night to prepare them for your arrival. Everything should run remarkably smoothly from here on out. Especially now that you have struck a deal with them.'

'A deal that I doubt either Cordelia or Pandora intend to keep,' Roman said.

'I've spoken to Pandora,' Olivia said. 'She's going to try and behave.'

'How reassuring.'

'It's the best I can do.'

'This is new territory for all of us,' Ariel interjected. 'As of now we have a plan that allows everyone here to leave this alive. Let's focus on that. What comes next can wait.'

Their breakfast came and they ate in tense silence. At quarter to eight, Ariel took them up to the roof to wait for the helicopter. Olivia hugged her jacket tighter around her. Once again, Roman offered her his jacket but she turned it down. She had quickly learned that when Roman did these things — offering her his coat, or holding the door open for her — he wasn't doing it because he cared. They were behaviours that he had learnt to help him fit in. It was almost a kind of manipulation.

You're so bloody stubborn.

The chopper touched down and they said goodbye to Ariel. He shook hands with Roman and pulled Olivia in for a brief embrace.

'He's not all bad,' Ariel murmured in her ear before pulling away.

Olivia felt uneasy in the helicopter, even more so as it took off. It felt unstable, and every gust of wind rattled it. It was as though it was at risk of plummeting from the sky at any moment and her stomach churned as they swept across the high rises of London.

Roman remained infuriatingly unperturbed by it all. He looked out of the window, making idle chit chat with the pilot via the headset they each wore. His small talk came easy — easier than Olivia had ever found it — and he smiled when he was supposed to smile, nodded when he was supposed to nod, and reacted perfectly human to everything that was said. It irritated Olivia to no end. Not because he was so good at it, but because he was better at it than her.

He's been studying humans his whole life. Every moment has been a learning opportunity. You, however, have never had any interest in learning about others. Who's the psycho now?

Olivia crossed her arms and looked out her own window. She didn't know exactly where Ashmoore was located, but she could tell they were heading South West. After forty minutes they began their descent just on the outskirts of Devon. They landed on a private strip. An armoured car was already waiting for them. Olivia tensed and Roman looked over at her.

'We're their guests,' he reminded her. 'Not their prisoners.'

'No, we're definitely their prisoners,' she said. 'We're just stupid enough to hand ourselves over.'

'You're not going to die, if that's what you're worried about.'

She looked at him. 'Whether I die or not, shit is still going to hit the fan.'

'The English are so poetic.'

The pilot helped her down onto the tarmac, Roman following. A man in a dark grey suit emerged from the car smiling widely. His skin was copper, his eyes dark. They stopped a good two metres in front of him and ignored his offer to shake hands. He didn't seem offended.

'Good morning!' he said, cheerfully. 'I'm Zaid Ramzi, VP for the UK sector of the Brotherhood. President Cordelia sent me to collect you.'

'I'm Spears and this is Aguilera,' Roman said, nodding at Olivia. 'We'll be your entertainment this evening.'

He grinned. 'Cordelia said I would like you.'

'Which is utterly baffling because she didn't mention you at all, Vice President Ramzi.'

Zaid merely laughed good-naturedly and beckoned towards the car. 'Come. We can talk at Ashmoore.'

The car was roomier than it looked from the outside. Zaid slipped in behind the wheel protected by the Perspex partition between himself and the back. Roman and Olivia looked at each other as the car doors locked automatically. Her chest heaved, an anxiety attack threatening to join them in the backseat.

'*Breathe*,' he mouthed to her.

She closed her eyes and took a deep breath.

You're not in any danger. Right now you're literally gold dust to them.

Zaid put the radio on as they drove. 'Any preference?' he asked.

'80s FM,' they both said.

He laughed and switched stations. The rest of the drive was quiet, save for the radio and Zaid's occasional off-key humming. Olivia looked out the window, looking for any road signs indicating where they were going, but they stuck to country lanes and back roads. Nothing but empty fields, horse paddocks, and greenhouses rolled by for a solid twenty minutes, and even those became sparse. The roads became narrower and closed in by the trees on both sides. It gave Olivia a nauseating sense of claustrophobia and the same anxiety attack from before perked up. A hand settled beside hers, pinky fingers touching.

She looked over at Roman but he was watching the trees go by. He seemed to know how and when to comfort people, without really caring about what he was doing. It occurred to her that he would make a good doctor. Good enough at feigning empathy to comfort his patients but still far enough removed to not let it get to him.

Don't admire the psychopath, Liv.

They turned down a side road and before them a crumbling old building rose up, as imposing as it was unsightly. Ashmoore Asylum was decrepit to say the least. The brick work was old and uninspired, and the roof was falling in. Across the windows were heavy, rusted bars, and one of the walls in the yard had been completely knocked down. By age or by accident, there was no telling. It sat alone in the overgrown grass as the end of a long gravel drive with an empty water fountain out front. The water feature was an angel with big black crosses spray painted over its eyes.

Zaid saw their faces in the rear-view mirror and laughed. 'It's nicer inside, I promise.'

There were guards outside the main entrance, dressed in armoured clothing with guns secured at their hips. They didn't even look at them as Zaid led them into the building with a key card. Olivia immediately saw what he had meant the moment they stepped inside. The crumbling exterior was a mere façade. The inside of Ashmoore was a fortress, clinical and cold with exposed brick walls and metal floors. More guards stood inside, lining the corridors as Zaid led the way through the maze of hallways. Olivia tried to keep track of how many turns they made but it was impossible.

'I'll show you to your quarters first,' Zaid said, leading them up a flight of stairs. 'Cordelia and the Twelve are in the amphitheatre waiting for you. There is much to arrange before the Awakening ritual tonight. Do you have any questions?'

'So many,' Roman said. 'Who are the Twelve?'

'The Twelve Disciples,' Zaid said. 'The most loyal twelve followers of the Brotherhood chosen to worship here at Ashmoore. They help make up the UK counsel with myself and Cordelia.'

'I see. And what preparations are needed before tonight?'

'The Wicked One must be cleansed,' Zaid said.

Olivia frowned. 'I'm not dirty.'

'It's a cleansing of the soul.'

'Well, my soul isn't dirty either.'

Zaid laughed with ridiculously high-spirited mirth. 'Plus we must prepare for the Bacchanalia.'

Olivia and Roman shared a bemused glance.

'By Bacchanalia,' Roman said, slowly, 'do you mean those ancient Roman sex parties the gladiators used to have?'

'What happens at Bacchanalia stays at Bacchanalia,' Zaid said as they reached the third floor. He led them down another hallway which seemed more like a hotel corridor. 'But mostly it is just to celebrate the Awakening of Pandora. This is how it would have been done in the days of the First.'

'And how does one prepare for a demon orgy?' Roman asked.

'You leave us to worry about that. You're our guests, Mr Wylder. We want you to relax and enjoy your stay.'

He stopped outside a door and opened it with the same keycard as before. They were ushered inside a room that had most likely once been a patient's room, but was now redesigned as a lounge. It reminded Olivia of a posh doctor's waiting room. Not that she had been in many of those, but she could imagine.

'If you need anything, just buzz,' Zaid said, nodding towards the intercom that sat on the coffee table.

With that he left them. Olivia heard the sound of the door locking behind him. She glanced around the room. No windows. No other doors. Not even a clock so you could tell how long you'd been in there.

'This is a power play,' she muttered. 'And not a very subtle one either.'

Roman nodded. 'Tactical too. Leaving us here without a sense of time is supposed to unnerve us.'

'Well, it's working.'

Roman took out his phone and tapped at the screen. He nodded. 'Signal is blocked.'

He sat on the modern-looking sofa and picked up a magazine from the coffee table. On the front cover was an actress that Olivia kind-of recognised, along with subheadings that read *Why We Need To Be Kinder To One Another,* and then underneath it, *Meghan And Harry: The Worst Thing To Happen To The UK Since Hitler.* Roman opened it and began methodically from the start, with every intention of reading it back to front.

She sighed and sat beside him, picking up her own magazine, opening it to an article with the heading *Multiple Orgasms: Myth Or Legendary?*

They waited.

They had both finished reading their own magazines and had time to swap before Zaid returned to collect them. The walk down to the amphitheatre was just as convoluted as their walk up to the waiting room had been and Olivia quickly lost count of how many rights, lefts, and staircases they had taken. They were definitely going lower, past ground level. The air grew colder, and the sleek modern lines of Ashmoore gave way to the original gothic architecture. The hallways reminded Olivia of old wine cellars.

Eventually they arrived at a pair of large, ornate wooden doors. Two guards stood either side, visors down on their helmets. They let

Zaid pass without question, and the double doors opened up into a grand covered arena. It was vast, to say the least, and their footsteps echoed on the stone floor. It was oval-shaped, and rows of seats rose all around them — all empty at present. The ceiling was domed and made of stained glass, depicting images of fire and death, and all things hell.

In the centre of the amphitheatre stood Cordelia in a beautiful emerald green pantsuit that matched her eyes. There was no shirt beneath her open jacket, only a gold chain keeping it from threatening her modesty. Her high heels were a similar golden colour, and her hair fell over her shoulders in loose curls. Olivia was sure that, had they met at The Betsy, she would have bought Cordelia a drink.

Behind her, all bald and wearing brown robes, eyes cast to the ground, were twelve men and women. Six of each. All as unremarkable and stripped of identity as each other. They were pale and sickly-looking, their frames thin. They made Cordelia look even more radiant. Maybe that was the point.

Cordelia smiled brightly as they approached. 'Welcome! I trust Zaid has been looking after you?'

'He left us in a room with nothing to read but back issues of *Femme* magazine,' Roman said. 'I took a quiz to find out which season I'm most like.'

'What were the results?'

'Apparently, I'm a spring.'

'Fascinating.'

'I like to think so.'

Cordelia turned to Olivia, beaming. 'We are beyond thrilled to have you here, Olivia.'

Olivia nodded at the people behind her. 'You sure look it.'

'Oh, don't mind them. They're the Twelve. They swore an oath of silence when they were welcomed onto the council.'

'Doesn't that defeat the point of having them as council members?'

Cordelia simply smiled again. 'They know their place.'

'So,' Roman said, looking around the arena. 'This is needlessly ostentatious. Even for an evil cult.'

'It has its uses,' Zaid said. 'As do all our facilities. For example, tonight's Bacchanalia.'

'Ah yes. The sex party.'

Cordelia barked a laugh. 'If that's what you chose to indulge in, then sure. But mostly we will focus on the Awakening ritual.'

Olivia cleared her throat, arms crossed tightly over her chest. 'Which consists of?'

'You will be presented to the court,' she said. 'I will perform the Evigilationem Significasse chant, and we will let some of your blood to allow Pandora to pass through you. It's all very straightforward.'

'And the prep?' Roman asked. 'I hardly doubt it's going to be mani-pedis and aromatherapy?'

Another laugh. 'It's just a few simple steps to ready the Wicked One—'

'Olivia,' they both growled.

Cordelia's mouth twitched with amusement. 'To ready *Olivia* for the evening. She will be given the mark of the First and detoxified. Naturally, her demon form will be temporarily bound to prevent it from appearing during the ritual.'

Olivia arched an eyebrow. 'A mark? Like a tattoo?'

Cordelia's smile turned wolfish. 'Well. Not exactly.'

13.

Olivia shook her head. 'No! Nope! Fuck no! Absolutely not!'

Zaid gave her an appeasing smile. Olivia wanted to punch it off his stupid face. The member of the Twelve holding the cattle brand looked between them nervously, the iron rod shaking in his weak grip. At one end of the lab were a group of scientists in lab coats dissecting what looked like — but what Olivia hoped wasn't — a myriad of human organs. At the other end, another group were discussing a series of x-rays of a creature that looked suspiciously like Bigfoot. And stuck in the middle with Olivia was a man with a cow poker. Hardly ground-breaking.

When they had been escorted to the lab, Olivia had been expecting some kind of shot, or maybe that stuff they did for MRI scans where they injected ink into your body so that it would show up in your blood. What she *wasn't expecting,* however, was to be poked with hot sticks that had been heating up over an open Bunsen burner flame.

'It's only small,' Zaid said. 'It will only hurt for a moment.'

Olivia folded her arms tightly. 'Absolutely not. I'm not a cow.'

'Well…' Roman murmured from across the workbench, fiddling with a blood slide.

A scientist plucked the slide out of Roman's grasp and glared at him. Roman gave the young man a warm smile and Olivia watched him melt into a puddle. Roman was, seemingly, instantly forgiven.

She shook her head. 'Tattoo me. Draw on me in Sharpie. Do absolutely anything else because I'm *not* letting you stick me with that.'

The brand was simple, just an upside down crucifix, two inches long. They wanted it to go on her sternum, just over her heart. It hadn't escaped her that meant taking off her top, and that just made her even more adamant that it was going absolutely nowhere near her.

'It will be over before you know it,' Zaid promised.

'I'll be scarred forever.'

'We can pick up some Bio-Oil on the way home,' Roman said, not taking his flirtatious gaze off the scientist whose cheeks were flushing pink.

'Roman!' she snapped. 'Put your dick away and help me!'

He dragged his eyes away from the young man and looked at her. 'If my dick was out, you'd know about it.'

She glared at him and he sighed, straightening.

'Zaid, is there any other way to do the branding without actually branding her?' he asked.

Zaid shook his head. 'Unfortunately not. Everything must be done the old way, like in the time of the First.'

'How do you know the First didn't have a magic marker?' Olivia asked.

Zaid's perfect façade of collectedness threatened to slip. She watched him take a deep breath and force another polite smile. He gestured at the member of the Twelve holding the iron rod.

'Number Two is very capable,' Zaid said. 'He's done many other brandings on Brotherhood followers.'

Roman frowned. 'Number Two?'

'Each of the Twelve gave up their names and go by numbers now.'

'Bad luck getting stuck with Number Two.'

Number Two looked nonplussed.

Roman shrugged. 'I suppose you're used to being the butt of people's jokes by now.'

'Roman…' Olivia warned.

'Always getting the bum end of things.'

'*Roman*…'

'No, no, I have a few more,' he said and paused. 'Your name means shit.'

'Roman!'

'Please,' said Zaid. 'We are already falling behind schedule. Let's get this done and move on.'

Olivia glared at him. 'Why should I?'

'Because,' Cordelia said, joining them in the lab. 'Without the branding there can be no Awakening. Without an Awakening there can be no Pandora. And without Pandora you are useless to us. Would you like to know what we do to things that are useless to us?'

Olivia didn't reply, merely crooked an eyebrow. Cordelia sighed. She looked over to the scientist Roman had been flirting with. Her eyes narrowed and suddenly the man doubled over, screaming. Olivia jumped back, eyes wide.

'What are you doing?' she asked. 'Stop it. *Stop it*.'

'Things that have no use to me don't end well,' Cordelia said, quietly.

The man crumpled to the floor, gasping and trembling. Roman rolled his eyes.

'Alright,' he said. 'You've made your point.'

'Not yet, I haven't.'

There was a loud crack, and suddenly the man stopped screaming. He went limp, his eyes glazing over. Olivia ran to his side and crouched beside him, feeling for a pulse. There was none. Around her, people continued about their business like this was an everyday occurrence. Maybe it was. She glared at Cordelia.

'You killed him!' she shouted.

Cordelia shrugged. 'I put him out of his misery.'

'Misery that *you* put him in in the first place!'

'Not me,' she said innocently. 'You, Wicked One.'

Olivia launched herself at Cordelia but Roman grabbed her and held her back. Cordelia simply smiled.

'If you don't want to suffer a similar fate, you will do as you're told,' she said.

'You're bluffing. You need me.'

'Perhaps. But I can certainly put you in agonising pain until you agree to follow orders.'

The two of them watched each other. Cordelia's face remained cool. Olivia's twisted into hatred.

'Alright,' she said through gritted teeth. 'I'll get the damn branding.'

Number Two nodded and pulled the rod from the blue flame. He stepped toward Olivia but she held her hand up.

'Not by you,' she said. 'Roman will do it.'

Roman looked surprised for the first time since she had known him. 'I will?'

Olivia snatched the rod from Number Two and held it out to Roman. 'Yep.'

'Can I ask why?'

'I don't trust these people.'

He frowned. 'Do you trust me?'

'Not really, but at least more than I trust them.' She looked over her shoulders at the others. 'Out.'

Zaid looked like he was about to protest but Olivia glared and he shut up before he'd even begun. Cordelia nodded at them and clicked her fingers, and everyone — including the lab techs — left. Olivia waited for the door to click shut behind them before pulling her top off.

Roman's mouth quirked. 'If you want to get naked with me you need only ask.'

'It's for the branding, idiot. Over the heart, remember?'

He watched her for a long moment. 'Are you sure?'

'Nope. But what choice do we have?' She tugged at the edges of her bra, exposing as much of her sternum to him as she could while keeping her modesty in check.

Roman put the rod back the flame for a few moments, making sure it was as hot as possible, and waited until the iron was glowing before withdrawing. He gave Olivia an uncertain look before pressing it to her chest.

Olivia screamed.

She looked at her reflection in the mirror, blanching. She had plenty of scars from fights. Demons healed quickly but they always left behind a faint trace of any wound that would have been fatal to a human. She still had the scar on her face from the accident all those years ago. But none of them had been self-inflicted. None of them had been put there on purpose.

The upside down crucifix was as ugly as it was deliberate. It had healed over almost instantly, but the pain lingered. She touched a hand to her chest, her fingers running over the raised bump of skin, and was horrified when a lump formed in her throat.

She closed her eyes and counted back from ten.

I'm really sorry, Liv.

There was a knock on the bathroom door.

'Olivia?' Roman called, voice uncertain. 'Are you alright?'

She swallowed hard, some of the tightness leaving her throat. 'Yes. I'm fine.'

'Shall we get going then?' Zaid called. It wasn't a suggestion, just a dressed-up command. 'We really mustn't fall behind schedule. We must detoxify and bind you.'

It won't be as bad as the branding. I promise.

Olivia unlocked the door, frowning at the faces peering back at her. Zaid wore a patient facade over his uptight body language. He had a tablet in his hand, his fingers drumming against the screen. Roman's face, however, was unreadable. Olivia thought she saw a trace of guilt in his eyes.

'Brilliant,' Zaid said, turning beckoning them to follow. 'We have a very tight schedule to keep.'

They followed him down the labyrinth of hallways. Olivia let his voice fade out, focusing only on the sound of her heart thrumming in her chest and her footsteps on the tiled floor. She could sense Roman watching her but she didn't look up at him.

They went down a flight of steps, and then another, and the modern architecture faded away once more into stone and mortar. They reached a corridor lit by oil lamps. The ground became earthy underfoot. There was a dampness in the air and a chill where the central heating couldn't reach.

The lamplight illuminated faces on the walls as they passed. It wasn't until she looked closer that Olivia saw that they weren't faces but skulls. Actual skulls. She jerked back, her flesh crawling at the realisation they were walking through a catacomb.

'What poor souls made up the décor in here?' she mumbled.

Zaid shrugged. 'Oh, all sorts. Devout followers, ancient members of the Brotherhood, enemies who crossed us. Nothing has been added to it for centuries, of course, but the history remains.'

She nodded. 'Creepy.'

They reached an open cell block door at the end of a passageway that opened up into a larger space than expected. Dozens of candles lit the round space, casting eerie shadows off the skulls. Antique Moroccan style rugs covered the damp floor, a low wooden table in the centre of it all. There were no seats around the table, but instead a mish-mash of cushions. Some were old and worn, some newer and overstuffed. There were throws and blankets, and the soft smell of incense burned in the liberal space. It was surprisingly cosy.

Sitting crossed legged at the table on a lumpy cushion was a beguiling woman. She dressed like a fortune teller and painted her face like a burlesque model. Her hair was all different shades of blonde — a tell-tale sign that it had been done herself and not at a salon. In some light she looked Olivia's age, and in another she seemed old and weary. Nevertheless, she smiled at them, and it was genuine and warm. Bizarrely enough, Olivia's throat constricted painfully again and she swallowed it down once more. Roman looked at her sharply but she ignored him.

'This is Sage Bishop,' Zaid said, standing at the cell door. 'Our Resident witch and an irreplicable asset to Ashmoore.'

'If she's such an asset why do you keep her in the basement?' Roman asked.

'She draws power from the earth and feels closer to it down here,' he said. 'She is allowed upstairs whenever she wishes.'

Olivia looked at Sage and smiled. 'Hi, I'm Olivia.'

Sage smiled and signed *hello* in sign language.

'She's mute,' Zaid explained, needlessly. 'She uses herbs and potions to perform her spells instead of words. She says—'

'I know what she said,' Olivia said, signing *How are you?*

Sage's face lit up, years dropping from her tired face.

Better than you, I'd wager, she signed back.

Something about the silent exchange seemed to irk Zaid, but he said nothing. Sage looked at him and gave him an unmistakable *shoo* hand gesture. Zaid's jaw worked in irritation, but he did as he was told and skulked back the way they had come. Sage waited for the sounds of his footsteps to fade before beckoning them both to sit down.

Is this your husband? Sage asked.

Olivia barked a laugh. *Not even a friend. But we can trust him.*

Roman arched an eyebrow. *I can sign too, you know.*

Why am I not surprised? Olivia asked and turned to look at Sage. *How does this work?*

I have a potion of herbs that can bring forth painful or sad memories, Sage signed. *You have to inhale the steam from it and the memories will be brought forwards like a vision. When this happens I have a banishing charm that will flush the trauma of these memories from your mind. This is how we will purify you.*

Olivia looked at her, sceptically. *Will you see my memories?*

Yes, but I won't judge you for them.

What about Roman?

He must stay. You will need an anchor while we search your mind. It is easy to get lost in your memories. He can help pull you back if you lose your way.

Will this get rid of my memories completely?

Sage smiled, softly. *No. But it will take away the pain they bring.*

Roman nodded. *Like therapy?*

Sage grinned at him. *Exactly!*

Olivia sighed, tensing. *Alright. Let's get this over with.*

Sage gave her a reassuring smile. They watched as she stood, crossing the room to a modest hearth where a small cauldron bubbled over an open flame. She was slight and frail, her legs looking like they might give out at any moment. While her back was turned Olivia and Roman exchanged a glance.

Is she a prisoner? Olivia signed.

Probably. Much in the same way we are.

Sage brought the cauldron over to the table and set it down. Olivia peered inside at the black liquid. She could see her reflection in its glassy surface. Thick, heavy steam rose and filled the cell. Something inside her desperately wanted her to touch it — practically begged her to dip her finger in and see what happened — but she refrained.

Lean over the steam and close your eyes, Sage signed. *Roman will translate for me.*

Against her instincts, Olivia let her eyelids drop closed. She immediately felt her hackles rise, her shoulders tightening.

'It's alright,' Roman said softly, translating Sage's unspoken words. 'Just listen to my voice.'

Olivia let out a breath she didn't realise she had been holding.

'Roman will be my voice, but I will be your guide,' he said, voice low. 'I am going to start now, if that's okay?'

Olivia nodded.

'Good girl,' he said. He began to recite:

'Body Be Still,

Mind Be Open,

Spirit Be Calm,

And Memories Unbroken.'

Olivia felt herself go limp. She fell backwards, but instead of landing amongst the pillows and throws she was falling through open air. Her eyes snapped open but all around her was blackness. She tumbled, limbs flailing as if she were a ragdoll. Part of her wondered if she should panic, but another, much larger, part of her told her to be calm. That everything was going to be alright.

She landed — quite suddenly and unceremoniously — in the backseat of her parent's old Subaru. She looked down at her hands, turning them over. They were different. She no longer had Fate's mark or her Libra tattoo. Her knuckles were free of scrapes, her palms bearing no calluses.

'You okay back there, Slayer?' a voice called.

Olivia frowned. The only person to ever call her that was—

She looked up into the eyes of her father, Jackson, who watched her in the rear-view mirror. Her face broke into a wide grin. Next to him in the passenger seat sat the most beautiful woman Olivia had ever seen. Her mother. Lorna was humming along to a Bee Gees song on the radio. She looked over her shoulder at Olivia and smiled.

'Alright, petal?'

Olivia nodded. Satisfied, her mum turned back around. Her dad reached over the console putting his hand on her knee. She took her hand in his and Olivia smiled.

It was alright. Everything was going to be alright.

She looked out over Sawyer River as they crossed Nelson's bridge. The water glittered peacefully in the moonlight.

Olivia...

She turned, starting when she saw Roman in the backseat with her.

'Roman?' she asked, her voice sounding far away. 'What are you doing here?'

He looked at her with uncharacteristically sad eyes and nodded to the windscreen. Olivia looked out just in time to see a dark shadow dart out in front of the car. Everything next seemed to happen in slow motion: her dad swerving, her mother screaming, the car sailing through the air. Olivia barely had time to scream before the car hit the water.

Suddenly, everything seemed to speed up. They were sinking. Fast. The water swallowed the Subaru whole. Her father was pushing against the door to no avail. Her mother turned in her seat, scrambling to reach her. Olivia felt ice at her ankles and looked down to see the water rising.

Panic rippled through her and she yanked at her seatbelt, gasping as it seemed to fight back, refusing to let her go. Her father tried to roll down the windows. He pounded on the glass and kicked at the windscreen. The front of the car was filling up faster than the back because of the angle they were at. The black water was up to her mother's waist. Lorna fumbled with her own seatbelt, trying to find the catch in the dark.

Her father roared, hefting all his weight against the car door. He screamed and shrieked and begged the damn thing to open. It didn't budge and the water was up to their chests now. Suddenly, all the life seemed to go out of her father. He turned in his seat and gave his wife a look that Olivia didn't understand. They nodded and both turned to Olivia. Her mother burst into tears and they both held out their hands to her. Olivia took their hands in hers, realisation dawning.

This was it. This was the end.

Then she was freefalling again. The darkness swooped in around her and she hurtled through the nothingness. She looked down at her clothes, expecting them to be drenched, but she was fine. As if it had never happened. As if—

—she landed abruptly in her teenage bedroom. Olivia sat bolt upright. It was just as she remembered it. The bed was unmade and a chair by the door had a huge pile of clothes draped over it that she knew she was probably never going to fold and put away. On the wall were posters of her favourite bands: *Blink-182, My Chemical Romance, Green Day, Panic! At the Disco*. Her desk had her GCSE maths homework sprawled out across it, not even started.

She stood and crossed to her full length mirror, looking at her young face. She still had her puppy fat around her cheeks. She looked so... *small*. In frame, bulk, posture. There was a knock on the door that stirred her. Her godfather popped his head round the door before she could answer. He smiled at her in a way that made her flesh crawl.

'Hello, poppet,' he said.

Olivia swallowed. 'Hello, Russell.'

Russell Hall invited himself into his goddaughter's room and sat down on the bed. He watched Olivia with a hungry gaze and patted the bedspread beside him. Against all of her instincts, she did as she was told, regretting it the moment Russell put his hand on her thigh. His other hand swept an errant strand of hair off her face and pulled her round to look at him by her chin. Over his shoulder, standing in the doorway, was Roman.

'Are you my girl?' Russell asked.

Olivia looked back to her godfather. She nodded.

'Say it. Say you're my girl.'

'I'm your girl,' she said quietly.

He leered and leaned at the same moment she was yanked back into the darkness. She tumbled blindly for what could have been seconds or hours — there was no way of telling — until she was thrown into the living room of her first flat in Dublin.

'Jesus, Liv, look at me.'

Olivia turned on unsteady legs, coming face to face with Cillian Hayes. Her heart leapt up into her throat. He was even better than she remembered. His hair was messy, his jaw stubbled. A look of exhaustion etched onto his usually chipper features. His blue eyes, once full of mischief, were red rimmed and glassy.

When she spoke, she had no control over herself. It was as if she were trapped in her own body. She realised, with a sinking feeling, that she was about to relive the worst moment of her life all over again, and there was nothing she could do to change it. All she could do was watch it all unfold.

'What do you want me to say?' she asked.

'Anything,' he said, desperately. 'Christ, I don't care if you scream at me. Just show me *something*. Let me in.'

'This is who I am, Cillian. You knew that when you fell for me. I can't change now just because it doesn't suit you anymore.'

Cillian looked at her despairingly. 'Baby, I'm not asking you to change. I just need you to talk to me. You're so closed. I can never tell what you're thinking. You're out at all odd hours, you come back with bruises and scrapes. Jesus, I found a *dagger* in your sock drawer!'

'I warned you there were parts of me that I couldn't share with you,' she said, her voice stoic. 'I don't understand why that's suddenly changed now.'

'Liv, baby,' Cillian said, taking her hands in his and putting them to his chest. 'I love you. So much. I didn't think love like this was real. Jesus, I'm mad for you. But—'

She pulled her hands away. 'Why does there need to be a *but*?'

'But, I'm *scared*,' he finished. 'Are you in some kind of trouble? You have to tell me what's going on so I can help.'

'I don't need your help, Cillian!' she exploded.

He put his hands up diplomatically, and stepped back to give her space. 'Alright, I'm sorry. Calm down and—'

'Don't tell me to calm down!' she shouted, anger swelling in her chest like a dam about to burst. Her shoulders heaved. She could taste something hot and bitter in the back of her throat.

He nodded. 'Okay, okay, sorry. I know you're upset—'

Her jaw clenched, her eyes widened. He knew immediately he'd said the wrong thing. Standing behind him, Roman knew it too.

'Please,' he said, softly, trying a new approach. 'Please, just talk to me.'

Olivia laughed but there was no humour in it. She knew what she was about to say. It would be the words that ended everything. The words that made her a murderer. She begged herself not to say it. At the very least she willed herself to look away. She couldn't watch it again. Please, not again.

'You know what, Cillian,' she said, quietly. 'If you can't accept me as I am, you can go to hell.'

She was yanked from her vision just as his body was engulfed in flames. She screamed — suddenly in charge of herself again — and reached out desperately for him, but she was already being swept away by the darkness. She screamed and cried and kicked at the void around her, but it was useless. She wasn't in control here. All she could do was watch and wait and remember.

Suddenly, she was being yanked up. The change in direction made her stomach somersault, and she wrapped her arms tight around her middle. She silently begged for it to end. For it to be over. She couldn't see anymore. She couldn't bear it.

Without warning, she seemed to explode up from the earth. She looked around for Roman and Sage, hoping it was over. Instead she found that she was standing on a dirt track on a crossroads. Around her for miles there was nothing and the horizon stretched out, as flat as it was fruitless. The only thing that gave it away was the wooden street sign, sticking out of the dry earth looking like a make-shift crucifix. On it, scrawled in black paint:

Dead End

'So, you're back,' said a voice.

Olivia turned and saw the man dressed like a cowboy from a mediocre spaghetti Western. His smile was lopsided, his stubble peppered with grey. He was almost handsome. It was the eyes, however, that caught her attention. They were completely white.

'You must've made your decision. So, little lady? What's it going to be?'

Wordlessly, Olivia held her hand out to him. The cowboy grinned and stepped forwards. He seized her hand in his and she started at his cold touch. His skin was like granite. He watched her with his blank eyes, but she had a feeling there was no part of her that he couldn't see.

The cowboy cleared his throat. 'Well, alrighty. I stand here today on behalf of Lucifer Morningstar. He has considered your offer and is willing to accept. In exchange for relinquishing your gift, he will bestow upon you a Devil's debt until such a time as you reclaim it. Do you accept?'

Her throat was hoarse. 'Yes. I do.'

The cowboy grinned. 'Pleasure doing business with you.'

He let go of her hand and a surge of pain swept over her. Her knees buckled and she cried out, falling to the hard ground. She looked up but the cowboy was gone. In his place stood Roman. He crouched in front of her, taking her face in his hands with a surprisingly gentle touch.

'I want to go home,' she whispered. 'Please. Take me back.'

He nodded. 'Alright, Olivia.'

Then everything went black, and stayed that way.

14.

Olivia woke with a start. She sat bolt upright, a scream ready to tear from her throat. Strong hands took her shoulders and guided her back down against the mattress, and held her there.

'It's alright,' said a familiar voice. 'It's okay. It's over.'

She blinked hard. Once. Twice. Her vision cleared and she realised she was looking up at Roman. He sat beside her on a double bed, watching her with a wary expression. She looked at his hands, at his position over her, and her insides went cold. He must have seen the fear flash in her eyes, brief but strong, because he pulled away. Probably remembering what he'd seen of her godfather in her vision.

'No,' he said. 'No, I wasn't. I would never. I just didn't want you to sit up too quickly and pass out again. Sorry.'

The fear faded from her face, quickly replaced by anger. She propped herself up onto her elbows, brows knitting together.

'What the bloody hell was all that about?' she asked. 'Where is Sage? She said this was going to help me! All she did was poke around in my head!'

'She said you did well,' Roman offered, 'and that you should feel better by the time the Bacchanalia starts.'

'Oh, well, fucking A then,' Olivia snaped, pulling herself upright. 'Christ, my head feels like it was hit by a John Deere.'

He offered her a glass of water and headache pills that had been waiting on the nightstand. She gladly accepted them and gulped them down. She swung her legs over the edge of the bed so that she was sitting beside him. She looked around at their room. It resembled something of an upmarket motel. Not exactly nice, but not completely terrible either.

'You were under for about an hour,' Roman said. 'It was weird. You were sitting up the whole time, eyes closed. I was there with you, but the steam rising over the cauldron acted like some kind of a hologram. I could see everything you were seeing in the smoke. I could hear it too. It was… bizarre. Then when it was over you just, kind of, passed out. You were out cold for another hour at least.'

Olivia looked at him. 'So… you saw everything?'

'Yes.'

She held his gaze for a long moment, before looking away. 'Okay then.'

Roman watched her. 'It wasn't your fault, you know. Cillian, I mean. Well, *any* of it. But especially Cillian.'

'It doesn't matter if it was or wasn't,' she said, quietly, staring at a fixed spot on the wall. 'He's still dead. All he ever did was love me and I killed him for it.'

Roman went to put a hand on her shoulder but decided against it. 'The past can hurt. But the way I see it, you can either run from it or you can learn from it.'

Olivia frowned, looking at him. 'Are you quoting *The Lion King*?'

He nodded sombrely. 'Yes. Yes, I am.'

To both of their surprise, she laughed. It was fickle, however, and fleeting. She rested her pounding head on his shoulder and sighed. They stayed like that for a while in oddly companiable silence.

'I'll kill him if you want me to,' Roman said, softly.

His voice was quiet, but unmistakably deadly, and when she turned to look at him she saw that his expression matched. A darkness had crossed his face that she had only seen once before when he killed Zara, the moment his knife had plunged into her chest. He watched her, his jaw tight with rage.

'Your godfather,' he said. 'I'll kill him. If that's what you want.'

Olivia let out a long breath and smiled sadly. 'What are you going to do, Roman Wylder? Kill every man who's ever sexually assaulted me?'

'Yes,' he said without thinking.

A lump caught in her throat. Oddly touched, she rested her head on his shoulder again. 'Let's not borrow trouble. For now, anyway.'

He nodded. 'Alright. For now.'

Olivia looked down at the simple silver bracelet on her wrist with a glittering blue pentagram pendant. It was plain and delicate, and if she yanked hard enough she was sure it would snap. She arched an eyebrow and looked at Zaid. It was the last thing she had been expecting when he showed up to their room.

'This is it?' she asked, sceptically. 'This is the binding spell?'

He nodded. 'Sage bewitched it herself. The pendant is made with Lapis Lazuli. It's a precious gemstone with magical properties. It protects the wearer from negative influences.'

'Like my demon form,' she said.

'All the while you wear this, your dark form won't be able to come forward. Once the Awakening is over and Pandora is raised you are free to take it off. Although we must ask that you return it before you leave.'

Olivia nodded. 'Trust me, I'm in no rush to keep it.'

Roman took Olivia's hand in his and studied the bracelet. 'It seems too… simple.'

Zaid shrugged. 'Sometimes simplicity is best.'

Roman shrugged and let Olivia's hand drop. 'Fair enough. Is it demon orgy time?'

He scowled. 'It's not a *demon orgy*. It's a Bacchanalia. It's—'

'—the Roman festival of Bacchus,' Roman interrupted. 'Yes, so you keep saying. But let's be real, it's an excuse to get wine-soaked and rowdy. Even in the time of the First, it was basically just a very drunken sex party where people paid homage to the god of wine. Look, I'm not saying I'm against it. Actually, I'm all for it. I'm just saying that if it looks like a duck, sounds like a duck, and smells like a duck... it's probably a demon sex orgy.'

Zaid sighed, quickly losing his patience — a response that Roman seemed to bring out in most, if not all, people. 'People are, of course, encouraged to have a good time. Before the Awakening, people will want to celebrate and let loose. However they choose to do that is up to them entirely. Nothing is off limits. Nothing is shamed.'

Roman quirked an eyebrow. 'When in Rome.'

Zaid didn't talk to them as he led them down another modern corridor. He seemed to have run out of patience for them — mostly thanks to Roman — and apparently saw no further need to make nice with them. Neither of them minded.

Roman and Olivia hung back a few paces behind Zaid as they walked, like two teenagers sulkily following behind a teacher who had just caught them graffitiing the school car park.

She gave Roman a sly look. 'So,' she said conspiratorially. 'Demon orgy, huh?'

'Apparently so.'

'Planning to partake?'

'Yet to decide. You?'

Olivia snorted. 'Impending sacrifice doesn't exactly put me in the mood. Anyway, what's the social etiquette for a Bacchanalia? How long do you have to mingle and pretend to be interested in the canopies before you can start bumping uglies?'

Roman shrugged. 'I would imagine it's somewhere between the speeches and the blood ritual. Like, there's a very small window of opportunity when you can go up to someone and say: *hey this is a great demon soiree and all, but would you like to go somewhere and get* really *horny?* You know?'

Olivia frowned. 'There won't be speeches will there?'

Roman mock shuddered. 'Perish the thought!'

'I can hear you both, you know,' Zaid said, glancing over his shoulder.

'We know,' Olivia said. 'We're purposefully speaking loud enough so that you can hear us.'

Roman nodded. 'We're actively trying to make you feel uncomfortable. Is it working?'

Zaid ignored them. They rounded the corner and he ushered them through an archway. The glamourous space unfolded before them and Olivia realised, with a sinking feeling, that they were in a salon. She turned her glare upon Zaid.

'What is this?' she asked.

Zaid gestured around them. 'This is the last stage of prep, Olivia. You need to look the part.'

Roman snorted. 'Unlucky.'

She crossed her arms over her chest. 'Why? What's wrong with me?'

'Nothing at all. But the Bacchanalia is a formal affair. Hair, makeup and correct attire is essential. Roman will be undergoing the same treatment.'

Roman frowned. 'Wait, what?'

'It's not negotiable,' Zaid said, firmly. 'As long as you're our guests, you will follow our rules.'

After more disagreement and a few threats that Olivia knew Roman fully intended to keep, they were separated. Olivia was taken through to an overly flamboyant stylist with bee-stung lips and pink hair. He fussed over Olivia, insisting that she would look beautiful as a blonde. The responding glare she gave him was enough to stop all further notions involving bleach. Reluctantly, he settled with giving her a wash and blow dry before pinning it up into a soft — though not overly-elegant — updo with pieces hanging down to frame her face.

When the makeup artist came to take over she looked at the scar running the length of Oliva's cheek with anxiety. She tried, in vain, to persuade Olivia to let use something that she called "heavy duty" foundation, but Olivia refused. The simpler the better. She ended up with a natural look that she didn't actually mind. She thought of Tadgh and how he would absolutely die if he saw her now, in full glam — or, at the very least, as full glam as she could stand.

When she was moved into the dressing room however, she paused. The garment hanging in front of her was surprisingly gorgeous. The fabric was satin and a deep shade of wine red. It was backless with thin straps and a low neckline. For the most part it was skin tight, until it reached the knees where the fabric relaxed a little creating a mermaid effect.

Jesus. You're going to show me up at my own Awakening.

'I can't wear this,' Olivia mumbled. 'This is too much. It's too nice for me to just die in.'

You're not going to die, Liv! For the last time, I'm going to make sure you pull through.

'They're going to let my blood,' she said numbly. 'They're going to sacrifice me and let my blood run until you rise. I could be dead long before you can even do anything about it.'

Trust me, I'm not going to be hanging around any longer than I need to be. I can't wait to stretch my legs.

'Can this even work? Can we both exist at the same time? Isn't this like some Harry and Voldemort paradox? One cannot live while the other survives?'

Why should only one of us get to live? We're both real people — well, demons. We both deserve to exist. I've been stuffed into your head long before you were even born. I was just hanging in limbo waiting for you to come into the world. We're two completely separate people.

Olivia smiled but it was hollow. 'I can't believe I thought you were my conscience. You don't even sound like me.'

Be real, Livvy. You never really thought that.

'No, I guess not.'

Shall we get dressed then?

'I suppose we shall.'

Unsurprisingly, the dress fit her like a glove. She imagined Ariel had a hand in that. They were, if nothing else, a fashion guru. Olivia knew as much after they had picked out that black dress for her. Thankfully, they had also picked out a pair of flat shoes to match her ensemble. The dress was floor length and you wouldn't be able to see them anyway.

Once she was decent, a stylist came in to adorn her with accessories. She was given a silver choker and earrings to match the style of her bracelet. Rings were placed on the fingers of her calloused hands, and a sparkling hair slide was fastened securely into her locks.

When she was all done, there was a knock at her dressing room door. Cordelia invited herself in before Olivia could answer. She wore a black glittering ball gown, her hair tousled into romantic waves and pinned back off her face. She smiled at Olivia with genuine warmth that did nothing to ease her nerves.

'Are you ready, Wicked One?' Cordelia asked.

Olivia bit down the annoyance at her refusal to call her by her name and nodded. 'Where is Roman?'

'Waiting for you in the foyer. I must warn you, he's looking especially delicious tonight. I'd stake a claim on him, if I were you, before someone else does. Bacchanalia can bring out the most carnal urges in demons.'

Olivia arched an eyebrow. 'Roman is more than welcome to have his claim staked by anyone he likes.'

'If you say so,' she said in a voice that implied that she did, in fact, know better.

Olivia resisted the urge to slap her. Instead, she let Cordelia lead her down into a new part of Ashmoore that she had yet to see. The modern surroundings gave way to something that resembled the interior of a stately home. It seemed more befitting of a duchy than to be stuffed in the recesses of an abandoned-come-upscaled asylum. They rounded a corner and the hallways opened up into an extravagant foyer that dripped with pomp and circumstance.

But the real sight was the man standing beside the fireplace, flute of sparkling water in hand. His tuxedo was black, as was his shirt and bowtie. His bronze hair had been somewhat tamed and combed back so that it wasn't falling into his green-gold eyes. His jaw, however, was still familiarly stubbled, and his smile was gloriously wicked.

Roman Wylder smiled at her, looking her up and down. 'Well. Aren't you the exact opposite of Quasimodo?'

Olivia grinned and looked down at her dress. 'This old thing? Had it for years.'

'How nice of you to dust off the cobwebs for me.'

Cordelia cleared her throat. 'If you both would like to follow me, I will get you ready for your entrance.'

The smile immediately left Olivia's face. 'What do you mean *entrance*?'

'Our guests want to see you arrive. You *are* the Wicked One, after all. Tonight is all about you.'

'Yeah, but can't I just sneak in a side door?' she asked. 'I don't like it when everyone looks at me at once.'

'Hate to break it to you, Olivia,' Roman said. 'But I think everyone's going to be looking at you in that getup regardless.'

'Naturally. But I don't want to act like some big guest of honour.'

Cordelia laughed. 'But you *are* the guest of honour.'

'*Prisoner* of honour,' she corrected.

'Nevertheless, tradition is tradition,' Cordelia said. 'All special guests make their appearance on the grand staircase. Come along, now. The night is young but not for long.'

Cordelia turned on her stiletto heel and escorted them to the ballroom. Olivia fidgeted as they walked, fussing with her jewellery and repeatedly tucking a strand of hair behind her ear and then pulling it free again. Roman sighed and grasped her hand, looping her arm through his.

'Relax,' he said softly. 'You look like you're having a fit.'

'How are you so calm?' she muttered. 'I feel sick.'

'Probably because I'm not the one who is going to be sacrificed.'

She nodded. 'That'll be it, yeah.'

Roman looked at her. 'You really do look stunning, you know.'

She smiled. 'Likewise.'

They approached a set of ornate double doors flanked either side by two men in suits with ear pieces. Cordelia turned to them, smiling.

'The doors will open when we're ready for you,' she said. 'Come out, smile, and make your way down as the music starts.'

Olivia frowned. 'What music?'

'Don't be dense, Olivia. All parties have music.'

'I get that, but—'

'I have to go. Even I don't get a grand entrance like this. I'll see you in there.'

Olivia opened her mouth to question further, but Cordelia was already purposefully striding away. So instead, she turned to Roman.

'What music?' she asked.

'They asked me if there was any particular fanfare you would like playing on your arrival,' he explained. 'They have an eighteen-piece orchestra in there. Cordelia recommended *Chariots of Fire*, but I steered her away from that.'

All the blood drained from Olivia's face. 'Oh God. Oh God, no. What did you pick?'

He patted her arm. 'Have a little faith. I spoke to the orchestra and it's all sorted.'

'Is it awful?' she asked. 'What is it? Wham? Ace Of Base?' She blanched. 'Rod Stewart?'

He smiled at her, but there was a wicked glint in his eye. 'Just trust me.'

The fidgets came back as Olivia turned to the door. Her nerves jangled and she bounced on the balls of her feet, the fingers of her free hand clenching and unclenching over and over. One of the guards put a hand to his earpiece and confirmed something. He nodded to his buddy and together they each seized a handle. There was a long painful moment where nothing happened.

Then they opened the doors.

15.

The ballroom was something from a Jane Austin novel — or so Olivia assumed. She had never actually read the classics. Nevertheless, she felt like a noblewoman being presented to court as all eyes turned to her. And God, there were a lot of them. They turned their gazes upon her, expressions ranging from awe to suspicion. Her legs immediately jellified. Roman's arm wrapped around her waist to subtly hold her up. Then the music started.

A classical version of *After Dark* by Tito & Tarantula drifted up from the orchestra and Olivia's mind was filled with images of Salma Hayek barely dressed with a giant snake wrapped around her shoulders. To her surprise, a blush crept up to her cheeks.

Roman leaned in to whisper in her ear. 'Come on, Slayer. Let's go.'

Taking her arm once more, they descended the grand staircase. She was grateful not to be wearing high heels, because she was one hundred percent sure she would have tripped and broken her ankle.

'Excellent song choice,' she murmured. 'Albeit a little inappropriate.'

He smiled. 'Much like yourself then.'

Cordelia waited for them at the bottom of the stairs. The music softened as they approached and Zaid passed her a microphone. She smiled at Olivia and Roman, and then her guests.

'Ladies and gentlemen,' her soprano voice reverberated throughout the PA system. 'Now that our guest of honour has arrived, let the Bacchanalia begin!'

Everyone cheered and Cordelia ushered them both through to a roped-off VIP section where herself and Zaid were seated. The music started up again, this time a classical rendition of *True Faith* by New Order. Olivia gave Roman a look and he shrugged.

'I gave them a set list,' he explained. 'Strictly eighties only.'

'You really are the best frenemy a girl can have.'

He winked at her before turning to Cordelia. 'So, what do we do now?'

'Smile,' Cordelia said. 'Mingle. Eat. Make nice. There will be speeches to come, then dancing, and any other activities you choose to partake in. The Awakening will begin at midnight. Once it's over you are free to leave.'

'So, it's… just a party?' Olivia asked.

'A Bacchanalia,' Cordelia corrected. 'But essentially yes. Until the ritual, it's just a ball.'

Roman and Olivia looked at each other.

'Hungry?' he asked.

'Famished,' she replied.

The buffet table wasn't far, but it seemed to take an age to reach it. The other guests swarmed her the moment they left their VIP section. They bowed and curtsied. Some glared. Others dropped to their knees. People were eager to talk to her. Some of them tried to touch her, but Roman politely refused them, acting as her bodyguard. She felt like a claustrophobic bride suffocating at her own wedding. By the time they reached the food, she felt as though she was going to keel over.

'Jesus Christ,' she muttered, grabbing a plate and filling it up with one of everything. 'I could understand if I was a celebrity, you know? If I was Cher or Kate Bush. But this is ridiculous.'

Roman frowned. '*They* were the only two celebrities you could think of?'

'Regardless,' she replied, testing the integrity of her small plate by adding another hors d'oeuvre to it. 'They're acting like I'm the second coming.'

'Well, you are.'

'Not really. I'm basically just like passport control for the *actual* second-coming.'

She went to reach for another canapé and he waved her hand away. She glared at him.

'No one in their right mind should eat that many mini quiches,' he said.

They took their food back to their VIP section and a waiter came over to offer them both a flute of champagne. They opted for the sparkling water instead. Olivia took stock of the ballroom and saw Roman doing the same. It was vast and dripping with finery. The floor was polished to a gleam, the ceiling mirrored to double the number of guests. The walls were decorated with intricate illuminations depicting all a manner of gruesome yet beautiful images from the Satanic Bible. There was a stage where the orchestra was set up, and lining the far wall were several ornate doors, each of them with a Roman numeral on them.

'Private sex rooms,' Roman said when he caught her looking.

Olivia frowned. 'They don't just screw on the dancefloor? That's not very Bacchanalian of them.'

'I'm sure they do. Just as I'm sure some people also like their privacy.'

'Why is it always the crazy ones who are great in bed?'

He shrugged. 'Believe me, I have strived to find an answer to that hypothesis. But, alas, to no avail.'

Olivia nodded to a buxom young woman in a black cocktail dress. 'What do you reckon her kink is?'

Roman thought about it for a bit, then said, 'She's a furry, for sure.'

'And him?'

Roman looked at the portly, middle-aged man she was referring to. 'I bet he likes to dress like a giant baby.'

'*Interesting.*'

Cordelia fixed them with an indignant stare. 'Those people you're making fun of are highly esteemed guests and good friends of mine. Would it be too much to ask that the two of you show a little decorum?'

They turned to look at Cordelia and then at each other.

'Does it in front of the mirror,' Roman said.

Olivia nodded. 'One hundo.'

Cordelia pretended like she hadn't heard them and stalked off to mingle. Roman and Olivia hung back and continued to judge the other party-goers. To her surprise, Olivia found herself laughing. A *lot*. To her even greater surprise, she was actually having a good time. Roman, when he was on top form, was actually very funny and remarkably good company. She knew that none of it was real — that this was just the perfect façade he had created after years of pretending to fit in — but nevertheless, it calmed her down.

'I know what you're doing,' she said, after Roman flagged down another waiter for two more sparkling waters.

He arched an eyebrow. 'Oh? What am I doing?'

'You're trying to distract me from worrying about the Awakening.'

'Is it working?'

She looked at him and smiled. 'Yes. Thank you.'

There was a humming sound over the PA system and the orchestra brought their playing to a quiet and abrupt close. Olivia looked up at the stage to see Cordelia holding a microphone. She smiled and it was radiant.

'Esteemed guests,' she began. 'Friends, family, and followers. Thank you for joining the Brotherhood here tonight for Pandora's Awakening.'

The screen behind the stage flickered and lit up with a single image. A charcoal sketch of the First, dated 117 AD, looked down at them all, a perfect clone of Olivia. There was polite applause at the portrait. Roman and Olivia exchanged wry glances.

'The tale of the First is legend,' Cordelia continued. 'The first demon that Lucifer Morningstar ever created, Lilith, was his connection to the mortal realm. She was his eyes and ears amongst the humans. She lived for centuries, but eventually grew lonely.

'Lilith fell in love with a mortal. They married and loved with passion, but she could see him ageing before her eyes. In her desperation not to lose him she made a deal with a witch who, in turn, bestowed immortality upon him.

'The witch's spell worked, but it came at a price. Nature always demands a balance. What immortality gave, nature took away. Where he was given strength, the sun made him weak. Where he was given power, dwellings no longer welcomed him inside. Where he was given influence over the minds of the weak-willed, he was given an aversion to anything touched by the Lord. And above all else, he was given the insatiable hunger. And thus, the first vampire was born.

'Naturally, when Lucifer heard what Lilith had done, he was furious. And jealous. He wanted to be the only one who held Lilith's affections. He dragged her back to his side in hell and never let her return to the mortal realm. Together they had a child as Lucifer's way to remind her that she belonged to him and him alone.

'In the world above, the vampire yearned for his family. Left to his immortality alone, he gave up his soul so he no longer had to feel any pain. He became cruel, and dark, and vicious, spreading his disease everywhere he went.

'Lilith resided in hell with Lucifer, watching it all but never able to intervene. In a final attempt to be with him again someday, she split her soul in two. Half of it stayed with her, and half of it she gave to her child. After begging Lucifer to let her child travel to the mortal realm, he relinquished. The child carried her mother's half-soul to the walking world and, through her, the First's bloodline lived on.

'But Lilith was smart. She knew that her and her true love were destined to find each other once again. One day, when the universe was ready to reunite them, the doppelgänger would be born into the bloodline. She would be the Wicked One, the one to carry her half soul within her. She would nurture the half-soul and nourish it. And when it was ready, it would emerge as the First's successor. As Pandora. The Antichrist.'

Raucous cheers filled the ballroom. The guests clapped with unnerving enthusiasm at the twisted fairy tale and Olivia felt something like ice water settle in the pit of her stomach. Roman glanced at her but remained silent.

'And there she is today!' Cordelia said, sweeping her arm over to where Olivia and Roman were sitting.

With almost robotic synchronicity, the crowd turned to look at her. Olivia blinked back at the sea of adoration, fear and hatred, and her hand immediately gripped Roman's. She squeezed and he squeezed back, out of practice more than anything else.

'What do I do?' she muttered.

Roman shrugged. 'Smile and look beautiful?'

Olivia forced a smile. 'How's this?'

Roman peered at her. 'The smile is a little bit creepy, but you're definitely beautiful.'

However creepy it was, it, at least, appeased her audience. Cordelia cleared her throat, calling everyone's attention back to her.

Jesus, she nearly let someone else have the limelight for a whole thirty seconds!

'And now, dear guests,' she said, smiling. 'I invite you to drink, dance, debauch, and enjoy Pandora's Awakening!'

Everyone cheered and the orchestra started up again, immediately going into a classical rendition of *Werewolves Of London*. Olivia turned to Roman, brows furrowed.

'Was that story true?' she asked. 'About Lilith and the First Vampire and the kid?'

Roman shrugged. 'As much as any religious story is?'

'So, I've got a two thousand year old vampire out there looking to fall in love with me?' she asked. 'Because I won't lie to you, Roman, I'm not ready to move to Forks, Washington.'

He frowned. 'Why would you move to Forks, Washington?'

'And if there *is* a two thousand year old vampire that the universe is supposedly trying to unite me with, where is he, hm? I think the first thing I'll buy him is a watch because he is *late*.'

'Okay, firstly, he's not meant to unite with you, he's meant to unite with Lilith's soul living within you, AKA Pandora Morningstar.'

'Which, in and of itself, is gross, right? It's like setting your husband up with your great-great-times-one-thousand granddaughter.'

Roman blinked. 'Your maths is astonishing.'

She glared. 'Even so. Isn't it a bit… incesty?'

'Not a word,' he said. 'And no. You are not the vampire's kin. And besides, he will be drawn to Pandora not to you.'

'Oh great. So even when I'm destined to find love, it won't work out. He just wants me for my *insides*. That's all you men care about, isn't it? What's on the inside.'

Roman frowned. 'I'm so confused.'

She patted his leg. 'Good thing you're pretty.'

'Are you just making jokes because you're nervous?'

She nodded. 'Nervous *and* terrified.'

Werewolves Of London ended and a new song took over. Olivia recognised it on the first note and she looked at Roman, gawping. It was the song he had invited her to dance to at The Betsy. *As The World Falls Down* by David Bowie. The song her parents had danced to at their wedding. That night in The Betsy seemed like a lifetime ago now.

Roman grinned and stood, holding a hand out to her. In his tux, with his hair combed back, he looked like a rich 19th century heir. His green eyes sparkled with unashamed mischief.

'Would you like to dance?' he asked.

'Yeah,' she said, a little breathlessly. 'I actually really would.'

She took his hand and he guided her to the dance floor. The crowd had thinned out now that the orchestra had resumed, with some people either too shy or too sober to dance just yet. Roman led Olivia to the very centre and pulled her into his strong arms. One hand sat comfortably against her back, the other clasping her hand and holding it against his chest. She settled her other hand on his shoulder and he pulled her close, their bodies almost touching.

He arched an eyebrow. 'Is this okay?'

'As long as you don't try to lead,' she said.

He grinned and led anyway, letting their bodies fall into a comfortable sway in time with the soft music. It was simple and they didn't cover much ground, but it caught the attention of the other party-goers and encouraged them to join, nonetheless.

'We seem to be trend-setters,' Roman said, nodding at the other dancers.

'It's our natural charisma and magnetism,' she replied. 'We can't help it. People are drawn to us.'

'Well you *are* the messiah.'

'And you *are* the Demon Hitman Extraordinaire.'

'To name just one of my titles.'

She smiled but it was fleeting. 'I'm going to die tonight, aren't I?'

Roman frowned, holding her imperceptibly tighter. 'Of course not. I won't allow it.'

'I know, I know. If you can't fulfil the sire you'll get sucked into hell.'

'No,' he said. 'Because I just won't allow it.'

She met his eyes. 'I feel like I can't breathe.'

'And yet here you are, doing it so flawlessly.'

'I'm scared.'

He pulled her closer. 'Olivia McQueen. I will not let you die tonight. Do you understand me?'

She nodded. 'Alright.'

They danced. Around them others danced too. That's when Olivia began to notice the kissing. The touching. Couples and threesomes — and even more — skulking off to dark corners of the ballroom to grope each other, others slinking off to the private rooms with a glint in their eyes. The dance floor, at least, seemed to be sacred ground. Strictly for dancing and nothing more.

Weirdly polite but okay.

Roman saw her looking and cocked an amused eyebrow, the corner of his mouth twitching. 'Interested?'

'You don't have to stay here and play nice,' she said. 'If you want to go off and… you know… *debauch* then you can. You don't have to entertain me.'

'Are you trying to get rid of me?' he asked. 'Do *you* want to do some debauching yourself?'

Olivia looked around at the other guests, a sea of Boomers, and pulled a face. 'I'm okay, thanks.'

'Really? There's no one in here that draws your eye? No one at all?'

She looked back at him, suddenly very aware of how close their bodies were, of his hand on her back, of his heart beating under her hand.

'You're flirting with me,' she said, more of an accusation than a question.

'Of course I am. You're beautiful.'

Olivia frowned as little red flags popped up in her head. She wasn't arrogant enough to think that she was *so* ridiculously beautiful that Roman had forgotten that he'd wanted to kill her just a couple of days ago. That he probably still did. And she wasn't *so* ridiculously horny that she was about to forget the fact that she kind of didn't like him. What she was, however, was just pretty enough, and just horny enough, to suspect that this was a genuine come-on. And honestly, suspicions aside — of which there were plenty — she was also fairly sure that she could handle it if it was.

'You're not interested in me,' she said, carefully. 'You don't even particularly like me.'

Roman lifted his arm and twirled her under it before pulling her back into his arms. 'Do I have to particularly like you to think that you're beautiful?'

'I suppose not.'

'And you?' he asked, his gaze never relenting as he looked down at her. 'Do you not find me devilishly good looking and charming?'

She grinned. 'I very much doubt you need me to tell you the answer to that. I'm human, aren't I? Well. Half human.'

'And yet here we are, dancing like very civilised non-humans.'

She watched him. 'Why? What else would we be doing?'

Something in his eyes flickered and Olivia felt a charge spark between them.

'Well,' he said, voice low. 'Supposed we weren't merely *business* partners, and our being here was through choice and not obligation, I suspect I would find this all rather… intimate. Wouldn't you?'

Olivia swallowed. 'I suppose…'

Their bodies were so close they could hold a pencil between them without it falling. Roman's hand was on her back but if it dropped lower it would be on her waist. Or her hip. She could feel his heart beating beneath her palm but it wouldn't take much for him to bring her fingertips to his lips and kiss them. It would be so easy. Almost natural. And of course, there were their hips. If they brought them together there would be nothing but a few thin pieces of fabric to keep them from touching. Something hot and tight coiled in her stomach at the thought of Roman's hips pressed flush against hers.

Um… wait, sorry. What's going on? What's happening here?

As if he could read her thoughts, his hand slid to rest on her hip. He pulled her flush against him grinning at the little gasp that escaped her lips. Slowly, he brought her hand up to his mouth and kissed her palm and then her fingertips in turn, sending a flurry of tingles down her arm. He returned her hand to his chest and she could feel his heart thundering there.

He bowed his head, his cheek brushing hers and purred next to her ear, 'Is that better?'

Her breath caught and she found herself unable to speak so she nodded.

'You're so stoic,' he murmured, his voice sending soft vibrations through her body. 'So calm and collected. Everything about you is completely guarded. I couldn't even begin to imagine what you look like when you're coming undone.'

Well now. *That* was a thought. Not an entirely terrible one. And of course now she was thinking about it, about Roman's hands on her, making her unravel as he promised he could. *Would*. If she wanted him to. And she suspected that she wanted him to. Like, *really* wanted him to. If the ache in her stomach was anything to go by, and it usually was.

Alright, I'm switching off. Let me know when you're done.

'Is that something you think about?' she asked, voice thick. 'Watching me… come undone?'

He drew back and looked at her with a bemused expression. 'How many times must I tell you? You are beautiful.'

'But you…' she struggled to find the words. Struggled to *think* when his body was pressed to hers like that. 'You don't have… feelings. You're a serial killer.'

He shrugged. 'I have wants. Needs. *Urges*. And I can always appreciate a pretty face.' He lifted his hand to her chin, his thumb brushing her cheek with surprising gentleness. 'And yours is exceptionally pretty.'

She studied his face. 'So, this wouldn't mean anything to you?'

'Do you want it to?'

A pause. Not quite a pregnant pause, but definitely a *few-weeks-late-but-totally-not-panicking* pause. 'I guess not.'

'And do you want this?' His hand tightened on her hip. 'Don't be afraid to say no, I don't have any feelings to hurt.'

Her mouth was dry. 'I don't know.'

His hand immediately moved away, sliding back up to rest between her shoulder blades. He put distance between them once more. He smiled politely, although his gaze remained heavy and heated.

'Then we'll stop there,' he said. 'I misread the room. I apologise.'

She shook her head. 'You didn't misread anything. It's just…'

Roman watched her. 'Yes?'

'The last person I was involved with… it didn't end well.'

'Tell me what you want, Olivia McQueen. I will give it to you.'

She hesitated.

'I want you,' she said softly.

He was on her instantly, his hands capturing her face, lips meeting hers with unexpected tenderness. Her hands found his waist and she bridged the gap between them once more. Their hips met and she gasped again. Roman moaned and tentatively traced her lower lip with his tongue, relishing as she shuddered in response. Olivia ran her hands up the strong planes of his chest feeling the solid wall of muscle beneath his shirt. She could feel how badly he wanted her, could feel it straining beneath the fabric of his trousers, pressing against her.

She pulled back for breath and her knees went weak at the look of unabashed desire in Roman's eyes.

'Private room,' she said. 'Now.'

16.

The moment the door closed his hands were on her, pulling her against him. His mouth found hers and he kissed her with such an intensity that she felt sure her lips would bruise. Her hips bucked forward of their own volition and he held her against him, showing her just how much he wanted her. She moaned against his mouth and he deepened the kiss, tasting her tongue with his.

He pulled back, but before she could protest, he was leaning in to trail fiery kisses down her neck. He bit down on the soft skin at the hollow of her throat and she cried out, head tipping back. Roman purred and she could feel his smile against her thrumming pulse.

'Oh, I like that noise,' he murmured, coming up to gaze at her with hooded eyes. 'But I bet I can make you scream.'

Olivia trembled and pulled his face back down to hers. Or at least she tried. He stopped, barely a centimetre away, unrelenting. He grinned. She groaned and tried to meet him halfway but he caught her chin in his hand and held her steady. The strangled sound that escaped her throat made his breath catch.

'Please…' she whispered. 'Touch me.'

He growled and finally kissed her. His hands desperately gripped her waist, travelling slowly up her sides. They cupped her breasts and she gasped against his lips. Her hands were suddenly at his shoulders, pushing off his jacket. She started on his shirt buttons and he shivered as her knuckles grazed his skin.

The shirt fell open and Olivia swallowed hard. Slowly she let it drop to the floor and she placed her hands flat on his chest. Beneath her palm, his heart hammered. He was chiselled and solid, his stomach taut. She ran her hands down his bare body and he shuddered. It was then she noticed the scars. They were everywhere. Almost so faded that they were barely visible, but she could just about make them out.

She walked around him, trailing her fingertips across his stomach and then his back as she went, looking at them all. She came back to face him and met his dark gaze.

'I'm sorry,' he said.

She frowned. 'What for?'

He looked down at himself. 'I know I'm not—'

She cut him off with a kiss, then moved her lips down to a patch of traumatised skin on his collarbone. He sucked in a sharp breath.

'Your skin tells a story,' she said, lips brushing his sternum. 'And I want to read it.'

He caught her chin in his hand once more and looked at her with serious eyes. 'I can never love you, Olivia. You have to know that.'

She suspected that most girls would be upset hearing that, especially right before sex, but to her it sounded like a blessing.

'I don't want you to,' she said.

Olivia pulled him down into another kiss, parting her lips as an invitation for him to taste her. He pulled her close, his hands hitching up the fabric of her dress. She shivered as her legs were exposed to the cool air, inch by inch. Roman grinned and leisurely stroked her hip bones with his thumbs, keeping the dress bunched up around her waist. His fingertips inched under the fabric of her panties and she squirmed in his embrace, silently pleading for more. He obliged.

She moaned, legs shaking, as he slipped his hand between her thighs. His fingers moved in slow, tantalising circles and she writhed against him. He didn't speed up, even when she begged him to. His free arm circled around her to support her as she trembled, her head lolling back, eyes fluttering closed.

He kept the same, agonisingly slow pace, and as she began to protest he withdrew his hand and spun her around, pinning her to the wall. She gasped as his hand found her again and she moaned, pressing back into him, feeling how rigid he was. He grinded his hips into her from behind and her knees almost buckled.

'Please,' she breathed. 'Please. Roman, I—'

She cried out as he parted her, pushing two fingers inside. He worked fast now, lips on her neck, biting down hard. Her breaths came in short, sharp intakes and he could feel her body winding tighter and tighter, aching for release. When she came she cried his name, her body quivering. He turned her gently in his arms and picked her up, wrapping her legs around his waist. He carried her to the bed and laid her down, kissing her affectionately.

His hands went to the dress rucked up at her waist and he slid it up her body and over her head. It was immediately forgotten as he lowered his mouth to her bare breasts. She gasped, hands bunching in the bed sheets as his tongue traced over her nipples. He stayed like that awhile, teasing her until she was writhing beneath him. He drew back slightly and looked down at her. They locked eyes, something unspoken passing between them. Some kind of acknowledgement that they both needed this.

He lowered his mouth to her chest once more, kissing the fresh scar against her sternum. He murmured a soft apology against her skin that went unnoticed. Then, he began to kiss his way down her body. Knowing what was coming, Olivia groaned in anticipation. His lips brushed over her navel, across her hip bones and against her shaking thighs.

'Roman...' she said, softly.

He kissed her through her panties and her hips rolled of their own volition. He could feel how ready she was for him through the thin fabric. He kissed her again and she cursed softly, hips wriggling in a silent protest for more.

Teasingly, tantalisingly slowly, he hooked his fingers under the hem of her panties and waited. She looked down at him with an expression halfway between need and annoyance. Roman grinned and yanked them down in one fluid movement. He kissed her again where she wanted him most and her body fell back against the mattress.

His tongue started slowly, learning what she liked, what she responded to. He found a rhythm and pace that made her hands fly to his head, fingers lacing through his hair, and he stuck to it, revelling in the way she squirmed beneath him. He brought her to the edge over and over again, never letting her fall over the precipice. It was only until she was a quivering wreck, begging for him to release her that he obliged. When she came this time, she screamed, her back arching, her head turned to press her face into the sheets.

She looked up in time to see him standing, unbuckling his belt. She let out a soft moan and his gaze darkened. His trousers dropped to the floor and she could see the large shape of him beneath his boxers. Drawing herself up and to the end of the bed, she reached for him, cupping him through his underwear. He swore, his hands clenching at his sides. She reached for the waistband of his pants and he caught her wrists, holding her firm but gentle. She looked up at him, frowning.

'You don't have to,' he said, voice thick with desire. 'We can just focus on you if you'd like.'

She arched an eyebrow. 'And let all this go to waste?'

'We don't have to,' he repeated.

'I know. I want to.'

He let go of her wrists, sighing as she pulled his boxers down. He watched her eyes widen slightly as she drank in the sight of him. She took him in her hand and he let out a low, guttural moan. Olivia worked her hand up and down, her other hand resting on his tight abdomen. His eyelids fluttered closed, his head tilting back. His hips moved with her, his chest heaving. Olivia leaned forwards and pressed a gentle kiss to the tip and he quickly caught her hands again.

He looked down at her. 'If you keep doing that, this will all be over far too soon.'

Olivia grinned and laid back on the bed, holding out her hand to him. He joined her, climbing over her frame and kissing her. She pulled him down flush against her and they both gasped as his length pressed into her hip. Insistently, she pulled his mouth back to hers and he kissed her like it was all he knew how to do. His hands raked down her sides and grabbed possessively at her thighs. His lips found the hollow of her throat again and he placed a hot, open-mouthed kiss over her pulse as it thrummed.

'Roman,' she said. 'I want you. Inside me.'

He drew back to look at her with a gaze so intense that her breath caught in her throat. She watched, chest rising and falling as he positioned himself between her thighs, gently nudging her legs open wider. He took himself in his hand pumping once, twice, before lining himself up with her entrance. He paused and she resisted the urge to scream in frustration. She looked at him, saw him watching her with darkened eyes. His breath was ragged with the exertion of control.

'Are you sure?' he breathed, voice heavy.

'Yes,' she said.

Olivia cried out as Roman filled her to the hilt, their hips meeting in long-awaited ecstasy. She breathed hard as she adjusted to the feeling of him inside her. She wrapped her legs around his waist, her hands finding the hard planes of his shoulder blades. Roman drew himself almost all the way out before pushing in again, making her body arch with pleasure. He took this opportunity to wrap one strong arm around her back, anchoring her to him, his other hand holding her hip as he drove into her over and over again.

She clung to him as he thrust into her, her nails raking down his back drawing blood. Roman hissed in pleasure and pain, burying his face in the crook of her neck to muffle a groan. His strokes were long, and slow, and delicious. She pulled him deeper into her with her legs and he growled, biting down on her neck.

She gasped. 'More.'

The noise that came from his throat was more animal than human. He seized her wrists and pinned them above her head, his hips driving hard and fast. She writhed and bucked beneath him. The ache between her legs throbbed as the pleasure at her core tightened. Her thighs shook with the promise of release.

Roman's moves became frantic. He bore down on her, hips slamming into her. She could see his muscles bunching, his body coiling. His breath came in rags, every other exhale a soft curse. She angled her hips up and with every stroke he hit the perfect spot.

She came with a guttural scream, her eyes screwed shut, her toes curled. Her whole body shuddered and that was all Roman needed. He cried out her name as his climax rippled through him.

He panted in her arms for a few moments before untangling himself from her. Olivia shivered at the sudden lack of warmth and Roman thoughtfully pulled the sheets over her. She mumbled something that could have been a thank you as she revelled in her post-orgasm bliss.

They laid in companiable silence, eyes closed. For a long, happy moment, the world was still. And then—

Well, now you're fucked.

17.

Olivia avoided Roman's gaze and she slipped her dress back on. She struggled with the zip but still slapped his hands away when he tried to help. This just seemed to amuse him, much to her irritation. The private room had a small vanity table with a mirror and she checked her reflection. The makeup was holding up but the elegant up-do was falling apart around her face. She impatiently removed all the bobby pins jammed into her scalp and shook her hair free. It sat in loose tousles around her shoulders and she decided that it would have to do. When she turned, she saw Roman grinning at her.

'What?' she snapped.

'You're very tetchy for someone who just orgasmed three times,' he said.

'And you're very smug for someone who has to attend a human sacrifice.'

'Of course I'm smug. I made you come three times. You were *very* responsive.'

Olivia felt her cheeks burn. 'Stop saying it!'

His grin only widened to the point it looked like he was going to swallow his head. 'Are… are you blushing?'

'No!'

'Oh my goodness. I am making the unflappable Olivia McQueen blush!'

'Shut up!' she glared. 'We are not talking about this. Ever again. Understand me?'

'About how we had incredible, mind-blowing, three-time-orgasm sex?' he replied. 'Sure, my lips are sealed. Until the next time, when they'll be—'

'There won't *be* a next time,' she interrupted. 'This was a one-off, alright? It's probably my last night alive, and we're at a Bacchanalia, and you were doing that *thing* with your eyes. It's not happening again.'

Roman looked at her, gaze alight. He took a step forwards. 'What *thing* with my eyes?'

'That thing! There! Stop it!'

'I have no idea what you mean,' he said, reaching out to touch her face.

She caught his hand and turned it over, looking at his watch. 'It's almost midnight,' she said, letting his arm drop. 'Cordelia will be having kittens.'

Roman frowned. 'I didn't realise dragons could have kittens.'

'And considering she's the one who is going to be performing the bloodletting, I really don't want to piss her off.'

She turned and walked towards the door but Roman caught her arm and gently turned her to face him. His expression was guarded, all traces of the earlier humour gone. She searched his eyes but he had gone back to his true self. The façade was gone, the serial killer was back.

'I won't let her kill you,' he said, flatly. 'If she tries, I'll kill her first.'

She watched him for a long moment, then nodded. 'I believe you.'

'Good.'

Back in the ballroom, the scene was much the same as it had been then they'd left: an orgy. They weaved their way through the throng of writhing, gasping bodies. Olivia murmured apologies as they passed that went completely unnoticed. They reached their booth and a waiter came over, two sparkling waters ready for them. Olivia accepted gratefully. She wasn't sure where to look, so she looked at Roman.

'How long does it take for someone to bleed out?' she asked.

He cocked an eyebrow. 'Your pillow talk is terrible.' He saw the look she gave him and sighed. 'You'd have to lose around fifty percent of your blood for your organs to fail. Providing you don't hit an artery or a vital organ, haemorrhaging could take anywhere up to five minutes.'

'Five minutes,' she said. 'Five minutes for Pandora to rise. If she takes any longer, I'll die.'

'For the last time—'

Roman was cut off as Cordelia approached. Her smile was wide but tense, her shoulders stiff. Olivia imagined she could almost hear her teeth grinding.

'The Twelve are almost done setting up the altar,' she said, gesturing to the stage.

Olivia glanced over and saw the orchestra now pushed into a tight corner to make way for the ceremony centre stage. A large marble slab had been set up, sitting on top of a pentagram painted on the varnished flooring in what Olivia hoped was red paint. There were shackles and chains that brought out her claustrophobia. Atop the slab sat a long, ugly dagger that looked like her own. The blade was jagged, the handle made from gnarled bone.

An Infernal blade. So your cuts won't instantly heal.

She nodded. She had her own strapped to her thigh beneath her dress. Perfect for bloodletting a demon.

Half demon. That half a soul makes all the difference.

It certainly did. It was the entire reason they were here tonight.

Cordelia turned her tight smile back to them. It was then that she took in Olivia's dishevelled hair. She looked between her and Roman and smirked. Olivia's hand twitched with the urge to slap her.

'I see you've been enjoying the festivities,' she said. 'Thank Satan this ritual doesn't need a virgin sacrifice.'

'Or a virgin officiator,' Roman said, giving her a pointed smile.

Cordelia's smile wavered for a moment, but she pulled it back, flawlessly. 'Playground insults. How mature.'

He shrugged. 'You started it.'

Cordelia turned her withering glare upon Olivia. 'I'll call you when it's time.'

Olivia nodded. 'I can barely contain my excitement.'

Cordelia rolled eyes and left them to it. They sat in tense silence listening to the orchestra play. A classical version of *Take On Me* merged seamlessly into *Superfreak* and then *Never Gonna Give You Up*. Olivia wondered, idly, what eighties song would be the soundtrack of her death.

You're not going to die! I'll be out of you faster than you can say human sacrifice!

She hoped it was something good. Something by Whitesnake or Dolly Parton.

First off, wow, *that is a broad spectrum. Secondly, oh good grief, you're* not *going to die.*

There was the sound of noise over the PA and Olivia looked up to see Cordelia on the stage, microphone in hand. Olivia drew in a long breath, feeling her chest tighten. She could feel Roman's gaze on her but she refused to look at him. Cordelia cleared her throat, instantly commanding the attention of everyone in the ballroom.

'Ladies and gentlemen,' she began. 'The Awakening ceremony is about to begin. I ask that you please either cease your current activities or take yourself to a private room to finish. This area is now a sacred space.'

The guests obediently obliged with most of them redressing and composing themselves, only a handful of them slinking off to private rooms to continue what they'd started. Within a matter of minutes, the thriving, moaning orgy had stopped, looking like it had never happened — save for the mussed hair and regretful expressions.

Cordelia smiled at her now attentive audience. 'Members of the Brotherhood. Esteemed Guests. Brothers and sisters. Thank you for joining me on this most auspicious night. The time has now come to begin the Awakening ceremony and bring forth Pandora.'

Polite applause. Eager smiles. Sideways glances at Olivia that made her skin prickle.

'I would like to welcome to the stage,' Cordelia said, dramatically sweeping her arm out to Olivia, 'The Wicked One.'

A spotlight found her and she winced. There was more applause as everyone swung round to look at her. She found that her legs couldn't move. That was when she felt Roman's arm linking with hers, pulling her to her feet. The spotlight followed them as Roman led her out of the booth and across the dancefloor to the stage. The orchestra played a soft, melodical version of *I Think We're Alone Now*. Olivia was too sick to even appreciate it.

Climbing the steps to the stage felt like walking to the gallows. Her executioner smiled at her, radiantly. The spotlight all but blinded her as Roman turned her to face her audience, the applause a loud roaring in her ears. Her legs started to shake. Roman slid a strong arm around her waist, keeping her upright.

'I'll go to hell before I let you die, Olivia McQueen,' he murmured against her ear.

She turned her head to look at him, and the look he gave her told her that he meant it.

Cordelia continued, 'The Wicked One has been branded and detoxified. Her demon form is bound by Lapis Lazuli. All that is left to do now is call on Pandora. Let the Awakening begin!'

Two of the Twelve came forward from the side of the stage. They peeled Olivia away from Roman and guided her to the marble slab. For an awful moment, Olivia thought she was going to be sick, but she held it back. Her movements were stiff as she laid back on the altar. One of them reached for her ankles to shackle them to the slab, another grabbed her wrists.

She was spread-eagled and secured down, and she felt the first dregs of panic stir within her. Her chest swelled, her breaths coming fast. A scream sat in her throat threatening to rip free at any moment. She realised, mortified, that she was whimpering — nearly crying — and that alone was enough to send the panic reeling.

Then she felt the rough hand in hers. The calloused skin. The strong fingers. She looked up to see Roman holding her hand. He looked down at her and mouthed, *I've got you.*

Olivia swallowed the scream before it could free itself and closed her eyes. She took a deep, shuddering breath and felt Roman squeeze her hand. They were in this together. If she died, if he couldn't hold up his end of their bargain before the seventy-two hours were up, he was going straight to hell. There was as much riding on this for him as there was her. That alone was weirdly comforting.

The orchestra died down, the music fading into something Olivia didn't recognise. It was no longer soft and lyrical, but harsh and menacing. The instruments shrieked and squealed as the bows dragged severely across their strings, low and ominous.

Olivia turned her head and saw one of the Twelve bringing Cordelia a long, crimson red robe, draping it around her shoulders. In her perfectly manicured hands, Cordelia held the dagger with the Infernal blade. The audience had gone silent.

Cordelia approached Olivia, shooing Roman away. He stepped back but stayed in Olivia's line of sight, and for that she was grateful. Cordelia smiled down at her. It was a bizarre cross between adoring and pitying and Olivia wondered, genuinely for the first time, if Cordelia was more than a little bit unhinged.

'Wicked One,' Cordelia said, tone soft and serious. 'I call on you. Do you answer?'

Olivia swallowed. 'I do.'

'Do you give yourself over to me willingly? Mind, heart, body and soul?'

'I do.'

'I call forth Pandora Morningstar, child of Lilith and Lucifer Morningstar. Is she ready?'

Yes.

Olivia let out a long, shaking breath. 'Yes.'

Cordelia smiled. 'Let it begin.'

18.

Cordelia brought the knife down to Olivia's chest and cut away at the delicate fabric of her dress, exposing a long sliver of skin over her sternum. The branding she had been given just hours before sat exposed, the skin already healed and leaving behind a neat scar. She realised that she was shaking, her whole body trembling against the marble slab.

Olivia had always considered herself brave — almost to a fault. She rushed head first into danger because she was a demon — well, half demon — and she healed faster than humans. She was more difficult to kill too. It had to be the head or the heart to finish her. Anything else would heal. But this dagger, with it's Infernal blade, one strike could kill her. She had never been so close to death.

She also realised that she had never before been so helpless. Since she was old enough to move out of her godfather's nearly ten years ago, she had decided that she would never be helpless again. She had trained hard at the gym and taken self-defence lessons. She had gotten strong, and powerful. She'd taken on her parents' legacy, hunting down rogue demons and casting them back to hell.

And yet here she was: strapped to an altar about to be cut open. Part of her couldn't believe how stupid she was. How completely idiotic to allow herself to get into this situation. She had dedicated almost a decade of her life to self-preservation, to becoming strong and surviving, and now here she was. Probably about to die.

It's better I come out this way rather than tearing you to shreds one day when it's too late.

Olivia couldn't say she agreed. In fact, she couldn't say much at all. Instead, she stayed quiet and watched Cordelia loom over her, dagger in hand. She began to chant:

Saviour come forth,

Pandora awaken,

Body be given,

And blood be taken.

She repeated it over and over again as she slowly brought the dagger down to Olivia's chest. Olivia held her breath, determined not to scream as the blade made contact with her skin. That determination, however, was quickly side-lined as Cordelia cut open her branding scar. The cry that ripped from her throat echoed around the ballroom.

Cordelia wasn't deterred, though. She was methodical and precise as she followed the lines of the scar, seemingly unperturbed by the blood that welled and trickled down Olivia's torso, pooling in her belly button and the hollow of her throat. Olivia dimly realised why her dress was red.

When the scar was open, and a fresh wound once more, Cordelia pulled the dagger back. She watched Olivia with wide, glazed-over eyes as she repeated her mantra over and over. Olivia's chest heaved and she turned her head to look at Roman who watched her with an unreadable expression. His hands, however, at his sides were balled into tight fists, his knuckles turning white.

The pain didn't stop when Cordelia stopped cutting, as Olivia assumed it would. It had dulled somewhat, but it was still there, burning hot. The blood pooling at the base of her throat overflowed, trickling down the sides of her neck, matting into her hair. She wasn't sure how much time had ticked by, but she could feel herself weakening. Her arms and legs had a strange sensation like pins and needles. Her breaths were shallow. Her vision swam and she felt like she was lying in bed after a heavy night drinking.

She looked at Roman and he mouthed the words, *hold on.*

She wanted to hold on. She wanted, so desperately, to fight. She wanted to see this through to the end. She wanted to take Cordelia's perfect face and slam it as hard as she could into the nearest wall. But another part of her was ready to let go. She was so tired. So completely and utterly drained. It would be so easy to close her eyes. To drift off. To sleep. Her parents would be waiting for her. They could finally be together again.

Don't you dare, Liv. I'm almost there. I can feel it. Just hold on for a bit longer.

Just as Olivia felt her eyelids fluttering closed, a sharp, jagged jolt of pain shot through her. Her eyes snapped open and she screamed, her entire body arching. Roman instinctively stepped forwards but Cordelia thrust out an arm to hold him back.

'It's working,' she whispered. 'Pandora is rising.'

Olivia looked down at her chest. She wanted to vomit. From the cut in her sternum, she could see the tip of a bloody finger poking out. Then another joined it, then another. She watched in horror as a blood-stained hand pushed its way out of her torso. The hand strained upwards revealing a forearm, then an elbow, then a bicep. And just when Olivia was sure it couldn't go any further, she saw her entire mid-section tear open as a shoulder pushed through.

She shrieked. Tears filled her eyes and streamed down her pale cheeks. Roman was reaching for her but four of the Twelve were holding him back. She could hear him screaming her name, hear him cursing Cordelia, demanding that she make it stop. Olivia watched as Cordelia looked at him, dispassionately. She shrugged, murmured something about semantics, and turned her attention back to Olivia who writhed and sobbed.

Another arm emerged from her stomach, and another shoulder and the crown of a head of blond, blood-drenched hair. The bloody hands found the edge of the slab and began to haul the rest of its body free. There was a chest, a stomach, and hips. Olivia shrieked as a long, toned leg unfolded itself from her stomach, then another. And then it was standing over her. *She* was standing over her — a six foot, blonde-haired, blue-eyed goddess. The antichrist.

Pandora.

The room fell silent, save for Olivia's screams. The audience watched in silence — some in awe, and some in horror. Some guests had fainted or emptied the contents of their stomach. Cordelia simply looked up at her messiah, tears brimming in her blue eyes. Behind her, Zaid and the Twelve looked much the same, gazing upon their saviour with unabashed adoration.

Pandora stepped down from the altar and looked at her surroundings with childlike wonder. Cordelia suddenly dropped to her knees, hands in the air as in surrender. The guests quickly followed suit, as did Zaid and the Twelve. Free of their grip, Roman ran to Olivia's side. He ripped the shackles from her wrists and ankles and gathered her up in his arms, unsure what to do with her.

'She's dying!' he shouted at Cordelia. 'Help her! Do something!'

But Cordelia wasn't paying attention to her. She only had eyes for Pandora.

Roman growled and pulled the binding bracelet from Olivia's wrist, desperately hoping that as her demon powers flooded back to her that she would heal. Nothing happened and he snarled, pulling her protectively into his chest. He fished his phone from his pocket, trying and failing to find signal. A string of expletives exploded from him and he flung his phone across the room.

Olivia reached up with a trembling hand and gently touched his cheek. Roman flinched and looked down at her, face tight, eyes hard. She could see him at war with himself — a hundred emotions that he didn't understand, or even knew he had, swimming just beneath the surface. He had no idea which one to hold on to, which one to let take over. At that moment, he looked so unsure. Confused. Vulnerable.

'I'm so sorry,' she whispered.

He frowned. 'What for?'

'When I die, you'll go to hell,' she croaked. 'I didn't want this to happen. I'm so sorry.'

He blinked, genuinely bemused. 'How on earth can you be thinking of me right now?'

'I'm sorry, Roman,' she repeated weakly.

Her eyelids drooped and closed. She went slack in his arms and Roman felt lead settle in his stomach. He shook her gently.

'Olivia,' he said, sternly. 'Olivia, wake up. Olivia McQueen, *wake up.*'

She didn't move. Didn't wake. Something that Roman supposed might be panic caught in his chest. He shook her again, harder this time. She rattled in his arms like a ragdoll.

'Olivia!' he snapped, tone sharp like a school teacher. 'Olivia, enough! Wake up! Dammit, Olivia, *wake up!*'

A bloodied hand reached out and touched his arm. He looked up and found himself looking into the ice blue eyes of Pandora. Her hair was matted with gunk and something not too unlike afterbirth. She was naked, her body smeared with wet, sticky blood. *Olivia's* blood. Instinctively, he pulled himself and Olivia out of her grasp.

'Let me help,' she said.

Her voice was clear and soft like summer rain. It sounded as if it were from a different time. It captivated everyone in the ballroom and they looked at her with unflinching devotion, hanging on her every word.

Roman eyed her warily. 'You're the one who did this to her.'

'And I'm the only one who can undo it,' she said, nodding to his hands.

Roman looked down at himself, blanching as he saw his skin turning grey, black veins spreading out beneath.

'Let me heal her,' Pandora said. 'Or are you really so desperate to burn for all eternity?'

'How can I trust you?'

'You can't. But you have to.'

Roman hesitated. He looked down at his hands again, the ashen colour spreading up his wrists and under his jacket. He looked back to Pandora who held her arms open. With great reluctance, he passed Olivia's slack body to her.

Pandora looked down at Olivia's limp frame with pure love, like a mother cradling her baby.

'You gave me everything,' she said softly. 'A home. A body. A friend. A life. I owe you everything.'

Pandora bowed her head to kiss Olivia's forehead, her platinum hair falling over them both like a curtain. She stayed like that for a moment, unmoving. Just as Roman was about to yank Olivia back into his own arms, he looked down and saw the grey receding back down his wrists. The black veins faded and his natural pallor slowly returned. He held his hands up and turned them over in astonishment. Then he looked at Olivia.

Pandora drew back, her hair falling away to reveal Olivia in her arms, completely healed. Roman watched in amazement as she laid her unconscious form gently back on the slab. For a long, horrible moment, nothing happened. Then—

Olivia sucked in a long, gasping breath, her eyes snapping open. Roman collected her in his arms immediately, looking at Pandora who simply smiled at them both. Olivia's breaths were short and sharp, her hands grappling at Roman for purchase. She felt empty. Like part of her was gone. Missing. It hollowed her out and she gasped. Roman held her tighter, trying to stave off the impending panic attack.

'Thank you,' was all Roman said.

Pandora smiled. 'You're welcome.'

Cordelia scrambled to her feet, both hands clasped to her chest. She bowed her head as she approached Pandora, tears streaming down her cheeks, cutting through her flawless foundation.

'Pandora Morningstar,' she said, voice quivering. 'My Saviour. Your grace. I am but a humble servant. My life is your life. My breath is your breath. Please accept me as one of your followers. I would consider it the greatest honour if you would allow me to worship you.'

Pandora looked at Cordelia, smiling softly. 'You're so sweet,' she said.

Cordelia finally allowed herself to look up into the eyes of her messiah.

Just in time for Pandora to rip her head from her shoulders.

19.

There was a stretch of silence that seemed to go on forever. Then someone screamed. Then another. And another. Panic rose in the ballroom like a great wave crashing to shore, and everyone was quickly swept up into it. All but Olivia and Roman, who watched with something akin to disbelief.

Pandora looked at Cordelia's head in her grasp for a few, contemplative moments, then tossed it carelessly into the crowd. A poor woman instinctively caught it, then shrieked and fainted. Pandora's gaze swept over the sea of faces, before glancing over her shoulder, her eyes settling on Zaid.

Zaid's knees buckled, tears already welling in his eyes. Pandora smiled as she approached him, her grin widening as he started to beg. She seemed to indulge in it for a while, looking over him, bloodied and naked, while he whimpered. Then she ripped out his tongue.

Zaid tried to scream, but all that came out was a strangled gurgle. Pandora frowned at him, like the sound displeased her, and punched her fist through his chest. Zaid crumpled and she looked at the glistening red heart in her hand. She squeezed and it came apart in her grasp, lumps of muscle and flesh oozing between her fingers.

Then she turned her gaze on the Twelve. She strode towards Number One, her arm outstretched.

'Pandora, stop!'

Pandora froze. She looked at Olivia who was untangling herself from

Roman's grip. She slid off the altar and stood on shaky legs. The two women regarded each other, Olivia with hesitation, Pandora with interest.

'Stop it,' Olivia said. 'You promised you wouldn't hurt anyone.'

'Incorrect,' Pandora replied. 'I promised I would *try* not to.'

'Try harder.'

Pandora looked at the Twelve, huddled together and cowering like a nest of baby birds before a hungry cat, then back to Olivia.

'They had no qualms about killing you,' she said. 'Why do you care whether or not I kill them?'

'Because everything you do is a direct result of me,' Olivia said. 'If you kill them, their blood is on my hands.'

'Ah, so you're motivated by guilt. Well, not to worry. I am not so much a product of you as I am of two millennia of plotting and scheming.'

'Plotting for what? What the hell is the end goal here?'

Pandora smiled. 'When Lilith split her soul and hid it in her and Lucifer's child, it was with the sole intention of being reunited with her true love again one day. I laid dormant for over two thousand years in the Morningstar bloodline, waiting patiently, descendant after descendant, waiting for the Wicked One. The doppelgänger.

'The part of Lilith's soul living within you was supposed to merge with you. Wipe you out completely so that Lilith could live again. Instead it turned into me. And these idiots—' Pandora gestured to the party guests scrambling over each other to get out of the ballroom '—decided to worship me. I never said I wanted to be worshipped. All it took was one overzealous seer to announce my fate, and suddenly I had a whole religion of wannabe Satanists calling me their messiah.

'But I never wanted to be the antichrist. And I never wanted to be Lilith. The other half of her soul is still burning in hell with her body, and the First Vampire is still wandering the earth looking for you, hoping that Lilith has taken over you, mind, body and spirit. But where does that leave me?'

Olivia blinked. 'Please don't tell me that you actually expect me to answer that.'

Pandora laughed. It was a beautiful sound. It made Olivia feel sick. 'You've always had such a good sense of humour, Liv.'

'Yeah, I'm a real riot.'

Pandora walked over to Cordelia's headless body and yanked the robe off her limp form. She draped it around her own naked body, protecting her modesty — not that much had been left to the imagination.

'I'm not your enemy, Liv,' Pandora said. 'I saved your life.'

'And for that I'm grateful.'

'But I cannot allow you to get in the way of my true plan.'

'Which is?'

She smiled. 'For so long the Brotherhood assumed I would want to bring about the apocalypse. That I wanted to unleash hell on earth and watch the world burn. How wrong they were. I do not want to destroy humanity. Not even remotely.'

Roman cocked an eyebrow. 'That *is* reassuring.'

Pandora smiled beautifully. 'I want to rule it.'

'Ah.'

She tilted her head. 'I suppose you're going to tell me that I can't do that?'

Roman shrugged. 'I'm not the boss.'

'I can't believe I thought I disliked you.'

Olivia stepped forwards, hands up. 'Hold on. Everyone just fucking *hold on*. No one here is taking over the world, alright?'

'I didn't say I wanted to take over the world, I said I wanted to enslave humanity. To do my bidding, and such what.'

'That's kind of the same thing.'

Pandora looked at Roman who shrugged and said, 'It kind of is.'

'And you can see,' Olivia said, 'why I can't let you do that.'

'Livvy, you're not a hero,' Pandora said, giving her a pitying look. 'Now that I'm not a part of you even more, you're not even special. You're just a half-breed, mongrel. You always thought that having half a soul made you special, but, in actual fact, it made you worthless. Not quite a demon, not quite a human. The only other thing that made you interesting, aside from me, was your gift and you gave that up too. Stop trying to play Wonder Woman and go home. It's all over now, anyway. The Brotherhood is gone. I'm out of your hair. Go focus on yourself or, at the very least, your feelings for Roman. Oh, don't look so shocked. We shared a brain for over two decades. I know you, Liv. And I know when you should give up.'

Pandora turned back to the cowering Twelve and Olivia moved to stand in her way, face determined. Most of the ballroom guests were gone, apart for the ones passed out or injured in the stampede to get away. An eerie silence had fallen over the ballroom replacing the harried screaming and crying that had filled it only moments ago. Everything suddenly seemed far too still.

'You're not killing anymore people, Pandora,' Olivia said. 'It's over.'

'Olivia, come on. I know you. You don't care about them. Not really. These morons don't deserve your pity or your guilt. Let me kill them and I'll be on my way.'

'On your way to do what? More killing?'

'What if I was? Why do you even care?'

'Because you can't just kill people!' Olivia exploded.

'Yes. I can. And I will if they get in my way. So I advise you, Livvy, to move aside.'

Roman took a step towards Olivia. 'She has a point. It's over now. This doesn't concern us anymore.'

Olivia looked at him, incredulously. 'How can you say that? If we let her go then people will *die* because of me!'

'Worse things have happened than a few assholes being killed,' he said.

'And what about the next person she kills?'

'We don't know that she will.'

'We don't know that she *won't*.'

'It's not our problem, Olivia. Our part is over.'

Olivia's jaw tensed. 'Not if I say it's not. That means you're with me whether you like it or not.'

Roman's eyes hardened. He stepped up to her, the façade falling away, and looked down at her with something not quite hatred, but close.

'We are done here,' he said quietly. Dangerously.

'I say we're not,' she replied, tone equally venomous.

'And I say enough,' Pandora said.

She side-stepped Olivia and flung an arm out, almost lazily, at the Twelve. Olivia barely had time to shout before they each crumpled, falling to the floor completely boneless. Olivia staggered back at the sight of them. They were like skin sacks. Like "human" costumes that you could slip on and wear. Bile rose up in her throat and she nearly choked on it.

Pandora turned to her, grinning. 'Get it? Because they were spineless.'

'A tad on the nose,' Roman murmured.

'Pandora, what have you done?' Olivia whispered.

'Oh, don't give me that look,' she said, dismissively waving a hand. 'The world is no worse off without them.'

'You just killed twelve humans.'

'And yet no one is crying about it.'

Before she knew what she was doing, Olivia charged at Pandora. One look, however, and Olivia was sailing back through the air, colliding with Roman. They rolled, limbs tangling. Olivia's head hit something — probably the ground — and she saw stars.

Pandora's smile was gone now. She looked at Olivia with open hostility.

'That,' she said, 'was a very silly thing to do. Now I'm angry. Who knows what I'll do when I'm angry.'

'Pandora… please…'

'Goodbye, Olivia McQueen.'

Pandora gave them one last parting sneer before lifting her arms above her head and rocketing up off the ground, crashing through the roof. Olivia ran to where she had been standing and saw she had already gone through the floors above and was flying off into the night sky and out of sight. She turned back to Roman who was on his feet and shaking debris from his hair. They locked eyes.

'Well,' he said. 'I guess that answers the question whether or not she can fly.'

The flight back to Dublin was tense. Ariel seemed pleased to see Olivia was still alive, but his smile had immediately disappeared once they had told him what had happened. Before they'd left, they'd searched the catacombs for Sage and found her holed up in her quarters. Ariel had arranged for someone to take her somewhere safe and called his pilot to prepare the plane. Now they were on his private jet, just the three of them and an air hostess who this time — thankfully — wasn't trying to kill them. Not yet, at least.

Olivia sat as far away from Roman as she could, which unfortunately, wasn't far. Ariel sat somewhere between them, a smartly-dressed mediator in a fine suit and tie. Not that there was much to mediate, beside the odd snarky comment or sly look.

Thankfully, Ariel had brought them a change of clothes. Olivia wanted to burn that red dress and bury its ashes. She sat in a pair of comfy jeans and a Prince t-shirt, fiddling with the zip on her leather jacket. Her mind was disconcertingly quiet without Pandora providing commentary on everything she did. There was an emptiness inside that unnerved her. She hadn't realised her leg was bouncing until she felt Ariel's newspaper tap it.

'You're making the plane shake,' he said, slipping into the seat opposite her.

Olivia sighed and scrubbed at her face. She was tired. 'Sorry.'

'So…' Ariel began. 'Roman's good in bed, huh?'

Olivia paled. 'How did you know?'

'I didn't. Thanks for confirming.'

Olivia closed her eyes, pinching the bridge of her nose. 'It's not my proudest moment.'

'But still one of the best?'

Olivia gave him a look but didn't reply. Ariel sniggered.

'I don't mean to tease,' he said. 'Only sympathise. I've been burned by Roman Wylder too.'

'More like scorched,' Olivia muttered.

'The way he looked into my eyes. The way he held me. *Touched* me. I was convinced he was in love with me. And then…' Ariel shrugged.

'Then there's the awkward silence as he goes back to being a serial killer?'

'Pretty much.' Ariel paused. 'I just don't want to see you get hurt.'

Olivia smiled, but it both looked and felt forced. 'I don't have feelings for him, if that's what you mean.'

'Of course you do. They might not be particularly *happy* or *positive* feelings. But they're there nonetheless. Just… don't let your guard down.'

'More than I already have?'

Ariel smiled. 'You have more to give than just your body.'

Ariel patted her hand before returning to his seat. Olivia turned her focus back to the window. The clouds were far below them, the sky orange and pink. They'd be landing in Dublin just after dawn, and Olivia wondered how many more sleepless nights she could take before it all snuck up on her. Probably not many.

A shadow fell over her and she knew it was Roman without looking. He carried a sort of energy with him. The space around him seemed to crackle wherever he went. It was electric, and thrilling, and dangerous all at the same time. When she refused to look at him, he sat down in the seat beside her. Their thighs brushed and Olivia sucked in a sharp breath.

She wished she still had Pandora in her head, telling her to get a hold of herself. Yes, Roman was gorgeous. Yes, they'd had the best sex of her life. Yes, the thought of him touching her made her body ignite. Yes, yes, yes...

She realised she'd lost her train of thought.

'We need to talk,' Roman said, softly.

'So talk.'

'Face to face, preferably.'

Olivia turned her head and started at how close he was. Their noses were nearly touching. She scooted back, putting some room between them. The air suddenly felt very hot. She resisted the urge to reach up and turn the overhead AC on.

'I'm listening,' she said.

Roman looked at her. 'It's about what Pandora said.'

'That narrows it down.'

'About you and me,' he said. 'She said you had... *feelings* for me.'

'Yes. Many. Disdain, repulsion, hatred—'

'Olivia.'

Olivia watched him, jaw clenched. 'She was trying to goad you. Looks like it worked.'

'I just want to make sure that you—'

'That I what?' she snapped. 'That I don't have a huge crush on you? Trust me, we're good on that. Most times I can't even stand the sight of you.'

He paused. Then, 'You're upset.'

She gaped at him. 'You're infuriating.'

'You're projecting.'

'You're deflecting.'

They watched each other for a long moment.

'Look,' she said, letting out a long breath. 'You're handsome, okay? You are. Let's not beat around the bush. You're handsome, and the guy you pretend to be when you're trying to convince the world that you're not a serial killer, is actually a really nice guy. Maybe that's the person you could have been if life hadn't completely fucked you over. Plus, we had sex. Really, *really* good sex. All of that, plus the fact we've been in dire peril for the last forty-eight hours is bound to create some kind of a spark. So yeah, Roman, I'm attracted to you. *Physically*. But that's it. So please, enough with the Ted Talk. It's all fine. Really. We're good. You're still a *dickhead*, but we're fine.'

Roman let her words sink in, his expression exasperatingly blank. Then his lips quirked into a smile.

'What?' Olivia demanded.

'Nothing,' he said. 'You're just the most incredible person I've ever met.'

Olivia nodded, looking back out the window. 'Damn straight.'

20.

Shenanigans offered the warmest welcome it could muster, which, as it turned out, wasn't that warm at all. Nevertheless, Olivia was beyond relieved when Alastair put a steaming mug of tea in front of her. He joined her, Roman, and Ariel at a table, a mug of microwaved blood in his hands. Ariel seemed to be having a hard time with this fact and was doing his best to avert his eyes anywhere but the vampire's hands. His gaze settled, instead, for Alastair's face. Which, in turn, made *Alastair* unsure of where to look.

No one spoke for an awkwardly long space of time. They each nursed their drinks in silence, catching each other's gaze and then looking away. Olivia and Roman accidentally brushed hands on the table and she stiffened as a flush of heat rose through her. That, naturally, did not go unnoticed.

'All right,' Alastair said, eventually. 'Who's going to tell me why everything is so weird between you two?'

'Nothing,' she said—

—at the same time Roman said, 'We had sex and now it's awkward.'

Olivia turned fully in her seat to face him, eyes wide. 'Jesus shitting Christ, why don't you just tell everyone while you're at it?'

Roman frowned. 'I just did.'

Olivia imagined herself punching him in the face. Before she could make it a reality, there was the sound of a bell ringing as someone entered the pub. They each turned to see Imelda Crane, clad in a black dress, fishnet tights, and Doc Martens. Her pink and purple dreads hung freely round her strong shoulders, and matched her bright pink lipstick. She smiled at them all and it was a welcome distraction.

She locked eyes with Roman and said, 'This had better be good, Wylder.'

Alastair pulled up another chair beside him, and nodded for her to sit down.

'This is Imelda Crane,' Roman said. 'Old frenemy and local witch.'

'Not a witch,' Imelda corrected. 'Seer.'

'Nuance.'

Ariel extended his hand to Imelda across the table and they shook. 'Ariel Levine of Levine Corp. Also an old frenemy of Mr Wylder.'

Alastair nodded. 'Alastair Knox. Vampire. Same here.'

Roman scowled at them each in turn. 'Why don't any of you think of me as a friend?'

'Because we've met you,' Alastair said. 'Now tell us why you called us all here.'

Roman filled everyone in on the events of the last twenty-four hours — mercifully leaving out the part where he and Olivia had sex — and every gory, traumatising, sickening moment leading up to them all being called to Alastair's bar.

'Plus,' he said, looking at Imelda. 'Olivia and I had sex.'

Olivia went to stand again but Ariel put a hand on her arm, and she stayed seated.

Imelda looked between Roman and Olivia, then shrugged. 'Who here *hasn't* has sex with him, honestly.'

Alastair frowned. 'I haven't.'

'Never say never,' Roman said, kissing the air in his direction.

'Do that again and I'll sink my teeth into your throat.'

'Don't threaten me with a good time, baby.'

Ariel put his hands up, like a school teacher requesting a noisy class to settle down. 'Let's remain focused, shall we? Roman, you still haven't told us why we're all here.'

Roman smiled brightly. 'Are you ready for the good bit?'

'While we're young,' Imelda said.

'Pandora is alive and kicking, with plans for world domination,' Roman said. 'And as much as I'm content to let her go on her merry way, Olivia thinks that would be a bad idea.'

'A horrible idea, really,' Olivia interjected.

'And seeing as how the sire bond is good until 11:57pm this evening, I'm still under obligation to bend to her every whim and will.'

'Which means finding Pandora and shutting her down,' Olivia said.

'Exactly! Which is why I've called you all together. We, a motley crew of misfits may we be, are going to work together as a team to capture Pandora, detain her, and foil her evil plans to enslave the human race. Or at least until 11:57pm. Whatever comes first, I'm not fussy.'

Olivia glared at him. 'You're an asshole.'

'I'm a psychopath,' he corrected. 'Don't look for any redeeming qualities in me because you won't find them.'

'Ain't that the truth.'

Imelda frowned. 'Hold on… so where is Pandora now?'

Roman shrugged. 'She killed a few devout Satanists and flew off into the night. Haven't seen her since or checked her socials.'

Alastair nodded, arms crossing tightly across his broad chest. 'So let me get this straight: the antichrist is on the loose. She has all sorts of unparalleled powers — which we can assume we've only scratched the surface of — *and* she wants to take over the world?'

Olivia nodded. 'Pretty much.'

'And you want *us* to help you?'

'Ideally, yeah.'

'I can't say I'm exactly eager.'

'I completely understand,' Olivia said. 'The only problem is, she wants *world* domination. Last I checked, we also live in this world. Therefore *world* domination would not be great for any of us.'

'I can also see your point.'

Roman tilted his head. 'Come on, do you really think she's going to stick to plan A? How many people have tried to take over the world before? Hitler, Napoleon, Alexander the Great. Sure, even you British had a crack at it! No one ever actually sees it through.'

'Because someone always stops them,' Olivia said. 'Do you honestly think Pandora is just going to get bored and give up on her lifelong dream?'

'She's your age, which makes her a millennial. So yeah, pretty much.'

'How can you be so sure?' Imelda asked.

'She's been cooped up in Olivia's head for the last twenty-five years,' Roman reasoned. 'She's only seen the world through her eyes. Once she realises there's a whole planet out there she's going to want to see more of it. She'll go to Disneyland, meet Mickey Mouse, have a giant pretzel and hopefully chill out a bit. World domination sounds great on paper but in reality it's a lot of work.'

Ariel arched a perfect eyebrow. 'So you're hoping she simply... gets bored and complacent?'

'Yes, exactly.'

'My God, you are stupid.'

'He's not stupid,' Olivia said. 'He's being a twat. He can't be bothered to deal with this so he doesn't want to. What do you think Pandora is going to do when she's through with the rest of the world and you're left? Do you think she's going to give you a thumbs up and leave you to it?'

'That's what I'm hoping for, yes.'

'She already said she'll cut down anyone who doesn't bend the knee. And I can't see you anxious to be someone else's bitch any time soon. That, Roman, will leave you dead.'

'She'll have to find me first.'

Olivia's hands balled into fists, her knuckles turning white.

Alastair let out an exasperated breath. 'Even if we did help you — which I'm not saying I am — what could we even do? She is... well, she's the antichrist. A literal Goddess. I've been in a lot of fights with a lot of different characters, but a malevolent Goddess might be punching a bit above my weight.'

Olivia and Roman looked at each other, both coming up blank.

'Well...' she started. 'We don't really have a plan for that yet. All we know is that... we need you guys to help us.'

Ariel, Imelda and Alastair shared uneasy looks.

'Olivia... Roman...' Ariel began. 'I'm not like any of you. I'm human. I don't have strength or powers—'

'You have money,' Roman said. 'And resources. Imelda you have supernatural abilities. Alastair you have this place. Sanctuary.'

'Right,' Imelda said. 'And who has a god-killing weapon that can take the antichrist out?'

Roman took Olivia's wrist in his hand and raised it into the air, showing them the scar Fate had left along with her I.O.U.. 'We have a being from the Celestial realm on our side. And last time I checked the Bible—'

'Which was never,' Alastair mumbled.

'—The Celestial realm trumps the Infernal realm.'

'So... what?' Imelda asked, sceptical. 'We just call her and say "hey, wanna fight the antichrist with us" and hope she shows up?'

Roman nodded. 'Pretty much.'

Ariel fiddled with his diamond cufflinks. 'And if she says no?'

'She can't. She owes us.'

'She's already said no to us once before,' Olivia said, pulling her hand free.

'Yes, but now she *owes* us a favour. She can't say no.'

Alastair looked at Olivia. 'Do you think she would help us?'

Olivia chewed the inside of her cheek nervously for a moment before saying, 'I think so, yeah.'

He sighed. 'Alright. As long as she's in, I'm in.'

Imelda groaned and said. 'Fuck it, me too.'

All eyes fell to Ariel. He looked at Olivia, imploringly. 'I'm not supernatural. I don't know how to fight. My only talent is literally being rich.'

Roman shrugged. 'You have other talents, if I recall.' When no one replied, he elaborated, 'In bed, like.'

Olivia put a hand over Roman's mouth and looked at Ariel. 'You don't have to do anything you don't want to do. But I could really fucking use your help right now, and I actually trust you not to screw me over the moment my back is turned. So you don't have to stay. But honestly, I really need you to.'

Ariel groaned. 'Jesus. Fine. Yeah, alright. I'll help.'

Roman licked Olivia's palm and she recoiled, horrified.

'So, what happens now?' Alastair asked. 'You just… call on her?'

Olivia hadn't thought that far ahead. 'I suppose so.'

She looked at her palm, scarred with Fate's sigil. She suddenly felt very stupid. She traced its lines with the fingertips of her other hand, picturing Fate as she had last seen her in her head. She closed her eyes.

'I need you,' she said.

The bell over the door rang again, and they all turned to watch Salma Hayek walk in, clad in her costume from *Until Dawn*. Olivia thought she might black out.

'You called?' Fate asked, drawing a seat and sitting down between Olivia and Ariel.

Everyone stared. Imelda looked as though she was about to topple off her chair.

'You're Salma Hayek,' Imelda said, softly.

Fate smiled. 'Merely appearing in her visage so as to not corrupt your simple minds. Olivia called on me, and seeing as this is an image that she finds aesthetically pleasing, this is the face I am borrowing today. I can be someone else, if that helps you?'

They all quickly said no.

Fate delicately put her hands on the table and smiled at them in turn, her warm gaze stopping on Olivia. 'How can I help?'

'Well,' Olivia began, making a concerted effort to keep eye contact. 'I don't know how much you know about the situation—'

'Everything. I was just being polite by asking.'

'Right. Yeah. Of course.'

'You need something to kill Pandora.'

'Yes please.'

'She is unkillable.'

Olivia blinked. 'Oh.'

Fate patted her hand. 'I do apologise.'

Roman loaned forwards on his elbows. 'When you say unkillable…?'

'She cannot be killed,' Fate said. 'She is immortal.'

Alastair frowned. 'So am I, but I can still be killed.'

'The antichrist is a different kind of immortal,' Fate explained. 'She is one of the Ancients. The First Vampire, the First Demon, the First Witch — these three were created by Lucifer Morningstar to be eternal.'

'There must be something we can do,' Ariel said. 'Some kind of weakness she has?'

'None, sorry.'

Imelda drummed her fingers against the table. 'Is it too late to back out?'

'However…'

Olivia looked at her sharply. 'Yes?'

'There's nothing to say you can't trap her.'

'How do we do that?' Ariel asked.

Fate held out her palm. She closed it into a tight fist and when she opened it again she was holding a small wooden box, no bigger than an ice cube. On all sides were miniscule, intricate carvings in a language Olivia didn't recognise. It seemed harmless enough, but when Fate passed it to her she could feel the energy radiating out from it.

'What is it?' she asked.

'It's called a vinculum,' Fate said. 'Think of it as a tiny little prison, because that's what it is. Absolutely priceless on the supernatural market. You could practically buy yourself any favour for it with the right person. It can keep one entity captive at a time. It works on intuition so make sure you have a clear image of who you want sucked in there before you open the lid. When you've captured her you can call on me and I'll keep it safe.'

Imelda frowned. 'That seems too easy. We just think of Pandora, open the lid and aim for her?'

'Essentially yes.'

'What's the catch?' Alastair asked.

Fate smiled. 'There's already someone in there. Quite a nasty man, actually. Capturing Pandora will mean releasing him so that she can take his place.'

'Is he immortal too?' Ariel asked.

'Hm? Oh, no. Nothing of the sort. He's a demon. A serial killer named Enzo Claremont.'

Roman beamed. 'A demon? Easy! Olivia's got an Infernal blade. We stick him with the pointy end, he goes back to hell, and there's a vacancy for Pandora at Casa De Vinculum.'

All eyes went to Olivia.

Imelda arched a slitted eyebrow. 'You have an Infernal blade?'

'Uh,' she mumbled. 'Yeah. Kinda.'

'Sweet.'

'At any rate, it's all I can offer you,' Fate said. 'I hope it will suffice.'

Olivia nodded. 'It's great. Thank you.'

Roman plucked the vinculum out of Olivia's grasp and turned it over in his hands, eyeing it sceptically. He threw it up in the air and caught it with the other hand. Fate blanched.

'Please,' she said. 'Be careful. It's very fragile and the moment that lid comes off Enzo Claremont will be freed.'

Roman gave her a reassuring look. 'Don't worry. Careful is my middle—'

He sneezed, the box tumbling from his grip. It fell to the floor with a quiet clatter and bounced across the bar lino, coming to a stop as it hit the leg of a barstool. The lid toppled off. Olivia reached for Roman's wrist — for support or to crush it, she wasn't quite sure. The six of them watched the vinculum, waiting for something to happen. For a long stretch, nothing did. And then—

Black smoke poured from the open box. First in wisps, and then in great plumes. Suddenly they were all standing — Fate included — with nothing else to do but watch. The smoke rose up, billowing in a long column. Within it, Olivia thought she could make out the figure of a man. Someone tall and slender, but deceptively strong. Then, without fanfare, the smoke dropped and all that remained was a rakish man with jet black hair and grey eyes.

He smiled at them and said, 'Thank you.'

Then he disappeared, blinking from existence, and reappeared at Olivia's side. Before anyone could react, he grabbed her by the throat and disappeared again, this time taking her with him. A few long seconds passed. Then, slowly, all eyes turned to Fate.

'I should have told you,' she said. 'He's gifted.'

21.

Being a hostage, Olivia had decided, was neither preferable, nor was it particularly comfortable. It *was,* however, a kind of novelty. She'd never been abducted before, and this guy — Enzo Whatever-It-Was — was really pulling out all the stops. She was in a dank room, for one. It was dark and lit only by a single lightbulb overhead that swung madly every time a concerningly large moth bumped into it. Secondly, there was no décor, except a few dried splotches of blood on the tiled floor. She was even tied to a chair. *Tied to a chair!* If she wasn't in dire jeopardy — which she assumed she probably was — she might laugh at the ludicrousness of it all.

There was the sound of a door opening and closing, and then Enzo Something-Something stepped into the circle of light. He was lean and lithe, and had a face that looked like it got punched a lot. He wore ripped jeans, scuffed boots and a 1993 Nirvana world tour t-shirt. His smile was as arrogant as Olivia would have expected any serial killer's to be.

'You must be quite confused,' Enzo said in a Texan drawl. 'If you like, I can explain to you why you're here.'

Olivia sighed. 'You're going to kill me, I assume?'

'Well, actually, I—' Enzo paused. He frowned. 'Yes. Yes, I am.'

She blinked. 'You sound annoyed.'

'I'm not annoyed.'

'Well, you *sound* annoyed.'

'Well, I'm not.'

Olivia tilted her head. 'Did I steal your thunder? Is that it? God, I'm so sorry. I tend to do that. Jesus, you probably had a big speech prepared and everything, and I just completely ruined it for you. Look, how about this? We start over. You go back out there and come back in, and I let you get on with your opening villain speech before I start being witty and charming. Would that make you happy?'

Enzo's face twisted into a sneer. 'Oh. You're one of *them*.'

Olivia quirked an eyebrow. 'One of what?'

'A comedian.'

'Oh, well, *thank you*.'

Enzo crossed his arms and stepped up to her so that she had to crane her head back to look at him. 'You think that you can sit there and try to be funny—'

'—I don't have to try—'

'—and pretend that you're not scared, because I know you are. I know your shitting your pants right now, little girl, but you're making stupid jokes and pretending to be Billy-Big-Balls. It's not going to work on me.'

Olivia sighed and nodded. 'Wow, you see right through me. Do you have any idea how good it feels to finally be *seen*?'

He hit her. Hard. She felt her cheekbone crack beneath his fist. Her eyes watered.

'Still think you're funny?' he asked.

Olivia blinked the tears back and nodded. 'Kinda, yeah.'

He hit her again and she gasped. He roughly grabbed her face in his hand and pulled her round to look at him. The sneer was back. His fingertips dug into her crushed cheekbone and she winced.

'Listen here, princess,' he said. 'This is how it's going to go. You're playing *my* game now. Those ropes are spelled. It doesn't matter how much of a big bad demon you are, you're not breaking free. Not to mention that when you passed out after we teleported I searched you and found a *very* interesting little dagger. An Infernal blade. I've gotta say, I'm impressed. But I confiscated it, because little ladies such as yourself, shouldn't be carrying around such dangerous weapons. So, long story short, you're not getting out of here anytime soon.'

'Why on earth would I want to leave?' she muttered. 'I'm really digging this whole *Saw* bathroom vibe. I appreciate a man who knows his aesthetic.'

For a horrible moment, Olivia thought he was going to hit her again. If Pandora were still with her she'd be telling her to *shut her damn smart mouth*. But she wasn't here, and her damn smart mouth had free reign, and it was going to get her killed. But then, Enzo let go. He stepped back and visibly gathered himself, swallowing down his anger. He smiled.

'Here's the deal, sweetheart,' he said. 'I've been stuck in that box for longer than I care to think about.'

Olivia nodded at his shirt. 'I can tell.'

'So I need you to catch me up on everything that's happened while I've been indisposed.'

She frowned. 'Why pick me? Why not one of the others? Hell, why not go outside and pick up a newspaper?'

'Because I haven't killed anyone in a very long time, and you're a very pretty girl. And I only kill very pretty girls.'

'Aw, you're sweet.'

'So once you've told me what I need to know—'

'Wait, wait!' she interrupted. 'Let me guess! You're going to… kill me?'

'Yes.'

'With kindness?'

'No, with knives.'

Olivia shrugged as best she could with the ropes around her. 'Eh.'

Enzo stepped out of the light for a moment and when he returned he was dragging a chair behind him. He plopped it down in front of her and sat on it back to front, his arms crossed over the back, his stubbled chin resting on his forearms. He looked like one of Olivia's douchebag professors when they were trying to relate to their students.

'What year is it?' he asked.

'2050. The US president is a cat.'

'What country is this?'

'A new one. They built it back in 2032. It's called Greg.'

'What is your name and purpose?'

'Princess Leia, from the planet Alderaan. I'm an agent of the rebel alliance sent to bring about the destruction of the Death Star.'

Enzo's jaw clenched. 'I'm going to give you one more chance to start telling me the truth, darlin'. If you don't, I'm just going to get straight to the torturing and murdering part.'

Olivia sighed and nodded. 'Alright. Yeah, alright.'

'Why did you let me out of the vinculum?' he asked.

Olivia chewed her lip for a moment, then said, 'I thought it was a dice. We were going to play Yahtzee.'

He hit her again. This time with feeling. The whole left side of her face crumpled and stars exploded behind her eyes. She tasted blood and felt one of her teeth had broken. Enzo got to his feet, kicking the chair aside. He cracked his knuckles in a way that Olivia supposed he thought was menacing.

'Right then,' he said. 'Torturing and murdering it is.'

Olivia spat out her tooth and gave him a bloody grin. 'Let's go.'

Olivia was beginning to see the downside to demon healing. As useful as it was for when she got into fights — and she got into a *lot* of fights — it was not quite so practical, however, when being tortured. Well, she supposed, it depended on whose viewpoint you looked at it from. From the perspective of a torturer it was pretty sweet. You got to come up with new and inventive ways to inflict pain. Your prisoner kept healing and you could keep on hacking bits away at them. As the *torturee*, though, it sucked. She had time to consider this while her fingertips grew back.

It could have been hours. She had no way to tell. It felt like days, but she knew that couldn't be right. She wished she hadn't used up her I.O.U. from Fate. She could really use a *deus ex machina* around about now. She was scared that she was coming perilously close to begging for death. How embarrassing that would be. Her parents had trained her for just about anything. She could fight. She could disarm. She could keep cool in most dire situations. But she guessed they hadn't gotten around to negotiating a way out of a hostage situation before they kicked the bucket.

Enzo held her dagger in his hand, turning it over in his fingers. A promise of what was to come. Both her greatest fear and her desperate need. She mumbled something around the blood in her mouth, trying to imagine that she looked cooler than she knew she didn't as it dribbled down her chin.

'Hm?' Enzo said, quirking an eyebrow at her. 'What was that? Speak up, sweetheart.'

'I said…' Olivia croaked. 'I would like to speak to your manager.'

He hit her. She decided it was worth it.

'Why do ya'll do this to yourself?' he asked. 'You could have told me what I wanted to know and I would have killed you quick and easy, and this would have all been over with. But no, you make your pathetic jokes, and cower behind all that false bravado. What are you waiting for? Your friends to rescue you? Was that your boyfriend whose hand y'all were holding? Are you expecting him to come save the day?'

'Not really,' Olivia admitted, wincing at how hard it was to talk. 'He doesn't even particularly like me.'

'Clearly. It's been almost four hours.'

'Where even are we?' she asked.

Enzo shrugged. 'No idea. I pictured the kind of place I wanted to take you and… well the rest just takes care of itself. Teleportation is a very *instinctive* gift.'

'So we could be in Australia?' she croaked. 'Shit, I didn't bring any SPF.'

He snorted. 'Hardly. I get about a fifty mile radius on it.'

That was interesting. Fifty miles in any direction meant they were either still in Ireland or in the middle of the Irish sea. Considering the lack of fish around her ankles or saltwater in her lungs, she suspected it wasn't the latter.

'No transatlantic teleporting for you then,' she said.

'You're very chatty all of the sudden,' he noted. 'Realised your mistake have you?'

'Actually, I'm lulling you into a false sense of security. That way you'll never see it coming when I attack.'

'You just told me your plan.'

'Foiled again.'

To her surprise, Enzo laughed. 'I kinda like you,' he said. 'Shame I'm gonna have to kill you.'

'Then don't. Let me go. I'm hardly the ideal hostage. I don't beg. I don't scream. I don't even cry.'

'Yet.'

'You're a man with his eyes on the prize. I get that. I do. And I respect that. But I really am a lost cause. Wouldn't you prefer some college sorority sophomore? You can chase them, and they can scream and trip over something that isn't there. They get back up and carry on screaming. They fumble as they try to put their key in the lock and drop it completely. Then instead of picking their keys up and trying again, they run off in a different direction completely. All the while screaming and tripping over, until they eventually wind up in some dead end so you can corner them and gut them like a fish. Doesn't that sound nice?'

Enzo gave her a withering stare. 'I can't tell if you're stalling for time or if you just love the sound of your own voice.'

'Definitely both.'

'All you had to do was answer a *few* simple—'

'Oh, good *God*,' Olivia groaned. 'Alright, you really want to know what you've missed? Alright, fine, I'll tell you. The world is shit. It really is. America had a human Jaffa cake in charge for a while. Australia keeps setting itself on fire and for some reason no one cares. There was a deadly virus that kept everyone indoors for two years. Some giant fucking African bees started murdering people. The UK spunked it's good fortune with the EU up the wall for no good goddamn reason. It's still a criminal offense to be gay in seventy-two counties —and punishable by *death* in ten of those countries. Disney keeps making the most fucking awful live action remakes of its animated classics that literally *no-one* asked for. Plus the ocean is on fire. So yeah, that's about all of it. You really haven't missed out on much, buddy.'

Enzo blinked, obviously unsure of what to do with all that information. 'I… see?'

'So if I were you, I'd go back to your snuggly little box and go back to sleep for another thirty years because nothing is getting better anytime soon.'

'You have a… very bleak outlook on life.'

Olivia looked down at her bloodied and bedraggled self and then back to Enzo. 'Do I? My apologies.'

Enzo seemed to be weighing it all up in his head for a moment. Then he shrugged. 'It's not ideal, but it'll do. Alrighty, time to die.'

'Yep, thought so.'

Enzo stepped close to her, brandishing her own damn knife at her throat. The arrogant smile was back.

'Any last words?' he asked.

She shrugged. 'Jumanji.'

Enzo had a moment to frown before Olivia surged forwards and bit his hand. Enzo screamed and she bit down harder, tasting his blood in her mouth mixed with her own. The dagger dropped from his grasp and his other hand came to the back of her head. He grabbed a fistful of her hair and yanked but she held steady. She screamed around his hand as a clump of her hair tore out, scalp attached.

Realising he needed to change tactics, Enzo resorted to hitting her, heavy punches slamming into the side of her head. Her eyes closed as she absorbed each blow, her head rattling, her ear feeling like it was about to explode. Keeping her teeth sunk deep into his palm, she pushed back on her heels, toppling the chair backwards. She went down, pulling her with him. Beneath her, the wooden chair splintered, the ropes loosening.

She released Enzo's hand and slammed her forehead up into his nose. He howled and rolled off her, clutching at his stupid, punchable face. She shimmied out of the ropes and rolled onto her feet, ignoring the way every bone in her body screamed as she rocketed up to standing.

Enzo had rolled onto his knees and was looking at her with unconcealed hatred. 'You bitch! You broke my nose, you bitch!'

'It'll heal,' she said and ran at him.

The heel of her boot connected with his chin and he fell back onto his arse, his other hand coming up to grasp his broken jaw. Olivia snatched up the dagger and turned to Enzo as he tried to sit up. She strode over to him and he snatched up a broken chair leg and hurled it at her. She dodged and glared. Then he did it again with the other leg.

'Fuck *off!*' she shouted.

She picked up a chair leg of her own and threw it. The first one bounced off his beautiful, bloody face but the second one speared him right through the throat. His eyes bulged and he gurgled in surprise before falling back. His legs flailed as if independent from his body, his hands clawing at the make-shift stake in his windpipe. Olivia approached and grabbed him by the ankle. Enzo scrambled for purchase on the tiled floor as she dragged him back into the light. She wanted to watch the surprise on his face when she sent him back to hell.

Straddling his torso, she pinned each of his arms under her legs, her knees pressing into his inner elbows. She lifted the dagger high above her head and gave him a bloody, toothy smile, that she hoped looked as deranged as it felt, and brought the blade down.

She was right. The look of surprise was worth it. Enzo's mouth fell slack as the blade sunk into his heart. And then he was ash.

Olivia took a moment to herself. She slipped the dagger back into her boot and sat back on her heels, assessing the damage. The injuries would heal. The pain would fade. Her blood would replenish. She felt like absolute shit, and she was certain she looked it too, but she was okay. She was alive.

She realised, sickeningly, that she missed Pandora.

With a huge sigh and an even bigger amount of effort she hauled herself up off the floor. She turned and saw Roman staring at her from the doorway, looking impressed.

A beat passed. Then—

'Where the bloody fuck have you been?'

22.

It turned out that Enzo hadn't taken her far. They were barely out of Dublin city, at a long abandoned factory that now served as a home to rats and black mould. A quick sweep of the place confirmed that they were, thankfully, alone. It was then that Roman pointed out that it would be a perfect place to lure Pandora to.

'Think about it,' he said, shaking a rickety railing on one of the mezzanine balconies. 'It's big, open, plenty of hiding spots, room to set up a trap.'

Olivia nodded. 'Lots of space for activities.'

'Like, sure, there's some mould. Sure there are a few man-eating rats about. Sure, there's probably a dead body stashed around somewhere. But nowhere is perfect. And in this property climate, this is a *steal*. Literally. No one is here, we steal whatever we want.'

'Stealing *is* good.'

'Not to mention it's out in the boonies. Well, Wicklow. You could probably slaughter a whole army here and no one would know it! And the blood would wash right off the tiles.'

'Gotta keep things clean, that's for sure.'

She tried to sound more excited, but her head was elsewhere. Fucked right off. Out of office, please forward all emails to HR. Not to mention that she was exhausted. Totally fucking exhausted. She wanted to go back to her shitty flat, and curl up in her shitty, second-hand IKEA bed, and bundle herself up in her shitty moth-eaten blankets. And maybe have a cry? Or a scream? Or both? What she *really* didn't want to do was stand around making plans for her final showdown with the Big Bad.

Roman looked at her, frowning. Eventually he took the bait and said, 'Alright, what's wrong?'

Olivia turned to him slowly and looked down at herself. Her clothes were stuck to her body with her own blood. Her hair was matted and sticky. She felt like she'd been trampled by a herd   of elephants with knives for feet and she looked like it, too.

Roman followed her gaze and nodded. 'I see. Would it help you if I told you it's not that bad?'

Olivia's face darkened.

'I mean,' he said. 'You pull it off well. The whole *Carrie* look. It's very… Myspace goth era.'

'Roman,' she said quietly. 'In the last twenty-four hours I have been sacrificed, had the antichrist burst through my chest cavity like a goddamn scene from *Alien*, died, been brought back to life by the same antichrist, been taken hostage, tortured and nearly murdered again. If you can't say anything *nice*—'

'I am being nice!'

'—or even remotely helpful—'

'I'm *very* helpful!'

'—then please do keep your fucking mouth shut.'

Roman blinked. 'I'm sensing that you're… angry?'

'Yes, I'm fucking angry!' she shouted. 'I'm angry, and hurt, and tired, and fucking *sick* of this! I'm supposed to be studying for an exam right now! My life is supposed to be boring and normal! That's the reason why I made a deal and got stuck with this Devil's debt! Because I don't want to be doing shit like this!'

'Well, what *do* you want?'

Olivia let out a sound that was probably a laugh, but could just have easily been a sob. 'I want to sleep without having nightmares. I want people to stop trying to kill me. I want to be human. I want my parents back. I want Cillian back. I just want a normal fucking life where everything isn't a huge fight.'

Roman looked at her for a long moment. Then he said, 'How about a cup of tea and a bath?'

Roman's apartment was not what she had been expecting. First of all, there were books everywhere. The shelves were overflowing with them, piles of tomes stacked up and pushed into the corners of every room. There seemed to be something from every genre. Crime. Thriller. Comedy. Drama. YA. Romance. Erotica. LGBTQ+. Action. Roman, it seemed, was not a fussy reader.

Nor was he really into furniture. The apartment was minimalist at best, but she supposed that was good because it made room for all of the books. Everything was sleek and modern, all black and white. The book covers made up for the lack in colour and gave the place a surprisingly homey vibe.

She was also surprised to see he had a record player, and beside it a vast collection of music. Much like his reading material, there seemed to be something for everyone. To someone who didn't know him, it just looked like Roman had varied taste. But to Olivia, who was getting to know him *far* too well, she knew what it really was: an extension of the façade. He was covering all bases. Appealing to everything like the everyman he wanted the rest of the world to believe he was. Something about it caused a sharp pang in her chest as she wondered just how lost Roman Wylder really was.

To get to the bathroom, you had to go through the bedroom. Something about it made her stop. It was here that Roman's true self was really reflected. She didn't know how she knew, but she just felt it. It was unlike the rest of the apartment. Instead of clean lines and modest furniture, his bedroom was warm and cosy.

The walls were navy blue apart from the feature wall which was all exposed red brick. Instead of a duvet, the bed had a blue fleece blanket. There was a mahogany writing desk pushed up against one wall, and beside that a modest bookcase with only a few select tomes on its shelves. *Jaws. Misery. Dracula. The Woman In Black. American Psycho.* Over the bed was a framed movie poster of *Nightmare On Elm Street*, Freddie Kruger's eyes following her as she passed through the room.

She stopped at a picture on the nightstand. It was Roman and Alastair, except Roman was much younger — maybe seventeen — and dressed in casual jeans and an Irish rugby shirt. His hair was a complete mop and his smile was wide. Beside him, Alastair was completely unchanged, barely managing a grimace for the camera. He had his arm around Roman's shoulders.

Roman cleared his throat. 'Uh. Yeah. That's, uh…'

Olivia smiled. 'It's sweet.'

'Alastair gave it to me. Before he realised who I was and kicked me out.'

'And you kept it?'

Roman shrugged. 'It was a gift. You're not supposed to throw out gifts.'

The bathroom went back to the everyman façade. It was clean and clinical, but it had a tub and that's all Olivia cared about.

'How do you take your tea?' he asked.

'White, two sugars.'

She showered first to get all the blood off, and washed her hair with something that looked suspiciously like an all-in-one shampoo and shower gel and smelt overpoweringly of lemons. Roman did, however, have proper bubble bath, and Olivia added a liberal amount to the hot water. When she sunk down into the tub, she let out a long, satisfied groan. Her little flat only had a shower and she couldn't remember the last time she'd had a bath. She closed her eyes and let the hot water ease out the stiffness in her muscles.

There was a knock at the door and Olivia called for him to come in. Roman wandered in blindly with one hand holding a huge *Thundercats* mug of tea, the other hand over his eyes.

'Olivia, where are you?' he said. 'Am I close? Marco!'

Despite herself, she laughed. 'You can take your hand away. Everything is covered up with bubbles.'

Roman let his hand drop and cracked one eye open. He grinned and it proved infectious. 'You look cosy.'

'Your bath is incredible. I want to marry your bath. I want to buy a summer home in Majorca with your bath.'

He passed her the cup of tea. 'I think it's already romantically involved with the sink.'

'Just my luck.'

Olivia sipped her tea and moaned happily. Roman cocked an eyebrow at her and she laughed.

'I'll leave you two alone,' he said, turning for the door.

'Your flat isn't what I was expecting,' she said, suddenly.

He turned back to her. 'Oh? You thought there'd be more saran wrap and plastic sheets?'

'No. Not the saran wrap.'

He smiled. 'What did you expect?'

'I don't really know. It's very… generic.'

Roman shrugged and sat down on the edge of the tub. 'I didn't change anything when I moved in.'

'Have you read all of those books?'

'Yes. I didn't like all of them, but once I've started I always finish. I keep my favourites in my bedroom.'

'I saw,' she said, taking another sip. 'Your bedroom is more you.'

He smiled, softly. 'You think so?'

She nodded. 'Rugged but sophisticated. Shabby but chic. Cool but cosy.'

'And I'm all those things?'

She shrugged. 'It just suits you, is all.'

They sat in companionable silence while she drank her tea.

'Alastair means a lot to you, doesn't he?' Olivia said after a while.

Roman looked like he was choosing his words carefully. 'I would be... unhappy... if something happened to him.'

'That generally means you care about someone.'

'How peculiar.'

Olivia watched him for a long moment. 'You mean a lot to him too, you know. It's obvious. You're like a son to him.'

'That makes sense. He was like a father to me.'

'Are you mad at him for kicking you out?'

'No. I'm sure I would have done the same if I were in his position.'

Olivia felt that pang in her chest again. 'Did he teach you how to act, uh...' she trailed off as she searched for the right word.

Roman grinned. 'Normal?'

She returned his smile, sheepishly. 'Yeah.'

'Yes. He did. He didn't know he was doing it at the time, but ever since I realised that I wasn't normal, I looked to him for guidance. He was a good man. *Is* a good man. I knew that if I studied him, *copied* him, then I could pass for being a good man too. I learned every trait. Studied every mannerism. He was always kind and compassionate, if not a little rough around the edges. He was a gentleman, and a good friend, and a great father-figure to me. I knew that if I could make people think that I was just like him then no one would realise that I'm actually a monster.'

Olivia's chest ached, unexpectedly. The thought of a teenage Roman, lost and traumatised, desperately trying to mould himself in the shape of his hero made her throat close up. Every time she thought she was close to figuring him out, Roman Wylder surprised her. Not for the first time, she wanted to touch him. Hold him. She wanted to show him what it was to be comforted and to know that it was okay to let someone console you. Which was fucking ridiculous because that's what you did when you cared for someone. And the last thing she needed was to care for Roman Wylder. She wasn't in the business of borrowing trouble without good reason, and Roman was definitely trouble.

Olivia looked at him. 'I don't really know what to say.'

Roman smiled. 'You don't have to say anything. Just enjoy your bath.'

As Roman made his way to the door again, Olivia said, 'For what it's worth, I don't think you're a monster.'

He looked back at her. 'No?'

'No. I think you're an insufferable shit with a God complex and an overgrown ego. But I don't think you're a monster.'

Roman shrugged and smiled, and said, 'I'll take it.'

By the time she got out of the bath, Roman had washed and dried her clothes and they were waiting for her in a neatly folded pile on the bed. Olivia tried not to think of him handling her underwear and dressed, before following the scent of something delicious coming from the kitchen.

Roman stood at the stove, frying pan in hand. Olivia crossed to the kitchen and sat on the island counter to watch him. He moved with confidence and precision that Olivia could only dream of. Most of her dinners consisted of frozen meals and takeaways. Her master's degree, the gym, jiu-jitsu and her Devil's debt kept her so occupied that she was always too tired to cook by the time she got home in the evenings.

'I hope you're not vegan,' Roman said, not looking at her.

'Even if I was, that smells too good to turn down.'

'Attagirl. How was your bath?'

'Heavenly.'

Roman plated up the full Irish breakfast — even if it was late afternoon — and served it at the breakfast counter. They ate in silence and Olivia savoured every bite. Roman had made her another cup of tea to wash it down with, and for the first time in a long time, she felt perfectly content.

Reality soon came crashing back down on her though, when Roman said, 'We should call the others. I let them know you're okay, but we should tell them about the factory.'

Olivia sighed and nodded, eating her last forkful of scrambled eggs. 'Yeah, probably.'

Roman made the call and put it on speakerphone. Alastair picked up immediately.

'Are you done playing house yet?' he asked, gruffly. 'I thought you wanted our help killing the antichrist?'

'We're not playing house,' Roman said. 'Olivia needed to rest. And yes, we do still want your help, that's why we're calling.'

'So what's the plan?'

'The place where Enzo took Olivia is perfect for luring in Pandora. It's remote, quiet, big enough to lay a trap. It doesn't look like anyone's been there in at least twenty years. We can go there, set ourselves up and finish this.'

'Alright.'

'Olivia?' Imelda called. 'You there?'

Olivia swallowed a mouthful of tea. 'Yep. You okay?'

'Grand, yeah. Me and Ariel have a bet going about what Roman's apartment looks like. He reckons it's dark academia but I think he's got a secret cottage core aesthetic going on.'

'Everything's pink and he has posters from *The Birdcage* everywhere.'

'It's better than we ever could have hoped.'

'If you're quite done, children,' Alastair sighed. 'Roman will you text me the address?'

Roman promised to send the address and another separate address of something they needed to pick up along the way, but he didn't say what. Olivia looked at him, suspiciously. He didn't notice, so Olivia prompted him by kicking his shin.

'Ouch,' he said. 'What?'

'What are you getting them to pick up?'

'Don't you trust me?'

'Nope.'

He mock-gasped, putting a hand to his chest. 'You wound me.'

'You annoy me.'

Roman tilted his head and gave Olivia one of his thousand-kilowatt smiles. 'Our secret weapon,' he said.

23.

Olivia didn't really know what she was expecting the secret weapon to be, but Sage Bishop certainly wasn't it. She still had no idea if the witch was young or old — it seemed to change in different light. Her patchwork blonde hair was tied up into a messy bun and her grey eyes were alert and excited. Olivia realised, with sympathy, that this was the first time she had been asked to do magic whilst not under the duress of the Brotherhood. She was free and freedom really suited her.

They all took orders from Sage as she instructed them how to set up the space — even Roman allowed himself to be bossed around. Olivia could see a soft spot in his eyes for her. The same as he had for Alastair. She wondered, idly as she continued to purify the air with burning incense, if Roman just randomly picked out people that he liked. People that he considered worthwhile and different from the usual dredge of humanity. People that he could put on a pedestal and point at, saying *this person. I will make an exception for this person.*

There was so much about Roman that she had uncovered in the past few days, and yet there was still so much left untouched. She wasn't sure if she wanted to know more, and at the same time she knew that if the opportunity arose, she would jump at the chance to discover all his secrets.

The films and TV shows got it all wrong. They always portrayed the serial killers as self-destructive, singular-minded, laser-focused. But Roman wasn't any of those things. His way was far simpler: fulfil the need and don't get caught. He didn't bask in his own glorious purpose.

237

He didn't think he was better than anyone, or destined for greatness. There were no delusions of grandeur to him. He didn't revel in what he did. To him, it was as much a means to an end as the everyman's nine-to-five. A way to keep the darkness at bay by seeking out the demons in the shadows. Self-preservation. Survival of the fittest.

He was, she noted, remarkably self-aware for a psychopath.

They had agreed to set up in the main room. It was the biggest space and it had the most emergency exits in case it all went horribly, horribly wrong. Which it usually did. The plan was to use Sage as a medium and draw on Olivia's connection to Pandora. If Olivia could convince Pandora to come to her, they would spring the trap. A large binding circle had been drawn on the floor and spelled for security by Sage. Those who entered it couldn't leave unless someone outside the circle gave them permission. Then all they had to do was open the vinculum and let it suck Pandora inside. Then they could give the box back to Fate. It would be over. Done.

Except would it? She wasn't exactly certain of how Roman felt about her. She knew they weren't *friends* exactly, but she was fairly certain he didn't outright dislike her. He definitely respected her. Plus they'd had sex. You couldn't kill someone you kind of liked, really respected, and recently boned, right? She wasn't so sure. She hoped he wouldn't try to kill her, because then she would have to kill him first. And she didn't outright dislike him, either.

The factory floor had quickly gone from something from a torture porn movie to something akin to a Satanist starter-pack. Pentagrams had been drawn across the walls and floor in blood red chalk in an attempt to draw Pandora to the energy there. The lights were rendered obsolete with the sheer amount of candles lit. They were all different shapes and sizes. It didn't matter if they were different colours or scents, and — mixed with the burning incense — the whole place was starting to smell like a very flammable *Bath & Body Works* store.

The binding circle had been drawn in, much to everyone's utter dismay, pigs blood. Olivia decided it was best not to ask how Sage got her hands on a gallon of pigs blood at the last minute, especially since she'd only just been moved into her safe house provided by Ariel. Some things, Olivia had decided, were just not her business and should stay that way.

She looked around at them all. They weren't exactly an ideal team, but it would do. Roman dressed all in black and using the leftover pigs blood to write passages from the Satanic Bible on the walls. Ariel in his three-piece, pin-striped suit, strawberry-blonde hair pulled back into a bun. He was helping Sage light the remaining candles, careful not to stand on the hem of her long hippy skirt. Making sure the binding circle didn't have any gaps or imperfections was Imelda, looking every inch the punk rock chic. And lastly there was Alastair, busying himself with burning sage — the herb, not the witch — to cleanse the air around them, looking more like a potato farmer than a vampire in his flat cap and fleece .

Olivia realised, with a shock of clarity, that she actually really liked all these people. It absolutely terrified her.

I think we're about ready, Sage signed. *Olivia, are you ready to try and make contact?*

Her palms were sweaty. *I think so.*

Sage beckoned Olivia into the centre of the binding circle with her. They sat down on the hard tile floor, cross-legged, and Sage took Olivia's hands in hers. The others waited outside the circle. She could feel Roman's eyes on her. The sun had gone down over an hour ago and night was drawing in quicker than she wanted to think about. She only had a few hours left on the sire bond. After 11:57pm, Roman was free to walk away. Or kill her. Or both.

She hoped he would stay.

Here is how this is going to work, Sage signed and Roman translated. *You and Pandora have a connection. I know you can't hear her thoughts anymore now that she has been awakened, but that doesn't mean you can't tap into them. You have a psychic link to her. I can guide you to her. When you find her, you need to convince her to come find you here. Then we trap her.*

Olivia nodded. *Okay. How do I try and tap into her thoughts?*

The sage and incense will have helped to open your mind and clear your toxins. This leaves you more open to astral projection.

Olivia felt her eyes go wide. *Astral projection?*

Yes.

No way.

Yes way.

She felt herself grinning. *You mean like* Insidious, *and* Doctor Sleep, *and* Behind Her Eyes?'

Sage looked at her blankly, like someone who had very much spent the last decade in a catacomb beneath a secret Satanist headquarters, and shrugged. *Sure.*

'Okay that's cool,' she said, looking over her shoulder at Roman. 'Tell me that isn't cool.'

'It's pretty cool,' he agreed.

She looked back at Sage. *I thought it was going to be like a Ouija board or tarot cards, or something. This is going to be like in a movie. Oh my God, it will be like* Doctor Strange.

Sure, Sage repeated. *Now let's begin. Close your eyes and listen to Roman's voice.*

It was harder than Olivia had anticipated to clear her mind. More than half an hour later, her spirit and physical form were both still painfully one. Even with Roman's soothing voice trying to coax her off into a dreamlike state, all she could think about was how much time had passed and how little they'd achieved. And how closer it was to being 11:57pm.

By the time they hit the forty-five minute mark, Olivia let go of Sage's hands and ran her hands through her hair, frustrated.

'It's not working,' she said, relying on Sage to read her lips.

You're getting inside your head, Sage signed. *That's the opposite of what we want. I can feel the walls going up around your mind. You have to let them drop.*

'We've already wasted so much time. There must be another way.'

'We could put an ad up on Craigslist,' Roman said, unhelpfully. 'Have you seen this antichrist?'

Olivia pointedly ignored him. 'Is there anything else we can do?'

Sage shook her head. *Aside from hunting her down in person, this is our best chance at finding her.*

'But it's not working!'

Sage chewed the inside of her cheek. Her gaze flicked from Olivia to Roman. *I have an idea. Roman, take my place.*

Roman quirked a wry eyebrow. 'As in…'

Literally, take my place, Sage stood. *You've been saying the words out loud for me anyway. Might as well cut out the middle man. I'll still be here to guide you.*

'How will this help?' Olivia asked.

Your mind is putting up walls because you don't trust me, Sage signed, without offence.

'Oh. Sorry.'

It's fine. I thought you might trust Roman more.

Olivia looked sceptically at Roman as he sat down in front of her, crossing his legs. He held his hands out to her, palms turned up, and waggled his eyebrows in a way that promised trouble.

'I don't know if I do,' she mumbled.

Well, we're about to find out.

Olivia sighed and took hold of Roman's hands. How many times had they done that in the past few days? How had it become their *thing*? She closed her eyes and listened to Roman repeat the same few lines he'd already said over a dozen times. Only now his skin was touching hers. Now she could feel the heat radiating from his body. Now their fingers were intertwined.

'Olivia, do you hear me?' he asked, softly.

'Yes.'

'Do you trust me?'

'Yes.'

'Are you ready to leave your body behind?'

'Yes.'

'Sage says it's working,' he said, quietly. 'Your mind is opening, Olivia.'

Sage began to feed Roman the new lines, bit by bit. He said every word aloud as instructed, his voice smooth and velvety. His grip on her hands was light but firm. He was her tether — ready to let her fly free, but also there to pull her back to earth if she soared too close to the sun.

'Who are you looking for?' Roman asked.

'Pandora.'

'Why do you seek her?'

'I want to talk to her.'

'Can you picture her in your head?'

'Yes.'

'Good,' Roman said, still taking his lines directly from Sage. 'Keep that image there. Focus on her. Reach out to her with your mind. You should be able to sense her. It can be a smell, or a touch, or a feeling. Can you sense her, Olivia?'

She could. She could smell the metallic scent of blood that had filled the ballroom when she'd clawed her way out of Olivia's torso. She could feel Pandora's arms around her as she breathed life back into her. She could perfectly picture her icy blond hair and bluebonnet sky eyes.

'Yes,' she breathed.

'Go to her, Olivia. Let go of where you are. Let go of us. We will wait for you. Follow Pandora.'

242

Olivia was floating. Or at least, she thought she was. Her eyes snapped open and she looked down to see herself — or her *physical* body, at least — slumped on the floor, head in Roman's lap. She held her hands up to her face, turning them over. For some reason she had expected herself to be see-through, but she seemed solid enough.

She was definitely floating though, and soaring higher. She looked up and saw the factory roof approaching. She cringed, putting her arms over her head, bracing for impact. She was pleasantly surprised when she floated straight through. She surged up into the night sky. Wicklow county opened up before her, a smattering of human life amongst long patches of darkness in the rural areas.

Soon she was high enough to see the neighbouring counties. Rolling plains of pastures and farmland, interspersed with winding country roads and dotted occasionally with towns and cities. She had never really realised just how much of Ireland was just land. Completely untouched. Below her the artificial lights of civilisation twinkled like little clusters of fireflies. It was quite beautiful, actually.

Just when she began to wonder if she would go high enough to see all of Ireland, gravity grabbed hold of her once more. She fell back to Earth.

24.

Olivia landed headfirst back inside her own body. Except that she also didn't. But kind of did. She landed in another version of her body that was already waiting where she wanted to be. It stood, alone and unanimated, until she stepped inside herself and breathed new life into her familiar, but also totally alien bones.

She didn't know where she was or where she was going, but at the same time she seemed to know *exactly* where she was and *exactly* where she needed to go. The world around her was a normal street, not completely unlike the one she grew up on. *Foxglove Road*. It was dark and quiet, and between the gaps in the pulled curtains, Olivia could see the glow of lights and the flicker of TV screens.

She confidently turned to her left and started walking. New sounds drifted from each house as she passed: a couple arguing, kids laughing, the football match, another couple having sex and, quite honestly, really going for it. It all blended into the background. She reached the last house on the street. It sat right in the centre as the road came to an end, siding with neither side of the road. An impartial observer. Neutral. Switzerland.

It was also where Pandora would be waiting for her.

She climbed the steps to the front door, unsurprised to find it ajar. She knew Olivia was coming. From somewhere inside she could hear the TV. It sounded like an episode of *F.R.I.E.N.D.S.: The One Where Ross Is Fine*. Olivia let herself in, not taking the time to admire the perfectly nice, yet exceedingly plain mid-century décor. In the main hallway was bloodied lump of flesh and gusts that had probably once been a person. Now, however, they looked like oatmeal with teeth. Olivia stepped over him and moved on into the living room.

Pandora sat in an armchair, watching as Ross Geller cried into his margarita, insisting that he was, in fact, just fine. She was wearing jeans and a t-shirt with the logo for the *Scream* franchise plastered across her chest. Judging by a similar shirt for *The Thing* on a dead woman — who's top half lay strewn across the sofa, bottom half nowhere to be seen — Olivia could hazard a guess that the clothes belonged to the previous house occupants.

'I don't understand this man,' Pandora said, nodding to the TV. 'Why is he telling everyone he's okay when he clearly isn't? Who is that benefitting?'

Olivia quirked an eyebrow. That wasn't the ice-breaker she'd been expecting.

'He does it to spare everyone else's feelings,' Olivia said. 'Because he's a good person.'

Pandora's nose crinkled as she frowned. For a split second, Olivia could see her for what she really was. She was just a child. Albeit, a murderous, tyrannical, dictating child. But a child nonetheless. She was only just seeing the world and she didn't understand any of it. There was a kind of sick, twisted innocence to it all.

'Well, he's an idiot,' Pandora said. 'He's making himself miserable.'

'These are the things we do for our friends.'

Pandora finally looked at her. She looked younger without all the blood. Sweet-faced and dimpled. Her hair was fresh and had air-dried into natural beachy waves. Her eyes were an ocean. She was every bit the Californian surfer-girl-next-door. They couldn't be more polar opposites if they tried.

'Have you ever given up your entire happiness for the sake of a friend?' Pandora asked.

'No,' Olivia replied, honestly. 'But I don't have friends to do that for.'

'If you *did* then would you?'

'I'd like to think so, yeah.'

Pandora turned back to the TV where Ross was having a heart-to-heart with Joey. 'They talk about their feelings a lot.'

'Sure they do. They're human, after all.' Olivia risked stepping further into the lounge. 'You must remember? Didn't you experience all this through me before we were separated?'

'I did,' she said. 'And I didn't. I just watched you experience it all. And now it all seems like such a distant memory. I can barely remember how any of it feels. Love. Hate. Joy. Sorrow. Anger. Pleasure. They're all so... far away.'

Olivia didn't know what to say, so instead she nodded at the dead body. 'You do that?'

'Yes. I needed to borrow their home and they wouldn't give it to me.'

'So you took it?'

'It seems to be working so far, doesn't it?'

Olivia chose her words carefully. 'I suppose I don't need to remind you that murdering people is bad?'

'Oh, I'm sure it is,' Pandora replied, picking up the remote and switching channels to the news. Apparently they'd sent another white billionaire into space. 'But I don't remember what it's like to feel guilt. The longer that I'm away from you the more it all slips away. I suppose, really, I know I shouldn't have killed them. But also, like, meh? Who is that man?'

Olivia looked to who she was pointing to on the screen. 'I'm not sure. I think he invented a talking toilet.'

'Humanity really is the worst thing to happen to this planet.'

Olivia crossed over to the sofa and gingerly moved the dead woman's arm out of the way so she could sit down. 'True. Most things are terrible. Most *people* are terrible. But not everyone. Some people are worth saving. And fighting for. And living for.'

'Oh?' Pandora looked at her. 'Who are you fighting for? Who are you *living* for?'

'Myself,' she said, and before she could stop herself, 'and Roman. And Alastair, and Imelda. Sage and Ariel.'

'Ah. Roman,' Pandora smiled. 'You care about him more than you realise. Did you know that? Well, I guess not, because then you would know it. Anyway, you care about him. Quite a bit.'

Olivia kept her expression neutral. 'I suppose I do. We've been through a lot.'

'He's going to betray you, you know. Will he be worth fighting for then?'

'I guess I'll cross that bridge when I come to it.'

Pandora watched her for the longest time. 'Why are you here, Liv?'

'I want you to come home.'

'I don't have a home.'

'*I'm* your home,' Olivia said. 'It doesn't have to be this way. You said you're losing yourself the longer you're away from me. Come back to me. We can be on the same side.'

'You'd accept me after all the people I've killed, would you?'

Olivia hesitated for only the briefest of moments. 'Yes.'

'Liar. What trap are you trying to lure me into, Liv?'

'I'm not—'

'Wow, you're a bad liar.'

'Pan—'

'Stop lying to me!' she exploded, standing so fast that she knocked the chair back. 'You can lie to yourself as much as you like, but don't you *dare* fucking lie to me!'

Olivia carefully rose to her feet. She wasn't sure if she could be hurt — or killed — in her astral form, but she didn't particularly want to find out. Her hands went out into a defensive stance that looked like she was saying *hey, come on, let's talk about this*, but in actual fact it was more along the lines of *stay the fuck back.*

'Alright,' Olivia said, voice calmer than she actually felt. 'I'm sorry. Yeah, you're right, I was lying. And yeah, I'm here to lure you into a trap.' Right, well now she was *definitely* going off script. 'We have a God-killer weapon. Some kind of knife from the Celestial realm. I don't really know how it works but I was going to use it to kill you.'

Pandora's face contorted with rage. 'I warned you about what would happen if you tried to come after me. I don't want to kill you, Liv, but I will if I have to.'

'Or,' Olivia said, 'we can bury the hatchet right now. I'll call Roman and tell him the plan is off. You come find me. We can go off somewhere together and it can just be us.'

Pandora laughed. 'You're so full of shit.'

'I mean it. You're like a sister to me.'

'A sister that five minutes ago you were intent on killing.'

'I never wanted this,' Olivia said softly. She was surprised at the lump forming in her throat. 'For the longest time I lied to myself about what you really were. I kept calling you my conscience, but I knew that wasn't it. I knew you were something different. You were your own entity without me. But I was never scared of you. It was a comfort knowing you were always there. You've seen me through everything. Mum and Dad. Cillian. Our shit-head godfather. Even dying. And now you're gone and I miss you. I really fucking *miss* you. Fuck, I don't want it to be like this between us.'

Pandora took a step closer and Olivia's stance became less casual and more obviously defensive.

'What did you think was going to happen?' Pandora asked, voice rising. 'Did you think we'd be braiding each other's hair, and talking about boys, and bonding about our *feelings* over margaritas? Get a grip, Liv!'

'You were supposed to be my family!' Olivia shouted. 'You were the only fucking family that I had left! All we had was each other and you fucking *left* me!'

Somehow there was only an arm's length between them. Despite all her training and all her instincts, Olivia could feel her resolve crumbling. Her throat was thick. Her eyelashes wet. For the first time in her life she didn't want to be strong. She wanted to be small, and safe, and let all of this be someone else's problem. She couldn't fucking do this anymore.

Pandora's brows knitted together. She swallowed hard. 'We were never family, Liv. I was just hitching a ride.'

'Bullshit.'

'No. It's true. I had a purpose. You were the means to an end.'

Olivia barked a laugh. 'Is that why you spent mum and dad's entire funeral telling me that everything was going to be alright? Or why you talked me down every time I felt like I was going to end it all? Or why you were there for me every night that I cried myself to sleep after that fucking monster put his hands on me?'

'Liv—'

'That was a means to an end was it?'

'Olivia—'

'Because the truth is, Pan, that no matter what you do, or how you hurt me, or how many people you kill, I will always fucking love you like you're one of my own because you *are*.'

Pandora swung a punch but Olivia caught it and pulled her into a bone-crushing bear hug. The dam inside her suddenly burst. Over a decade's worth of suppressed emotions, repressed memories, guilt, self-loathing, fear and love came pouring out. She could feel it from Pandora too. They held each other, sisters in every sense of the word other than blood, and cried without fear of shame, or rejection, or judgement.

Pandora pulled back and held Olivia's face in her hands. Her eyes were glistening and red-rimmed.

'I'm so sorry,' she said.

Olivia put her own hands gently over the top of Pandora's. 'It's alright. It doesn't matter now.'

'No,' she said. 'I mean I'm sorry for this.'

Olivia frowned. 'For wha—'

Pandora snapped her neck.

25.

Olivia woke in her own body, head still in Roman's lap. Her eyes snapped open and she sucked in a long breath, sitting bolt upright. Her hands flew to her neck as she remembered the feeling of having it snapped. Some part of her brain registered that she, thankfully, wasn't dead.

Gentle hands settled on her shoulders. She turned and looked at Roman.

'What happened?' he asked.

'She's coming,' Olivia said with certainty. 'I pissed her off and she's coming here to kill me.'

'Attagirl.'

Olivia allowed Roman to pull her to her feet. She checked the time on her phone. 11:17pm. She'd been out longer than she'd anticipated. Looking over at Roman, his expression was typically unreadable.

'Let's hope she gets a move on,' Olivia said.

It was a tense twenty minutes. Olivia paced the circle like a stressed tiger in a zoo. Alastair and Ariel had fallen aside to discuss tactics. Sage was teaching Imelda the benefits of burning different types of herbs and incense in an attempt to take their mind off what was to come. Roman simply stood at the circle's edge, arms crossed, gaze never leaving Olivia.

It was twenty minutes of last minute prep, confirming the plan, ironing out details and, unfortunately, waiting. Olivia couldn't remember who had first said that waiting was the worst part, but she'd never understood. It was the worst part that was the *worst* part. When she had been waiting in the hospital to hear if her parents were going to make it, it was okay because she could still pretend that she didn't already know that they were definitely dead. When she was lying in bed waiting and wondering if her godfather would come into her room that night, that was fine because he wasn't actually there yet. When she was waiting in the funeral home to see Cillian's body one last time, it was peachy-keen because she could keep lying to herself that he was still going to look like himself and not completely unrecognisable.

But now she got it. The waiting really was the worst part. At 11:37pm, she heard the sound of footsteps on the roof and she was almost relieved.

'Places, people,' Roman said quietly.

They each quietly slunk back to the shadows. Roman crossed to Olivia and reached for her hand across the circle limits. He pressed something into her palm and she looked down. The vinculum.

'What are you doing?' she asked. 'You're the one going to spring it, not me.'

'The only problem with that,' he said. 'Is that you don't trust me. Not completely. And, to be honest, I can't be trusted. I don't know what I'm going to do when time's up but I want you to stand a chance either way.'

Olivia looked at him for a long moment. She gave the vinculum back to him. 'You hold onto it.'

'But—'

'I'm making a decision,' she said. 'A very stupid decision. I'm going to trust you, Roman Wylder. Because I want you to stay. With me.'

His eyes softened for the briefest of moments. 'I hope I don't disappoint you.'

'Me too.'

He gave her hand one last squeeze before retreating back into the shadows with the others. Olivia took a deep breath and listened to the languid footsteps as they slowly crossed the roof, passing over her head. There was a creak of old wood as their visitor jumped down, and a gentle thud as they landed on the marshy earth. A shadow appeared behind the frosted glass of the main doors.

Pandora didn't knock before she entered. Olivia watched her stride onto the factory floor with all the confidence of someone who couldn't be killed. She stopped just a few feet short of the binding circle.

'You're alive then,' was the first thing Pandora said.

'Apparently when you kill someone in astral form all you're really doing is pissing them off somewhere else.'

'Good to know for future reference.'

'Gotta say,' Olivia said. 'Disappointed but not shocked. I really poured my heart out to you back there.'

'I'm glad you did. You've had so much bottled up for so long. It had to be good to get it out.'

Olivia crossed her arms protectively over her chest. 'So, have you come here to kill me?'

Pandora nodded. 'Yeah, kinda. No offense.'

'Some taken.'

'You're just,' Pandora searched for the right words. 'In my way.'

'Seems like a legit enough reason to murder someone.'

'I can't focus on my work knowing that no matter what I do or where I go, you'll be tailing me, trying to lure me over to the good side with cookies.'

'We also have moral superiority, if that helps?'

Pandora smiled. 'Oh, I'm going to miss this. I'm going to miss *you*. Your humour. Your quick wit. How you use it as a defence mechanism when you're unsure or scared. God, you're just so *wonderfully* human. Even though you're not.'

Olivia sighed. 'Right, well, let's get it over with then. Let's hash it out. Come here and fight me.'

'And cross over into your nifty little binding circle? I don't think so.'

'Spotted that, did you?'

'Stuck out like a straight man at gay pride.'

'Ah.'

'Yeah, sorry. Also I can sense all your little buddies waiting in the shadows.'

Olivia sighed again. 'You can come out now.'

Her friends appeared, one by one, faces flickering in the candlelight. She locked eyes with Roman for a moment before looking away. The sudden wave of guilt that crashed over her was immense. If any of these people got hurt it would be all her fault. Had she even thought about that? About the danger she was putting them in? Honestly, no, she had not. And she hated herself just that little bit more for it.

'So, how are we going to do this?' Olivia asked. 'Let's keep it civilised, shall we?'

'No touching of the hair or face?'

'Goes without saying.'

Pandora looked around them all. 'This is your chance to leave. Go now and I won't follow you. I'll forget you were ever here.'

Imelda snorted a laugh. 'We're not going anywhere.'

Pandora arched an eyebrow at her. 'And what exactly do you think you can bring to the table? You're a low rent version of the Long Island Medium, Fangs over here is a pacifist, Ariel is about as useful as a landline phone, and Sage looks like she is going to keel over any minute.'

Olivia looked to Sage. Beads of sweat had broken out on her forehead. Her teeth were gritted.

'Did you cleanse the area?' Pandora asked. 'Spell the circle? Wow, it must have really taken it out of you. Maybe you should sit this one out?'

Sage lifted her chin defiantly, and Olivia could finally see who she really was. Sage was a young woman who had seen far too much, and been through worse. It had aged her on the inside and sometimes it shone through to the outside. At that moment though, she looked younger than ever.

When nobody moved, Pandora shrugged and said. 'Your funeral.'

Then she came for them.

It all seemed to happen in slow motion. Pandora lunged at Sage. At the same moment, Sage flung both of her arms wide, sending a ripple through the room that knocked her back. The air in the factory crackled, suddenly charged with energy. Olivia looked at the symbol Sage had drawn on her inner wrist in the leftover pig's blood. The same she'd drawn on everyone and then herself. She felt the skin beneath the symbol prickle. She felt some of Sage's power flood into her. Looking around at the others she saw they felt it too.

All together. All as one. Connected.

Pandora rolled to a stop, just on the outskirts of the binding circle. She looked between them all. She could feel the energy pulsing through them. Excluding her. Olivia almost felt bad. Almost. Then they started chanting and Pandora's face filled with such rage that Olivia thought she genuinely might explode.

It was a simple enough mantra. It was Latin so some of the pronunciation was hard, but Sage had managed to teach it to them in the twenty minutes they'd been waiting. It was old magic. Dark and powerful. It was their only hope.

Body be willing,

And mind obey,

Your will is mine,

Become my slave.

Pandora's body went rigid. Her eyes bulged in her head, her mouth distorting into a snarl, lips drawing back over barred teeth. Olivia stopped chanting, letting the others continue. The power thrummed between the six of them, flowing in and out of the binding circle, breathing energy and life into them. She could feel the air shimmering around her. It was intoxicating. And judging by the sweat rolling down Sage's face, it was also very limited.

'Pandora,' Olivia said softly. 'Come here.'

The tendons in Pandora's neck stuck out as she tried to fight the compulsion. Every muscle in her body strained and popped as she resisted it. But despite her best efforts, she lifted one foot and took a step closer to the binding circle. Then another. She let out an ear-splitting scream as she was forced closer and closer to the thing, the *person* going to end her.

The moment she stepped inside the circle, Olivia felt the energy change. It darkened. She felt her demon side prickle, quietly asking to come out and play. Pandora glared at her where she stood, just an arm's length away. They were volatile together like this: Pandora's ancient power and Olivia's raw energy. They were meteors on a path to collision. They were twin bolts of lightning hitting a rod at the same time. They were the sun and the moon crashing to earth together.

'You must feel pretty great about yourself right now,' Pandora spat.

'Not really,' Olivia said. 'I already told you that I didn't want this.'

'And now you're going to kill me are you? With your God-killer weapon?'

'Actually no. That bit was a lie.'

Pandora frowned. 'What? What are you talking about?'

'We don't have a God-killer weapon. Apparently, they don't actually exist. What we *do* have, however, is a God-proof prison.'

Roman stepped up to the circle, holding up the little box in his hand. 'This is a vinculum. Latin for prison. It can hold one entity at a time and a new vacancy has just become available.'

'So that's your plan?' Pandora asked. 'Trick me here and trap me in a little box. Is that really it?'

'It seems to be working so far,' Imelda said.

'Are you sure?' Pandora asked. 'Your witch is looking a bit stressed over there.'

'Sage can't hold this forever,' Olivia agreed. 'But I don't need her to. I just needed her to get you in the circle. The rest is all me.'

Olivia saw the others frown. Alastair and Ariel shared a questioning look. Olivia turned to Sage and nodded. The witch let out a long breath and let her knees buckle. She collapsed, the connection between them breaking. The compulsion on Pandora snapped like an overstretched elastic band and she trembled, before sinking to her knees. She gasped for air as her senses came back to her.

'Olivia,' Roman snapped. 'What are you doing?'

'I spoke to Sage while we were waiting,' Olivia said, not taking her eyes off Pandora. 'I realised that I couldn't let you all put yourselves in danger like this for me. I told her to break the connection once I had Pandora in the circle. This is how it has to be. This is how it has to end. Just me and her.'

'Fuck that,' he shouted. He strode forwards, trying to cross into the circle, but came up against an invisible barrier.

'I also asked Sage to spell it so that once Pandora enters, no one else can,' she explained.

Roman looked between Olivia and Pandora, still gasping for air on the floor. 'This is ridiculous. You could get yourself killed. You could get *both* of us killed.'

'I know what I'm doing,' Olivia said, stepping towards Pandora. She crouched so that they were at eye level. 'Sage warned me about what's happening to you right now. When compulsion breaks so suddenly it turns the brain momentarily offline. Your body is struggling to remember how to function. Your lungs are relearning how to breathe.

Your heart is relearning how to pump blood around your body. Your brain is relearning how to send messages to your synapses.

'Do you know why I wanted to do it like this? Because I wanted to give you one last fucking chance. One last chance to stop all this. I know you can hear me right now, Pan. And I know you don't want to be trapped in a box for the rest of eternity.' She held out a hand to her. 'Sage knows how to spell an unbreakable oath. Shake on it now that you won't hurt anyone else. Sage can make it official. We won't have to fight anymore. Pandora, *please*.'

Pandora looked up at her, slowly. 'My options are to either be trapped in a literal cage or a metaphorical cage? Surely you see the irony?'

'I see a solution to a problem. One that doesn't end with us murdering each other.'

'I would rather die,' Pandora snarled. 'Than cow to you.'

Olivia sighed and stood up. She turned to Roman. 'I tried. Throw me the vinculum.'

Roman reached into his pocket and pulled out the little wooden box. He turned it over in his hand a couple of times. 'Ready?'

Olivia cupped her hands and held them out. 'Yep.

Roman smiled. It was finally over. It was all *finally* over.

Then the alarm on Roman's phone went off.

11:57pm.

26.

'Roman,' Olivia said, slowly. 'Don't.'

Roman looked at her and for the first time she saw who he could have been if the whole world hadn't completely screwed him over every chance it got. The kid he could have been if his parents hadn't murdered his siblings in front of him. The man he could have grown up to be if he didn't have to kill his dad or be killed by him. The human he could have been if he hadn't been born into the curse of being a demon. Because he was looking at her, honest, and vulnerable, and so conflicted.

'Roman. Please. Don't leave me.'

He looked down at the vinculum in his hand. All he had to do was throw it to her. That priceless, one-of-a-kind, magical artifact. Something that would buy off any price that was on his head. Something that he could trade with the devil and still be *owed* a favour afterwards.

'Roman!' Alastair barked from the other side of the binding circle. 'Stop fucking around, kid! Give her the damn box!'

'Roman, please,' Olivia implored, her gaze flicking between him and Pandora, whose breaths were slowly regaining control. 'Please. I trusted you. I still do.'

'Jesus Christ, Roman!' Ariel shouted. 'Quickly!'

Roman and Olivia's gaze met. For someone who prided herself on the fact she didn't cry easily, she'd been on the verge of tears a lot in the past seventy-two hours. A lump stuck in her throat again now. She swallowed hard but it wouldn't go down.

'Please,' was all she could say.

Roman took a step back.

'No. Roman, please.'

And another.

'For fuck's sake, Roman! Don't!'

Another.

'You can't leave me!' she screamed. 'You can't fucking leave me, you bastard! *Roman!*'

Alastair was already moving, but Roman was faster. It all happened so quickly that Olivia was sure she would have missed it had she blinked. She'd never even considered Roman's demon form before now. He'd seen hers, of course, the first night they met in the alleyway outside The Betsy. When she changed into her demon form she was red-skinned, horned and taloned. Roman's dark side though — it was unlike anything she'd ever seen.

His skin was alabaster and almost marbleised in texture. Black veins spread under his pure white skin and bled from his blacked-out eyes. Antlers, almost half the length of him, sprouted from his brow at the same time two black wings unfurled from his shoulder blades, ripping his shirt in half. On his chest, the threads of black veins came together to form a symbol.

A pentagram.

The sign of the Beast.

Alastair reached for him, but Roman's wings unfurled and he shot up into the air. Dust and debris rained down on them as Roman left a hole in the roof in his wake. And, just like that, he was gone. The vinculum too.

Olivia felt something in her chest twist painfully. She let out a shaky breath and looked at her friends. Alastair, visibly seething, but beneath the rage was just more disappointment. Ariel, looking like he needed to sit down before he fell down. Imelda, still nursing the unconscious

Sage's head in her lap, eyes welling with tears. They all watched her helplessly.

'Liv…' Imelda said.

Olivia forced a smile. The same brave smile she had given a thousand times. It only wobbled a little bit.

'It's alright,' she said, voice thick. 'It's okay. You can go. I won't be upset.'

Ariel stepped up to the binding circle and gently rested his hands on the invisible barrier that trapped her. 'We're not going anywhere.'

Alastair joined him. 'We're here. Until the end.'

Imelda took off her jacket and gently placed it under Sage's head. She joined them at the circle, both hands and her forehead resting against the invisible barricade.

'Friends don't abandon each other,' she said softly.

Olivia mirrored her hands to Imelda's, marvelling at how the force-field felt like glass beneath her hands. 'Thank you,' she whispered.

'Well,' said a voice behind her. 'Isn't this just *touching*?'

Olivia swallowed hard and turned to face Pandora, who was standing tall, blue eyes blazing.

'You should have got me when you had the chance,' Pandora said. 'Instead you decided to appeal to my better nature. Wow, just how *stupid* are you?'

'I'm not stupid for wanting to assume the best of you,' Olivia said. 'Just human.'

'Barely.'

'I'm proud of the part of me that is half human. Just the same as I'm proud of the part that is half demon. And I'm proud of the part of me that was you. You were the sliver of Lilith's soul that was passed down my bloodline. Thanks to you, I actually *had* half a soul. If it wasn't for you I'd be born all demon, and my adoptive parents would have killed me right away. I would have been just like any other mindless monster. But you gave me hope. You gave me a moral compass. You gave me a fucking *purpose*, so I'm sorry if I thought you were worth saving, but you're the only reason that *I* was worth saving.'

Pandora laughed. 'You think I'm the reason you're not a total fucking monster? Where's the logic in that? I'm not in your head anymore, Liv. By your working, you should be fully demon right now. But here you are, still trying to save me.'

'Fate said something to me, the first time I met her. Do you remember?'

'She said a lot, Liv. You're going to have to narrow it down.'

'She said the people we carry in our hearts leave a lasting impression on us. I think she meant that literally. I've carried you with me for so long that even when you left, the half a soul you brought with you stayed. You'll be with me forever, whether we like it or not.'

'Maybe's that the reason I'm just a raging bitch? I left all my goody-two-shoes-ness in you.'

'Maybe, yeah.'

'Anyway,' Pandora said, resting her hands on her hips. 'Shall we get this over with, or…?'

Olivia nodded. 'If you're sure you're ready to lose.'

Pandora grinned. 'Bring it on.'

Olivia called her demon form forth. She was suddenly all red skin and black scales. Ram horns curled from her temples and fangs sprouted where her teeth had one been. Her eyes burned with fire.

'Let's fucking go,' she said.

Pandora was keeping her alive at this point just to toy with her. She healed even quicker in her demon form. She never usually transformed unless she really needed to. There was something about letting her dark side out that brought out her lizard brain too. Rational thought seemed to fade away. All that was left was fight or flight mode, and when she was in her demon form it was always to fight. Now, however, she kind of wished she could choose flight.

Pandora landed a kick to her side that sent her sailing across the binding circle. She crashed into the invisible barrier and fell in a broken, bleeding heap. The binding circle seemed to be keeping Pandora's magic down, but she'd been there for all of Olivia's training. So they were grappling, and throwing punches, and blocking, and falling, and getting up again. It was nasty, and bloody, and sweaty, and Pandora was at a clear advantage. She was stronger. Faster. More durable. Olivia was barely a demon.

She groaned, clutching her side. Alastair screamed at her to move. To get up. Ariel was beside him, hand tense on his shoulder, repeating a mantra of *she'll be okay. She'll be okay. She'll be okay.* His face, however, obviously hadn't gotten the memo, because he looked terrified.

Imelda was begging Sage to wake up. Break the binding circle. Let them help her. It was obvious she wouldn't be waking up any time soon though. Her face was ashen and gaunt. What Olivia had asked had nearly killed her. And now Olivia was going to die anyway. It was for nothing. It was all for nothing.

Still, she got to her feet.

There was a sharp jab in her side from a broken rib. She hissed through the pain and squared her shoulders. Pandora stepped in swinging a great haymaker. Olivia ducked under her arm and grabbed her around the middle clamping her hands tight. Driving her shoulder into Pandora's stomach, she powered forwards, forcing her backwards. Her back hit the barrier and Pandora retaliated by raining elbows down on the back of Olivia's head.

Olivia grabbed Pandora's ankles, pulled her legs out from under her. She went down and Olivia was on her in an instant. She hooked her ankles inside Pandora's thighs, her forearm going to her throat.

She pressed down with all the weight she had and heard Pandora gurgle beneath her as her airways were cut off. She couldn't kill her but she could hopefully knock her out for a few minutes.

Pandora's hands found Olivia's hair and wrenched. Olivia screamed as her head yanked back, exposing her neck. Pandora punched her in the throat and she gasped. Her grip loosened and Pandora bucked her hips, flipping them over. She was on top now. She had Olivia's arm wrapped up in an arm lock and wasted no time in freeing her shoulder from its socket.

Olivia screamed. Her good arm flew up and she sunk her thumb into Pandora's right eye socket. She felt her eyeball burst and tried not to gag as bits of blood and jelly dripped down her arm and onto her face. Pandora reared back, clawing at her face and Olivia drew both legs into her chest before kicking out. Her boot heels slammed into Pandora's torso and she sailed backwards, smashing into the barrier again.

Olivia helped her shoulder along by popping it back into place. She snarled at the pain that was somehow worse than when it popped out, and stood on wobbly legs. Pandora's eye was already healed, just a little bloodshot. She looked at Olivia with utter hatred. The feeling was mutual.

'That hurt,' Pandora said.

'Boo-fucking-hoo, bitch.'

Pandora ran at her so Olivia met her halfway. They met in what might have looked like an enthusiastic embrace to someone else. Instead, it was nasty and ugly. Fists slammed into ribs, into the back of heads as they buried their faces in each other's shoulders for protection. Knees slammed into thighs and fistfuls of hair were grabbed.

Olivia tried to sweep Pandora's legs out from under her with her foot but overbalanced and toppled back. Pandora tried to wrench herself free but Olivia held on and they went down together. Before they even hit the ground they were rolling, grappling for control. Pandora ended up on top, her hands finding Olivia's throat and squeezing. She bore down with all her weight and Olivia spluttered, her legs kicking.

'I am so fucking *sick* of you!' Pandora snarled, spittle flying from her lips.

Olivia grabbed one of Pandora's wrists in hers. At the same time she twisted her body and hammered a fist into the side of her head. She swung her outside leg up, hooking it over Pandora's neck. With a push, she was flipped over onto her back and Olivia had her in a perfect arm bar. Before Pandora could grab her foot and put her in an ankle lock, Olivia lifted her hips and at the same time yanked Pandora's arm down, using her groin as a fulcrum. There was the satisfying sound of her arm snapping, followed by a long howl.

Olivia slammed her heel into Pandora's face, her nose exploding beneath her foot. She kicked her again for good measure before rolling over and pulling her feet under her. She tried to stand but Pandora's good hand had wrapped around her ankle. She jerked hard and Olivia was pulled back to her. She tried to twist in her grasp but Pandora was already climbing over her body, her limp arm dragging behind her.

She tried to turn over, tried to be in literally any other position than on her belly, but Pandora already had her hooks in around Olivia's legs. She cursed herself. How many times had her instructor told her to never give your opponent your back. But she had gotten cocky. She had hurt Pandora — *really* hurt her — and she'd assumed she would have a moment to catch her breath.

Pandora wrapped her good arm around Olivia's neck and held on tight while Olivia bucked, trying to shake her. She felt Pandora's breath hot on the side of her face, and before her mind could even dream up a horrible scenario of what was about to happen, Pandora clamped her jaws down on Olivia's earlobe and pulled.

Olivia screamed as her ear ripped off. The pain was followed by a burning sensation that reminded her of all the times she'd got the curling tongs too close to her head as a teenager. There was rushing noise, although she wasn't sure how she was hearing it. Her head swam and her stomach rolled as Pandora spat her ear out, letting it drop right beside Olivia's face.

There was a loud crack as Pandora's arm mended itself, and it came up to support her as she locked Olivia in a choke. Olivia thrashed and squirmed, but the choke just came on tighter. She reached back with her hands, tried to scratch at Pandora's face or grab her hair or *anything*.

She could see Alastair's face at the barrier. He was screaming something to her but it was muffled. Her vision was clouding. Her head was pounding. She missed her ear. She missed how much it didn't hurt before her ear had been ripped off. She blinked hard. Thinking was becoming difficult. Keeping her eyes open was even harder. She gurgled, her throat stinging. Her lungs felt like they were on fire. Her head was a wasp's nest. God she was tired. She was so fucking tired. Her eyelids fluttered.

'Stay with me!' Alastair screamed. 'Olivia, stay with me!'

She fought to keep her eyes open. Out the corner of her eye she saw movement. Boots. Black boots. Striding confidently up to the edge of the binding circle. She looked up and saw an angel with bronze hair and green eyes. He was holding a small wooden box.

'Oi, beasty,' Roman said and tossed the vinculum into the circle.

The wooden box clattered to a stop in front of Olivia's face, on its side. For a horrible moment, Olivia thought the lid wasn't going to fall off. Roman stamped his foot hard and the vinculum wobbled and the lid, mercifully, fell open.

A great plume of black smoke gushed from the box. It was smoky and acrid, and Olivia winced as it engulfed them both. She felt Pandora's grip on her loosen and she sucked in a big breath, choking on the sour air but not caring. She rolled easily in Pandora's slack position and kicked her back. The black smoke followed Pandora as she rolled across the floor, and Olivia could finally breathe in fresh air.

The smoke clung to Pandora, buzzing around her like flies on a corpse. She screamed and flailed, trying to scramble back. But it just followed her. Olivia pulled herself up to her elbows and watched as the fog encasing her began to pull her back to the vinculum. Pandora shrieked and clawed at the floor, her fingernails bending back against the tiles. She met Olivia's gaze and for the first time she saw fear in her eyes.

'Liv!' she begged. 'Please! I'm sorry! *Please!*'

'Goodbye, Pan,' she said, feeling the hot tears cut through the blood on her face.

Pandora shrieked as the smoke reduced her to nothing but ash, pulling her remains into the vinculum. When the last plume had disappeared inside the wooden box, Olivia surged forwards. She scooped up the lid and slammed it down on the tiny prison, refusing to relax until she felt the energy around it fully retract. And then it was gone. Pandora was gone.

Olivia let out a sob and rolled onto her back. Her ear was already healing. She could hear the others calling out to her. She turned her head and saw Roman. He watched her with a concerned gaze that made her stomach flip over. She smiled a bloody, toothy smile and was rewarded with one — albeit unconvincing — in return.

'Fate,' she whispered quietly. 'You there?'

There was a ripple in the air beside her. Olivia turned her head and saw Fate crouching next to her. She wore Meghan Markle's face. Also her wedding dress. Olivia smiled again as she reached out and touched a bloodied finger to her perfect cheekbone.

'I did it,' Olivia said.

'So, I see,' Fate replied.

Olivia held the vinculum out to her. 'You can have your thingy back now.'

Fate took the vinculum and pocketed it. She gently swept a hand over Olivia's forehead. 'You look awful, Olivia.'

'I could have really used your help back there.'

'I can't interfere—'

'With earthly affairs. I know. S'okay.'

'If it's any consolation, I was rooting for you.'

'Me too.'

Fate smiled. 'Do you know that I have a soft spot for you, Olivia McQueen?'

She laughed but it was weak and curdled with blood. 'Course you do. I'm a delight.'

That, at least, made Fate grin. 'I'll see you around.'

'I'll take your word for it.'

Fate stood to leave but Olivia stopped her. 'Before you go,' she croaked. 'Do you think you can let me out of here? I'm kinda stuck and I really want to go home. Or to a hospital. Either or.'

Fate nodded. She looked over at Sage pointedly and smiled when the witch woke with a gasp. Imelda held her close, keeping her from flying into a wild panic.

'Sage can take it from here,' Fate said.

Olivia looked up at her. 'Thank you. Do me another favour?'

'What is it?'

Olivia nodded to the vinculum. 'Don't let her out of there. She's, like, *really* mad at me.'

Fate surprised everyone by laughing. 'I promise.'

'Hey, Fate.'

'Yes, Olivia?'

'I have a soft spot for you too.'

Fate looked at Olivia over her shoulder and smiled. 'Of course you do. I'm a *delight*.'

27.

Dublin city was just waking up. The sun was barely peeking over Temple Bar and already it promised an unseasonably warm autumn day. The roads were still empty but Olivia knew it wouldn't be long until they were filled with people braving the morning commute to work. Soon there would be the hum of a thousand exhaust pipes, the squeal of the brakes on the Luas tram line, and the honking of school bus horns. But for now, it was quiet, and still, and Olivia was at peace.

Her legs dangled over the edge of Shenanigans' roof, swinging happily. When you were as ridiculously tall as she was, you hardly ever had the chance to swing your legs when you sat down. But here, three storeys up, she could swing them to her heart's content. It was the little things, she decided, that could really make you happy. Well. That and not being dead. That was *always* a plus.

Roman dropped down beside her and passed her a steaming mug of coffee. For a while they didn't say anything. They just swung their legs, watched the world wake up, and caffeinated in comfortable silence.

'You're up early,' he said, finally.

'I slept well,' she said.

It was true. For the first time in years she'd had a blessed, dreamless sleep. It had been a week since they'd defeated Pandora, and every night since, she had slept like the dead. It probably helped that every night Roman was beside her. He hadn't touched her, not intimately, since the Bacchanalia, but there was comfort in feeling his warmth beside her as she closed her eyes. Sometimes they held each other. Sometimes they didn't. She had no idea what was going on between them, but she decided not to think too much about it. Roman Wylder wasn't the kind of guy you took home to your parents. Or anywhere. He was unapologetically himself and she admired that. He was still a serial killer though, so baby steps.

'How's the ear?'

She pulled her hair back to show him. 'Works just as good as the old one. Imelda even pierced it for me.'

'Did she tell you your future at the same time?'

'She said she can only do that with tattoos.'

'What a flake.'

Olivia nudged him with her elbow and went back to watching the city. Her coffee was hot, and bitter, and perfect. Somewhere in the distance she could hear birds singing.

'So,' Roman said. 'We haven't talked about it yet.'

Olivia sighed. 'Yeah, and we don't need to.'

'Olivia, I abandoned you.'

She looked at him. 'Yes. Yes you did. And it was a really shitty thing to do. And then you came back. So it's alright.'

'You *trusted* me—'

'And you came through in the end, didn't you?'

He watched her for a long moment. 'Why aren't you angry with me?'

She sighed again. 'You ever watch that awful documentary on Netflix called *Tiger King*?'

'Absolutely not.'

'Right, well, basically this guy in America has a bunch of tigers in his backyard and people pay to come see them. Everything is fine until one day one of his staff gets their arm ripped off by one of the tigers. Everyone is so shocked, but I was, like, why? Why are you surprised? It's a *tiger*, not a kitten. Why is everyone so shocked that the wild animal did exactly what the wild animal is supposed to do?'

'Olivia, does this story have a point?'

She frowned. 'The point is, you're the tiger. And I'm the staff member who got too close. You hurt me. Of course you did, you're a tiger. I knew that if I got too close there was a chance you could hurt me and I got close anyway, because the feeling that I get when I'm around you is worth the risk.'

Roman watched her, expression exasperatingly blank. 'I... see.'

'Do you?'

'Not really.'

She put her hand over his. 'Look, I don't know what's going on here. I know it's in your nature to be destructive. I accept that. Don't think I'm making excuses for you, because I'm not. If you fuck around I'll let you know you're being a twat. And I'll fucking take you out if I have to, without hesitation. But I accept the mortal peril I put myself in when I'm around you, and I accept any consequence that might befall me because of that. You're dangerous. But you're also fucking worth it.'

Roman grinned. 'You're the most exceptional person I've ever met.'

'Of course I am.'

'I'm going to enjoy not knowing what is going on. Together.'

'Me too.'

He pulled her into a searing kiss, his thumb brushing gently over her jaw. He pecked her once more and kissed the tip of her nose before pulling back. He fixed her with an unusual look, which Olivia was beginning to understand was what he looked like when he was being open with her but not knowing why.

'When I changed,' he said. 'Back at the factory. I... I don't usually do that.'

Olivia thought about his alabaster skin. The black veins. The pentagram. 'Want to talk about it?'

'I suppose so,' he said and sighed. 'I was born… gifted. It's one of the rarer ones, but it's called the Darkness. It allows me to transform into. Well. Exactly what you saw. Our demon sides aren't like yours. We are beasts. The original idea was that my kind would be soldiers to the antichrist, but our gift is too volatile. We have no choice over when we change. Our dark form only comes out when… well, when we are overwhelmed with emotion.'

Olivia watched him. He held her gaze, not looking away. 'What are you saying?'

'I don't know. But I guess it's somewhere along the lines of… I lost control of myself. My emotions. When I realised your life was in my hands, and I didn't know whether to stay or run. I couldn't handle it. I can't handle how I feel when I'm around *you*, Olivia. The only time I ever feel anything is when I'm around you. You simultaneously bring out the best and the worst in me. I guess it all just… came to a boiling point. Anyway, that's what that was. In case you were wondering, like.'

'Has it happened before?'

'A couple times. When I killed my parents. When Alastair threw me out.'

'And then with me.'

He nodded. 'With you.'

'Fuck.'

'Yeah. Fuck.'

Olivia rested her head on Romans shoulder and looked back out over the city. They stayed that way in silence, watching Dublin slowly wake up.

As much as Alastair pretended to hate having a full house, it was obvious that he was actually thriving. For some reason, in the week since the factory, no one had gone back to their regular lives. They all knew they had to eventually, but there was a finality to it that no one was willing to face just yet. Sage and Imelda usually sat together, heads bowed over a grimoire or witch's talisman as Sage taught her to draw from her powers. Much to Imelda's chagrin, and to Roman's childish delight, she was, in fact, a witch. She just hadn't fully tapped into her potential yet. Sage was going to help remedy that.

The most interesting friendship, however, had blossomed between Alastair and Ariel. When Ariel had walked into Shenanigans the day after the factory showdown in a pencil skirt, blouse and six-inch heels, all feminine curves and red lipstick, Alastair's mouth had fallen open. Then he'd smiled. And the knowing smile Ariel had given back had said it all really.

It was one lazy Sunday afternoon, when Sage and Imelda were practicing spells and sign language, when Alastair and Ariel were pretending not to gaze at each other over coffee cups, and when Olivia was sat with her laptop open, proof-reading her essay titled *The Sign Of The Beast: How Modern Culture Has Influenced Satanism*, that Roman strode into the dilapidated pub with a smile that not only suggested trouble but *encouraged* it.

He put a file down on the table Olivia was sitting at, and pulled her laptop from her grasp. She glared at him and tried to snatch it back but he strode across the pub and put it on the bar in a time out.

'Are you taking my MacBook hostage?' she asked.

Roman dropped into the seat beside her and grinned. He pushed the file over to her.

'What's this?' she asked.

'Open it and find out,' he said.

She tried to drag it out to annoy him, but she was low-key curious and ended up snatching up the file. She opened it to see a profile typed out in a blocky font with a polaroid photo paper-clipped to the corner. The man had dark curly hair, copper skin, and a crooked smile. His eyes were dark and guaranteed absolutely nothing good whatsoever.

LAURA JORDAN

Olivia was immediately intrigued. She read on.

```
Name: Caliban (surname unknown)
Age: 2000 years (approx.)
Species: Vampire
Crimes: Murder, conspiracy to take over the
world, probably jay-walking
```

Olivia rolled her eyes at the last one. Then she saw the last line. She froze, mouth falling open.

```
Aliases: The First Vampire
```

Olivia looked at Roman, mouth still hanging open. He put a finger under her chin and snapped it closed. It was him. The First Vampire. The original. The man Lilith had fallen in love with and turned all those millennia ago. The vampire who had been searching the world for her doppelgänger. The Wicked One. Olivia McQueen.

'You found him,' she breathed.

'I found him,' he said, still grinning.

'What happens now?'

'Well, I figured we'd go hunt the bastard down before he comes looking for you asking where his long lost love has gone.'

Olivia started. '*We?*'

Roman's gaze softened in that way it only did for her. 'I figured I could use the help. You know. If you wanted to tag along?'

Olivia couldn't help the grin that spread across her face. Her essay could *suck it*. 'Oh *hell* yes.'

Also by Laura Jordan

THE
DEAD KING

Prologue

THE FROZEN GIRL

The baby's cry echoed through the trees in Sacred Hollow, sharp and painful. It was the cry of death as the cold froze her bones, and frost sealed her eyelids shut. It was the last cry for help before winter eagerly took its helpless victim.

It was the cry that led the Dead King to the forest.

He gathered the baby up in his arms without hesitation. He could feel her light dwindling. Fading. He felt a pang of heartache in his chest — an unfamiliar feeling to the Dead King— and knew he could not let her die.

Placing a hand gently on her cheek, the Dead King let some of his life-force pass from himself into the baby girl. After a few moments, she stopped shivering. The blue in her lips faded and the icicles on her eyelashes thawed. He felt her heart beating stronger. Healthier.

The baby's cries stopped, and her eyelids fluttered open. She looked up into the blue, empty eyes of the Dead King, and, to his surprise, she smiled at him. To his even greater surprise, he smiled back.

"You are not to be taken yet," he told the baby girl.

1.

Rosalie had always been fascinated by death. She supposed you *had* to be when you were an undertaker's daughter; however, her real enthrallment hadn't properly surfaced until they arrived in Santorini. Back in France, the process of death, funerals, burials — it was all so tedious. You embalmed the body, cleaned and washed it, dressed it in fine clothes and then dropped it into a hole in the ground. In Greece, it was different. They had different rituals.

The body had already been embalmed. Rosalie spent the best part of the morning scrubbing the corpse clean and struggling to get it into a tight, corset-back dress. She coated its lips red with oil paint and rouged its cheeks. When she was done, the body didn't even look like a corpse. It looked like a respectable lady, sleeping soundly in her finery.

Rosalie looked down at her own dress. It was plain and pale, like herself, and made from basic fabric that her mother had hand-sewn. Not for the first time, she found herself envious of another corpse dressed in more frippery than she was.

She sighed and folded the body's arms gently across its chest and tucked a silver coin into its fist. A fare for the Ferryman, paid for by the dead's family.

"Cross safely," Rosalie said. "Let the Ferryman be your guide."

She closed the lid of the coffin and picked up the nails and hammer. She was careful not to catch her fingers as she sealed it closed. Usually, her father would be helping her but he was sleeping off a hangover. Victor Beaufort was never seen in the workshop until midday, sometimes even later. They were supposed to be a team. Mother and Yvette spoke to customers, and herself and father did the dirty work. And Agathe looked after Victoria.

Rosalie looked up when she heard footsteps coming down the cellar stairs and saw her sister's beautiful face — a face that Rosalie both loved and hated. Loved because Yvette was her sister, and an undeniable ray or unfettered sunshine. Hated because Rosalie knew that as long as she lived, she would never be as beautiful as her younger sibling.

"Yvette?" she asked, putting down her hammer.

"It's Agathe," Yvette said. "She's having another one of her..." she searched for the right word, "...outbursts."

Rosalie sighed. She followed her sister up to the ground floor that served as the shop, where her mother would talk to the grieving and the heart-broken. Above that, on the first and second floors, were their living quarters. It was not a big home, despite its many levels. It was tall and thin, and crumbling with age. Despite the turn of the century, their small corner of the little Grecian Island was still steeped in Ottoman architecture, and that meant stone walls and floors, and not a bit of finery in sight. Apart from Yvette, of course.

Agathe stood in the middle of the shop floor, pointing a crooked finger at a customer who was sobbing into her handkerchief. Rosalie's mother sat beside the weeping woman, glaring at her mad aunt.

"Your dead will never reach the afterlife!" Agathe spat. "Leave as many silver coins as you want! Fill the damn coffin up with gold and jewels, and all the money in Santorini, but the Ferryman will never take your husband! Or anyone else, for that matter!"

"Agathe!" her mother snapped. "Not another word from you, or so

281

help me God, I will ship you back to Paris myself!"

"We're all doomed!" Agathe bellowed. "You! Me! Everyone on this godforsaken island is doomed to spend the afterlife in unending Limbo!"

The crying woman wailed and smothered her face with her handkerchief. Rosalie watched as her mother tried to soothe the woman, patting her hair and murmuring something comforting to her.

"Come on, Agathe," Rosalie said, stepping forward and taking her great aunt by the elbow. "Let's go upstairs."

Agathe turned her beady gaze upon her niece. "Unhand me! I'm no invalid."

Yvette flanked her other elbow. "We know, Agathe. But you're being a nuisance."

"A nuisance!" Agathe looked like she was going to start spitting feathers. "How *dare* you! I'm just trying to warn her! Warn you all!"

"Well, consider us warned," Rosalie said, leading the way up to the first floor. "Come on, you're bothering mother."

"That girl bothers *me*," Agathe muttered.

They reached the landing and she shook her nieces off. She marched into the kitchen, surprisingly spritely for an old woman with a clubfoot and a cane, and sat down huffily at the dining table.

"You can't keep bothering mother when she's working," Rosalie scolded, gently. "It's bad for business."

"You know what else is bad for business?" Agathe retorted. "False promises. That woman's husband is about as close to finding peace as the Dead King himself."

Yvette sighed and rolled her big green eyes. She had less patience for Agathe than Rosalie did.

"Enough!" she snapped. "Enough of this *Dead King* nonsense. I'm fed up with it, and so are *maman* and *papa*. Even Rose grows tired of your stories!"

Agathe looked at Rosalie with hurt. Out of herself and Yvette, she had always been the one to believe her great aunt's fairy tales of the Dead King and the Ferryman, despite being two years older.

"Is that true?" Agathe asked. "Rosalie Valentina Beaufort? Do you think my stories are just *nonsense*?"

Rosalie gave Yvette a scathing look. "I'm sorry, Agathe. But I'm not a little girl anymore. I don't believe in the Dead King anymore than I believe in ghosts. And neither should you."

"It's sickening your brain," Yvette snapped. "And what about Victoria? She's only ten, she shouldn't have to be scared by your ramblings."

"Better her be scared than caught by the Dead King," Agathe mumbled.

Yvette held her hands up in surrender. "I give up! Rose, she's all yours."

She turned and marched up the stairs to the second floor, leaving Rosalie alone in the scalding glare of her aunt. Rosalie sighed and pulled up a chair beside Agathe. She looked at the old woman, looked at the tan on her wrinkled face from the Grecian sun — something they never had back in Paris — and at the lines creasing her face like an old piece of leather.

She hadn't been like this back in France — not that Rosalie remembered particularly well. They had sailed over when she was just four years old, but even still, she never remembered her aunt being so... muddled. She used to tuck Rosalie and Yvette in at night in their cots to fairy tales of princesses, and goblins, and dragons. Since they moved away so their father could escape his debts and restart, Agathe's mind had turned poisonous. It started slowly, with bedtime stories featuring fewer princesses and goblins, and more monsters, and vengeful Gods.

In the sixteen years that Santorini had been their home, Agathe had lost her mind. Only now, she seemed to have truly cracked. At least before she kept her madness within the family. Today was the first time she'd actually screamed her insanities at a customer. Mother was worried she was getting, what the locals called, moonstruck.

"Agathe," Rosalie said softly. "There is no Ferryman, no afterlife, no Heaven, no Hell… and there is no Dead King, either. You need to stop this before they take you away, do you understand?"

Agathe turned her head away from her niece, chin sticking out stubbornly. Rosalie thought she could see pain underneath that frosty exterior, though. Betrayal at her own niece thinking she was crazy for believing in stories that she herself hadn't given up until a few years ago.

Rosalie sighed again and stood up. "I have a coffin to seal. You stay up here and behave. *Papa* will pawn you for ale money if he sees you getting up to no good."

Rosalie turned to go back downstairs when Agathe spoke. Rosalie would have continued on if it had not been for her aunt's voice. Something in it didn't sound right. It didn't sound… whole.

"You put your faith in the wrong places, Rosalie," she said looking at her niece with hard, unblinking eyes. "You do not see what is right in front of you. Open your eyes or you will lose everything."

"I'll see you at tea, Agathe," she said.

She took one last look at her great aunt and didn't know whom she felt sadder for: Agathe for losing her mind, or herself for losing her aunt.

Rosalie tucked Victoria into bed, hoping her bedtime story would effectively drown out her mother and father's arguing, although they were all used to hearing that by now. Victoria was as matter-of-fact about *maman* and *papa's* screaming matches as Yvette and Rosalie were. Part of her hated her parents for taking her youngest sister's innocence away from her so early. A child who was used to a screaming household was no longer a child. Although, when it came down to bedtime, Victoria was *always* ready for a story.

She pulled Victoria's blanket all the up to the little girl's cherub chin and stroked her halo of golden hair. She and Yvette were doubles — the same blonde hair and sparkling green eyes. They got their beauty from their mother, and —thankfully— nothing from their father. The pouting lips, and olive skin, and a smile that could have given Aphrodite a run for her money — it was all something the three of them shared and kept secret from Rosalie. She was their complete opposite, with hair as black as parchment ink and dull brown eyes that didn't sparkle. If she cared about her appearance, she supposed she might have been jealous.

She kissed Victoria's brow. "What story would you like, *ma chérie?* The Princess and the Goblin? The Brave Knight? The Maiden and the Monster?"

"Tell me about the Dead King," Victoria said.

Rosalie paused stroking her sister's hair. "Why do you ask for that story?"

Victoria shrugged beneath her blanket. "If *maman* and *papa* are arguing about it, it must be a good story."

"Has auntie Agathe been slipping you bedtime stories on the sly?"

Victoria looked guilty. "Maybe."

Rosalie sighed. "You know that auntie Agathe's stories aren't real, don't you?"

"But neither are your stories."

Rosalie smiled. "I mean, you know that they're nothing to worry about, right?"

"Yes."

"Don't listen to your auntie Agathe too much," Rosalie said, resuming stoking her sister's hair. "Alright?"

"Why not?"

"Because she's a bad influence."

That made Victoria giggle.

285

"So it's the Dead King you want, eh?" Rosalie asked, softly. "Well, alright. But you must remember that it's all make-believe."

Victoria nodded her head, deadly serious. "I will."

"Good girl. It all began with Hades. Hades was the ruler of the Underworld, and he took in the souls of those who had passed on. He could be kind and fair, but also cruel and brutal. He was in charge of keeping the natural balance between this life, and the afterlife, but he could not do it alone. Hades, although King of the Underworld, was unable to set foot outside of his kingdom, so he demanded the help of the Ferryman.

"The Ferryman's duty was to carry the souls of the dead from this life to the next, across the River Styx, and deliver them to Hades. This partnership worked well for centuries, but the ferryman grew tired of being at Hades' beck and call, and he became lazy. He shirked his duties, and, without anywhere for the dead souls to go, they became stuck in Limbo.

"Limbo is a place between this world and the next. You are neither alive nor dead. You are in-between, and the souls trapped there became known as the Betwixt. They were lost and adrift, and they looked to the Ferryman for guidance. He became their leader.

"When Hades heard of this, he was enraged, but unable to leave his kingdom he could not punish the Ferryman. He could only wait. So that's what he did. He waited and waited, and one day, when the Ferryman came knocking, he took his revenge. He punished the Ferryman for undermining him, and for taking the Betwixt as his own. He fashioned the Ferryman a crown made of curling ram's horns and carved out a hole in Hell for the Ferryman to rule.

"The Ferryman begged forgiveness, but Hades had no mercy. He banished him and his Betwixt to their new home and gave him the title of The Dead King, for he would never set foot in the land of the living again —apart from the eve of Midwinter. And thus, the City of the Dead was born. The Dead King ruled his new kingdom with hatred and disdain. And as for Hades, he never called upon a new

Ferryman. Instead, he closed the gates to the Underworld and left the dead souls with a choice: wander Limbo for all eternity, or join the Dead King."

Victoria blinked her big, green eyes. "That story doesn't have a happy ending."

Rosalie smiled sadly. "Not all stories do, *ma chérie*."

"I don't think the Dead King is a bad man," Victoria said, yawning.

"No?"

"No. He seems… sad."

"Maybe he is."

"Maybe he didn't want to be the Ferryman."

"Maybe you're right."

"*Maybe* it's time for bed," Yvette said, appearing at the door. "Enough, Rose, you'll scare her. You're as bad as Agathe."

"I'm not scared," Victoria protested.

"But you *are* tired," Yvette said, kissing her baby sister before climbing into the bed that she and Rosalie shared. "And so am I. Come, Rose. Put out that light and be done with today."

Rosalie tucked Victoria in tightly. "Goodnight, *ma chérie*."

"Goodnight, Rosie."

Victoria's eyelids finally proved too heavy and drifted closed. Rosalie picked up the oil lamp off their dresser and carried it to her bedside table. She stripped down to her chemise and climbed into bed with her sister. It was cramped, but cosy —like everything in their home. But at least they didn't have to share a room with Agathe. Agathe slept on the first floor in what had used to be the pantry before it had become infested with mould. Unsuitable for storing salt and sugar, but perfect for storing an insane old woman.

Rosalie put out the oil lamp and their little bedroom was doused with darkness. She turned her back to Yvette, and looked out the paneless window, the night sky alight with stars. When she was younger, she used to pretend that it were fairies that illuminated the sky instead of stars, until Agathe had scolded her for being so silly.

"You shouldn't tell her stories like that," Yvette whispered. "If *maman* and *papa* heard you—"

"Well, they didn't hear me, did they?" Rosalie cut in. "Besides, she knows they're not real."

"Even the more reason not to tell them."

Rosalie turned over to face her sister. She could barely make out her shape in the dark, but a pair of green eyes glinted at her. "They're just fairy tales, Yvie. *We* grew up with Agathe's fairy tales and *we're* fine."

Yvette scoffed quietly. "Oh, sure. You stuff dead bodies with *papa* and I write obituaries with *maman*, and our great aunt is completely mad."

Rosalie reached out and took her sister's hand in hers. "This isn't our life forever."

"Yes, it is."

Rosalie pulled Yvette into a cradling hug. "Of course it's not. You are going to live a wonderful life, Yvie. You can achieve anything you want. You are strong, and smart, and brave. You can have the whole world, if you want. You just have to be ready to take it."

"And what about you?" she asked. "What do you want, Rose?"

"I already have everything I want," she lied. "Come now, I thought you were tired. Sleep now."

Rosalie waited until she could hear Yvette snoring before peeling her arms away from her sister, and turning over in bed to look at the sky once more. She watched the twinkling stars and allowed herself to be a child again, pretending they were fairies. It was the only thing that could take her mind off the sound of her parents arguing downstairs. And off the Dead King.

2.

Rosalie woke with the sun. She always did. Her room faced the east and was a suntrap in the morning. Yvette and Victoria never stirred until Adele woke her lazy daughters at seven A.M. sharp, and Rosalie had every morning to herself to do whatever she pleased, and what she always pleased was the same thing. Painting.

She couldn't remember when exactly she fell in love with painting, but it must have been a long time ago, because she couldn't remember a time when she hadn't felt the itch in her fingertips to pick up a brush and paint her soul. Even when she wasn't painting on parchment, she was painting in her mind. Sharp lines, soft colours, dramatic angles, lights and darks.

She was drawn to the macabre in her art. The darkness. The grim. But whatever gruesome thing she painted to life, she always gave it some light. Some relief. For painting, in her honest opinion, was about balance. Balance and harmony.

She set up her easel she had made from scratch from rotting wooden slats that had washed up on the Santorini coastline and constructed in her father's workshop. She unravelled a piece of yellowed parchment and clipped each corner to the easel. She wished she had a proper stand. She wished she had a canvas to paint on. But wishes were a fool's promise. They simply couldn't afford such things. As it was, Rosalie had to make her own paint from parchment wax. But she could make do. A true artist was merited on the quality of their work, not how expensive their oils were.

She looked at the parchment, illuminated by the morning sun filtering in through the window and over her shoulder. She didn't know what to paint. She never did. She picked up her brush that she had made herself from wooden pegs and cadaver hair, and dipped it in the dark blue. When she brought the brush to the parchment, she didn't hesitate. It was like the bristles lived separately to her, lived entirely of their own free will. Her hand took over, and her mind stopped whirring, and suddenly everything was harsh strokes, severe lines, and unforgiving colour.

She felt her consciousness leave her body, and it was like she stepped out of herself to stand back and watch herself paint. She wondered what on earth the painting would turn out to be. She couldn't wait to find out.

Rosalie stepped back to admire her art. Usually, she was never one to suffer vanity or pride in herself — Agathe used to cane the backs of hers and Yvette's legs for indulging in any of the seven deadly sins — but this, she had to admit, was beautiful.

She paused, studying the face looking back at her. He was alien in his beauty. High cheekbones and a jaw that could cut through glass. His eyes were pale blue, and his skin so fair it was like he was made of ice, yet he seemed the furthest thing from fragile. There was fire within him; of that she was sure.

He didn't smile though, and she wondered why. His lips were curled into a grimace of pain. Such an expression looked so out of place on something so handsome. It was like a scar that disfigured him. She began to wish that she had painted him with a smile, but remembered that this was how he was supposed to be. Whoever he was.

"Very handsome," Yvette said.

Rosalie looked over her shoulder at her sleepy sister, sitting up in bed. She smiled. "Thank you."

"Who is he?"

Rosalie turned back to the painting. "I don't know. I wish I did."

"He's angry."

Rosalie shook her head. "He's… sad."

"Sad?"

"Yes, I think so."

"That's a shame."

Yvette stretched her arms up in a triumphant V shape. She unfolded herself from the sheets and crossed to the window, breathing in the sea air. Rosalie turned away, back to the striking man in her painting. She imagined that he didn't care if she was unexceptional, but that didn't make her feel better.

"You should paint this," Yvette said nodding to the landscape.

Rosalie joined her sister at the window. The coast of Santorini was truly astonishing. The sun dominated a cloudless blue sky and bathed their little island in stark white, giving everything a heavenly glow, and the sea a blinding sparkle as though it were peppered with diamonds instead of driftwood and seaweed.

"I don't decide what to paint," Rosalie said. "The brush does."

Yvette sighed. "I'll never understand you creative types."

Rosalie frowned. "My type?"

"Don't be offended," Yvette said, taking hold of her sister's hands and kissing them. "I mean it as a compliment. Your dreams soar higher than shooting stars, Rose. You're wonderful like that."

Rosalie wrapped her sister up in a tight embrace. "*Je t'aime.*"

"Je t'aime aussi."

Rosalie held her sister at arm's length. "Anyway, why are you up so early?"

"You were singing."

Rosalie's eyebrows shot up in surprise. "I was?"

"You were. *The City Of the Dead.*"

Rosalie recalled the grim nursery rhyme from her childhood. *Between this land, and the one next, Lives the City of the Dead…* She couldn't imagine why that had been in her head.

"My apologies, *ma sœur.*"

"Barely accepted."

When their mother appeared at the doorway, hair pinned up in an already fraying mess, apron already dirtied from making breakfast, she was stunned to see Yvette, her laziest daughter of all, awake before seven.

"My Lord," Adele said. "Miracles have yet to go out of fashion." Before either of them could speak, their mother started again. "Rosalie, put those silly drawings away. Yvette, wake Victoria. There's a delivery at the dock, and I need you to collect it."

"What about *papa*?" Yvette asked.

Adele smiled but it was tainted with resentment. "Gaston is sleeping off a hangover."

Rosalie and Yvette gave each other an uneasy look. Their mother only called their father by his first name when she was exceptionally livid with him.

"Off you go, both of you," Adele prompted. "Hurry."

Their mother disappeared, a flurry of flyaway hair and exasperation. They could hear her heeled boots stamping down every step to the first floor. There was silence between them for a moment.

Yvette encircled her sister's shoulders with one arm. "Your art is magnificent," she assured her.

292

Rosalie rested her head on Yvette's shoulder. *"Merci."*

They walked to dock, arms linked. For all they squabbled, for all they fell out, and disagreed over the little things, Rosalie knew that Yvette was her best friend and always would be. She was the only one who understood her art, and respected her complete and utter disinterest in ribbons and frills. Yvette understood her fascination with death and didn't question it. She just accepted her in a way that their parents or Agathe could not. *Would* not.

They were as different as night and day as they walked the coastline. Rosalie's dress was a basic cream silk, unfitted, with no skirts or hoops, or silly appendages. It was modest, and functional, and fit for the warm weather with three quarter-length sleeves and a square neckline that showed off her collarbones, but nothing more.

Yvette, however, wore a beautiful lavender affair, made of silk and lace that she had sewn herself, with a white sash at the middle tied in a neat bow at the back. Her sleeves were capped, and her neckline scooped low in a curve to show off a cleavage that Rosalie would have died for. Her gown had so many skirts and hoops that Rosalie wondered how she wasn't melting under it all, but Yvette never seemed to break a sweat. Upon her crown of blonde ringlets sat a pretty bonnet fashioned at a jaunty angle. Her smile put the whole of Santorini to shame. For a moment, Rosalie wondered if she too should have gone into dress-making.

Her beauty didn't go unnoticed either. She turned the heads of both men and women in equal measure. People looked after her in lust, in jealousy, in awe. No one looked at Rosalie in that way, and she was used to that.

The dock of their little town was small and could only harbour up to three ships at a time. There was one pier, one cargo bay, and one pontoon that stretched out one hundred yards into the Mediterranean

Sea for fishermen who couldn't afford boats to cast their nets.

In the furthest bay, Rosalie spotted their usual business partner, Stavros. He brought over deliveries from the mainland for them and several other trades on the island. His tanned face lit up when he saw Yvette. Rosalie hung back and let her sister approach him alone. It was no secret that she had a soft spot for the sailor and Rosalie didn't fancy playing gooseberry. Besides, the parcel looked small, just a single crate.

She watched Yvette smile and extend her arm, and Stavros kissed the back of her hand. She giggled and her cheeks reddened, and Rosalie smiled at her little sister. Of all the men who desired Yvette — and there were a lot — Rosalie liked Stavros the best. He was a decent man. Hard working. He hadn't anything to offer Yvette other than his heart, and Rosalie believed that to be better than all the wealth in the world.

"Curious, isn't it?" said a smooth voice over her shoulder.

Rosalie started and turned. She came face to face with a tall man in a long black cloak that was far too warm for a day where the sun was splitting the stones. His hood was up, and she could see nothing of his face but a gloomy outline. She took a step back, but kept her chin indignantly high.

"Pardon?" she said.

Although she couldn't see, Rosalie thought she detected a hint of a smile in his voice when he said, "Your sister and her friend. Curious, isn't it? How humans work. All those emotions. Quaint pleasantries and stolen glances. They've barely spoken a word to each other, and yet they've somehow said so much."

Rosalie realised she could detect a faint trace of her hometown in his accent.

"You're from *Paris*," she said, more of an accusation than a question.

A laugh. *"Oui, madame.* You are surprised?"

"I've not met anyone here from my home," she said. "And I've been here a long time. Yet, I've never seen *you* before."

Another smile, somewhere in that silver-tongued voice. "I don't make it a habit of coming ashore."

"You mean you stay on the mainland?"

"Something like that."

"Who are you?" she asked.

A pause. "No one."

Rosalie arched an eyebrow. "Why would *no one* need to hide their face?"

"Who says I'm hiding, *madame*?"

"I do. And so does your cloak. So that's two against one."

He laughed. "I see. So, I'm outnumbered, is that it?"

"I'm afraid so."

He paused. Then said, "Very well."

Reaching up, Rosalie saw the pale skin of his hands, almost luminescent in the light. His fingertips looked rough and calloused, his nails neat. He hesitated for a moment, and then pulled the black silk away from his face. Rosalie immediately felt something catch in her chest and she stepped back.

The man was striking. His skin looked as if he had been carved from marble, and his eyes were moonstone blue. His hair, black as night, fell to his shoulders in soft tousles, tucked neatly behind his ears. He smiled and it was beautiful and terrifying all at once. He was the man from her painting. A man who she had thought, up until that moment, was imaginary.

"Who are you?" she asked, quietly.

"I am a friend, Rosalie," he said.

"I don't know you."

"Oh, but you do."

"How do you know my name?"

295

"I know everything about you, my dear girl," he said.

He took a step forward and she took a step back. She looked down the pier to Yvette who was still flirting unabashedly with Stavros. She looked back at the man.

"Who are you?" she demanded. "How do you know me?"

He smiled. "I am the one from your paintings, Rosalie — and not just the one from this morning. I am the one from your past, your dreams, your nightmares. I am the one you have been waiting for, whether you know it or not."

Her stomach knotted. "How do you know about the paintings? Have you been watching me? I'll tell my father."

"Your father doesn't scare me. That drunkard may scare you, and your sisters, and your mother, but not me. I can save you from him, you know."

Rosalie's face crinkled into a frown. "How dare you presume to know me or my family. I need saving from no one, and certainly not by you. You're a stranger in an ugly cloak, with ugly words and I wash my hands of this conversation. And of you."

"You owe me your life, Rosalie," the man said. "I have given you twenty years on this plane, and now I have come to claim what is mine."

"I don't belong to you. I don't belong to anyone but myself."

She looked at her sister who now held the small crate in her arms as she laughed at something Stavros was saying. She opened her mouth to call out to her, but the man wrapped his hand around her wrist and pulled her close. She gasped, as if she had plunged into ice water. The world around them fell away. The pier, the sea, Yvette and Stavros — it was all obliterated by a sudden rush of darkness. Nothing remained but herself and the beautiful stranger. Fear blossomed in her chest, snaked up her throat and caught her in a snare.

"You owe me your life, Rosalie," he said, softly. "You can either give it to me willingly, or I will take it, but I'd rather it not have to be the latter."

"Who are you?" she whispered, her breath forming clouds in the air, as if they were in the Arctic.

A beat passed. "I am the Dead King."

Rosalie huffed a laugh, but deep inside of her something twisted. "You must think me simple."

"I think you are lying to yourself. Nothing good is born of lies, Rosalie. Search yourself, you know it to be true."

"The Dead King is a fairy tale," she said. "I stopped believing in fairy tales a long time ago."

"Whether you believe in me or not, I've come for my payment."

"I have nothing to give. How on Earth do you expect me to pay?"

"With your hand, Rosalie. In marriage. I want you for a bride."

Her face twisted in horror. "No. Never."

"You will come with me," he said. "We will rule the City of the Dead together."

She tried to pull away from him. "You're mad. None of this is real. No."

"Yes," he said. "You haven't a choice in the matter."

"If you are really *Le Roi Mort*, then you know you cannot take me unwillingly," she said. "I know the Old Ways. My aunt always told them to me when I was a child. The City of the Dead only takes willingly. It never steals from the world above. And I will never surrender myself to you."

The Dead King smiled but there was nothing exuberant about it. "I have my ways, Rosalie Valentina Beaufort. Before sundown, you will give yourself to me, whole and true."

"In that case, I hope you enjoy disappointment," she said.

Another smile. "We'll see."

He let go of her wrist, and the real world rushed her like a bull at a red flag. The sun blinded her, and the sudden Santorini heat winded her. She would have fallen to her knees had Yvette not been there to catch her. She looked around, eyes darting like a rabbit looking for a fox, but the world was a blur.

He was gone. The Dead King was gone. She looked down at her wrist and saw a red imprint of where his hand had gripped her. Her skin still felt cold.

"Rose?" Yvette held her shoulders and shook her. "Rosalie? Can you hear me?"

Rosalie dragged her gaze to meet her sister's. She blinked hard, and her groggy eyes focused on Yvette's concerned face. Behind her stood Stavros, looking equally worried.

"Yes..." she said, quietly. "Yes, I think so."

"You were just standing there, staring at nothing," Yvette said. "Honestly, if you weren't standing up I would have thought you'd died."

"Died?" she asked.

"Yes. You went so pale. Your skin was like ice and you were so stiff. You didn't blink, not even once."

"Is *madame* okay?" Stavros asked.

Yvette replied in fluent, perfect Greek, that Rosalie was fine and declined his kind offer to walk them home. She assured him that they would be fine and not to worry, but her pretty face remained creased with unease. With the crate under one arm, and the other encircled around Rosalie's waist, they started a slow walk back home.

"What happened, Rose?" Yvette asked. "It's like you went into some kind of trance."

"I don't know," she replied, honestly. "I just... went somewhere else for a moment."

"Like a dream?"

"I suppose, yes."

"I could see your breath in the air like we were back home in the dead of winter," she said. "Your lips were turning blue."

Rosalie stopped walking and turned to her sister. "Yve, do you believe in *Le Roi Mort*?"

"The Dead King?" she asked, one eyebrow arched. "Of course not. Why do you ask?"

"Why don't you believe in him, though?"

Yvette blinked. "Because he's not real. He's a fairy tale, Rose. A story Agathe liked to tell us as children to scare us."

Rosalie shook her head. "Not a story. A legend."

Yve tucked a stray strand of dark hair neatly behind Rosalie's ear. "All legends are just stories, Rose. What's brought all this on?"

Rosalie started walking again. She took the crate from her sister who's arm looked like it was going to give way any moment. It was small but heavy. She peeped inside and was unsurprised to see more materials for the workshop. Herbs, embalming fluids, body paint.

Yve stayed close to her sister's side. "Rose, I'm worried. You're behaving strangely."

"I'm fine," she assured her sister. "I was day-dreaming. I'm a painter, it's what we do. We get lost inside our own minds, fantasising works of art yet to be. Please take that fretted expression off your face, you'll get worry lines."

Yvette hesitantly let her features smooth into placidity, but concern hung in her voice, reluctant to let go of the matter. "As you wish, *ma sœur*."

"I'm fine," Rosalie repeated, keeping her chin high and her gaze forwards. "I'm right as rain."

She had no idea why she was lying, not just to Yvette, but to herself. Glancing down at the red imprint on her wrist, she knew with full certainty that she was undoubtedly, and irrevocably not fine. Not fine at all.

3.

When they arrived home, Yvette ushered Rosalie to a seat at the kitchen table and fetched her a cup of water. She sat across her sister, studying her, looking for signs of abnormality. Rosalie quickly became fed up with her and told her to shoo.

"You're not right," Yvette said. "I can see it in your eyes."

"Well then, my eyes are liars," Rosalie replied. "I day-dreamed myself out of existence for a few moments, Yve. It happens. It's normal."

They watched each other for a few moments. Rosalie quickly became aware of something hanging between them. Something invisible. Unspoken. She gave her younger sister a disparaging look.

"Good God, Yve, what is it?" she asked.

"You…" she began. "You were talking to yourself. Having a whole conversation. Like… there was someone with you. You seemed scared."

Rosalie took a deep breath. "I promise you, *ma sœur*, I'm okay. But you must promise me you won't tell *maman* and *papa*. Especially not Agathe."

Yvette looked uneasy. "Rose…"

"Please, Yve."

She sighed. "Alright. I promise."

Rosalie reached across the table and grasped her sister's hand. "*Merci.*"

There was a shuffling noise, and then the creak of a floorboard. Rosalie turned to see Victoria at the doorway, her blanket clutched between her small hands. She took a step back, ashamed of having been caught eavesdropping, but Rosalie just smiled and beckoned her over.

"Come here, *ma chérie*," she said.

Victoria smiled and bounded over like a lamb in springtime. Rosalie pulled the little girl into her lap, blanket and all, and snuggled her. Victoria laughed.

"Why are you snooping, little one?" she asked. "Hmm?"

"You know what happens to little girls who snoop, don't you?" Yvette asked. When Victoria shook her head, she continued, "They grow up to be powerful women who know everyone's secrets."

That made Victoria beam.

Rosalie tickled her littlest sister's cheek. "Have you only just gotten up?"

She nodded. "I had a bad dream."

Rosalie gave her a tender look. "My poor sweet. What was it about?"

Victoria hesitated. "You, Rosie."

Rosalie and Yvette shared a guarded look.

"What on earth about me in this dream was so scary?" Rosalie asked, keeping her tone light-hearted.

"It wasn't you," Victoria said. "It was what happened to you."

A pause. "What happened to me?"

Victoria's little hands gripped her blanket tighter, he knuckles turning white. "The Dead King took you."

Rosalie felt her face go slack. "Pardon?"

"I dreamt he stole you away," she said, voice small, "and made you his bride. That's why I was spying — to make sure you were still here."

Rosalie wrapped Victoria up in a bone-crushing embrace. She kissed her hair and soothed her hand across the little girl's brow. Over the top of her head she swapped worried glances with Yvette who stayed quiet.

"Dreams aren't real," Rosalie said. "They're just stories our minds make up. Not all of them are nice. This is my fault, *ma chérie* — I shouldn't have told you that bedtime story."

Victoria looked up at her. "But I like that story. *Maman* only tells me stories about princes and princesses. And Agathe's stories are dull."

Rosalie smiled. "Even so. Go on, now. Wash and dress. Otherwise it will be *maman* you have to fear, not the Dead King."

Victoria obediently scooted off her sister's lap and headed for the doorway. She paused, then ran back to Rosalie's side. Reaching into the folds of her nightgown she pulled out a small rock, no larger than a silver coin, and thrust it into Rosalie's hand.

"For you," she said. "To keep you safe."

Rosalie uncurled her fingers and quickly realised that the rock was a blue moonstone. The image of The Dead King's eyes flashed in her memory, and she quickly closed her hand into a fist again. She looked at Victoria.

"Where did you find this?"

"On the beach," she replied. "When *papa* took me to see the boats come in from the mainland. It was amongst the shale. It makes me feel safe when I hold it, so maybe it will keep you safe too."

Rosalie swallowed down a lump in her throat that she hadn't realised was forming. She gave Victoria a smile of pure love.

"Thank you, *ma chérie*. I'll keep it always."

Victoria tiptoed up to kiss Rosalie on the cheek, and then scampered around the table to do the same for Yvette. They watched their youngest sibling disappear around the doorway before turning to look at each other.

"What did she give you?" Yvette asked.

Rosalie passed her the moonstone. Yvette rolled it between her fingers, watching it catch the light.

"I doubt this came to be on the beach naturally," she said.

Rosalie agreed. "Someone must have lost it."

Yvette passed it back to Rosalie. "Or someone left it there to be found."

"Must you be so suspicious?"

"She had a nightmare about you and the Dead King," Yvette said. "When you came out of your trance, you were *asking* me about the Dead King."

Rosalie tried to keep her tone disinterested. "What is your point?"

"You don't think the two are connected?"

"No, I don't. And I don't believe in coincidence either. Nor fate, nor luck, or anything like that. It is what it is. I told Victoria a scary story last night, and it just stuck in both of our heads."

Yvette sighed and stood up. "You're not telling me something, *ma sœur*."

"Because there is nothing to tell you."

Yvette looked at her for the longest time, then said, "I sincerely hope not."

After Yvette had finished interrogating her, Rosalie retired to the cellar to begin her work. *Papa* was still unconscious in bed, so she had the workshop alone, but she didn't mind that. She worked best alone. Her head was clearer, her thoughts sharper. She could fully concentrate on the task at hand without having to worry about socialising, or minding her manners in front of her father.

Miss Alina Vorshack had died young. Scarlatina. She was no older than twelve or thirteen, with a once-pretty face, now sunken and sallow with death. The family had requested that she not be mummified, so it was short work. Just a case of cleaning the corpse, rubbing the body down with herbs that postponed the smell of decay, and painting her up like a doll.

That was Rosalie's favourite part. Bringing them back to life. She powered Miss Vorshack's face with lead-based powder that Yvette begged *maman* to allow her to use on her own face. Of course, *maman* always denied her — warned her about the dangers of lead-based cosmetics— and Yvette always sulked.

Once Rosalie had taken the yellowish hue from the corpse's face, she set to work on rouging her cheeks and painting her lips a delicate, soft pink. She washed and dried her hair and twisted it into intricate braids of gold. When she was finished, she stepped back to admire her work. The dead girl looked as though she were merely sleeping.

Now, just to dress her. Rosalie turned to fetch the gown from where it hung on the clotheshorse. It was gorgeous, born of blue satin with pearly white embroidery embellishing the bodice. The sleeves were tailored blue lace, and the skirt adorned with tulle flowers. For an awful moment, Rosalie was tempted to try it on herself, but she quickly quashed that thought, admonishing herself. Her cheeks rosied with shame and she knew she deserved it. To even *think* of trying on the dead girl's dress was irretrievably dishonourable.

She hurried back to the body on the stone slab, keen to get the gown out of her hands and onto the cadaver. She dressed the corpse in its finery — which took some time because of the layers of petticoats in the skirts, and ribbons to be tied in the corset. When Miss Vorshack was finally decent, Rosalie moved her body into the coffin her family had chosen, and gently placed a silver coin over each eye.

"Cross safely," she said. "Let the Dead King be your guide."

She paused. Ice shot through her veins, and for a moment, the room gavotted.

Let the Dead King be your guide.

She had never said that before. It had always been '*Let the Ferryman be your guide.*' Always. Without botch. She'd said it hundreds upon hundreds of times to the countless corpses she'd prepared for burial, both with and without *papa* — so why now did it change? Why did *his* name pop into her head? More importantly, why did she *let* his name enter her mind?

"Because you can't stop thinking about me, Rosalie."

Rosalie spun and nearly toppled at the sight of the Dead King sitting on the old rocking chair in the corner. He smiled at her and she felt ice flood her body once more.

"You're not really here," she said.

"Well, if I'm not then you're losing your mind," he said. "Which one do you think is worse?"

"Why are you haunting me?" she asked, exasperated.

The Dead King laughed. "Come now, that's a tad melodramatic."

"Leave me be," she said. "I've done you no harm, I wish you no ill will. I have nothing for you; you're wasting your time."

"No, Rosalie," he said, standing. "You are the one wasting time. You need to give me an answer before sundown, and the longer you leave it, the more your loved ones will suffer."

Her jaw tightened. "Stay away from my family."

"I would, my dear, but you leave me no choice. Poor little Victoria having to endure nightmares because of her selfish big sister."

"That was *you*?" she snarled, taking a step forward.

The Dead King didn't retreat, and now they were almost standing breast to breast. She looked up at him with defiance. He returned her gaze with one of arrogance. Rosalie wanted to slap it off. So she did.

305

The smack of colliding flesh resonated around the small cellar. Rosalie refused to acknowledge the sting in her palm, although it did make her eyes water. What upset her most was how completely unfazed the Dead King seemed to be. He rubbed his cheek and shimmied his lower jaw from side to side as if checking that it was still connected. Then he laughed. It was an unkind sort of laughter.

"You don't know who you're dealing with, Rosalie," he said.

"No," she replied, voice as cold and dead as the corpse on her workbench. "*You* don't know who *you're* dealing with, *Le Roi Mort*. If you so much as even *think* of hurting the people I love, I'll—"

"You'll what?" he interrupted. "Kill me? *Me*? The Dead King?"

"I will give you a fate worse than death," she promised.

He smiled. "I'm already there."

And then he was gone.

"Agathe!"

Rosalie barrelled into her great aunt's chambers — the once walk-in pantry — breath short and face flushed. She didn't need to look for the cragged, old woman because the room was only big enough for a bed and an armchair. Today, Agathe was in her armchair, reading a red moleskin-bound edition of William Shakespeare's *Prince of Venice*.

Agathe looked up as Rosalie intruded and regarded her with irritation. "What is it, child?"

"I need to know about the Dead King," Rosalie said. "Everything. Anything. Tell me all of it."

Agathe arched a wild, white eyebrow. "Why the sudden interest in *Le Roi Mort*? I thought you were a non-believer."

"Well, perhaps I've changed my mind," she said. "I need to know more."

"I've already told you everything," she said. "All I know are the stories I tell, and I've told you them all."

Rosalie came and knelt at Agathe's feet, resting her hands on the old woman's knobbly knees. "No. Not everything. I always knew you were holding back. Hiding something. Only telling half the story. Agathe, I need to know more."

Agathe looked at Rosalie for the longest time, and the realisation dawned on her wrinkled features. For the first time in forever, Rosalie thought she could see fear etched into those furrows.

"You saw him," she said. "Didn't you?"

Rosalie tried to lie, but the look of unconstrained dread in Agathe's eyes stopped her. She sighed.

"Yes," Rosalie said. "What do I do?"

"There's nothing you can do," Agathe replied. "You're doomed."

About the Author

Laura Jordan is a 6ft Libran and cat enthusiast from the countryside in Kent, England. She grew up in her family cottage with her parents, brother and grandad Len. She studied ballet and performing arts for the majority of her adolescent life, thinking she would make a career of it, before realising she could neither sing, act, nor dance.

Sensing her talents may lie elsewhere, Laura set off to study creative writing at the University of Greenwich where she scraped a bachelor's degree. Laura then went on to put her degree to good use as a senior reporter and editor for a builder's merchant's magazine. However, she was fired after three months after likening her workplace to "riding a bike through Hell" on Twitter.

Then Laura tried her hand at teaching. She became a Special Educational Needs teaching assistant for secondary school children, and much to everyone's surprise —not least her own— she found she was quite good at it. She kept to this line of work for three years until moving to Ireland to be with her boyfriend.

Living in Dublin with Derek, their golden retriever, and a small army of borderline feral cats, Laura spends her time co-hosting a podcast and writing books that she is still astounded that people want to read.

She is also very fond of pizza.

ACKNOWLEDGEMENTS

To my parents (especially mum who proofread my manuscript), who pushed my debut novel so much onto their friends that the majority of my readers are middle-aged women called Susan.

To my nan, who doesn't read my books but buys them and gets me to sign them, nevertheless.

To my beloved, Derek, who, like I said before, is *really* good in bed.

To my friend, Jake, who beta-read this manuscript for me, giving me notes that both made me die laughing and also made me a better writer.

And to my editor, Sian, who had to read all that. You're the real MVP.

Thank you all.

Printed in Great Britain
by Amazon

82487346R00180